Wiggle Room

Darden North

SARTORIS
LITERARY
GROUP

"A traditional publisher with a non-traditional approach to publishing."

Sartoris Literary Group, Inc.
Jackson, Mississippi
www.sartorisliterary.com

Wear the world like a loose garment.
--- Anonymous

1

Balad, Iraq

2006

Shards of asphalt ripped the barricade against the thin-walled trailer, throwing Brad from his bunk and a near-comatose sleep. He scrambled for his watch as the burst of sandbags outside pre-empted the claxon's late warning. Another mortar shell erupted on the pavement, the sound muffled by a voice from the radio: *Your butt OK? Better be, 'cause I need it, or there won't be anything alive to transport outta here tonight.*

"Damn, Elizabeth, I think that makes number 38, doesn't it?" Brad asked. "Thank God for those sandbags."

"Enemy's been busy, Major. But surely this one's over. And, like I said, I need you here at the hospital."

Brad sat up on the bare floor, leaning his head against the bed, still below the level of the barrier outside. Another look at his watch: he was due two hours of daylight sleep, and last night's flight transporting military patients had drained him.

"Come on, it's only 3:00 PM, Cossar, and I was down pretty hard. Even if they hadn't hit us this afternoon, you probably would've waked me up."

"But that's why you doctors make the big bucks," she chuckled. "Oh, that's right, I forgot—you volunteered."

The two-way radio cracked a bit as the last insurgents' shell hit a random target within the base, the strike still close enough to pepper the sandbags and weaken Brad's grip on the casing. He found the radio on the floor.

"And my four months is just about up," he said. "Bet you called just to see if my guts were splattered across the Sunni Triangle."

"You trauma guys are really too smart, particularly the sexy ones. You can see right through a nurse like me, or at least you'd like to."

Brad grimaced. All he wanted to do was crawl back up into bed.

"Relax, Cossar, I'll make the next air transport to Landstuhl."

"Sounds like it's quieted down," Cossar said. "I need some help in the ICU, so head on in to the hospital."

"Why can't Haynes handle it?"

He stretched across his bunk and popped the pillow back into shape.

"Called in sick this morning. Said he had the flu, but if you ask me it's probably the rough morning-after virus. Besides, Colonel Haynes never seems to be much help in the OR, unless it's something simple. And if you add in this issue."

"What issue?"

"Last week after lunch, one of my nurses thought she smelled something on his breath, even through a surgical mask. She wrote him up. He bit my head off when I showed him the report."

"That's the Haynes from Mississippi I know," Brad said. "Continuing the party at work."

Cossar laughed. "Said he had a cold and the smell was from sucking on menthol."

There was quiet outside and from the radio. The shelling was over. "What about those two other docs, the ones from Miami that checked in last week…or did they call in sick today, too?"

"They were on the forward team sent to wipe up after the bombing and gunfire during the Mosul Religious Festival. They reported in about an hour or so before our little mortar attack: overloaded with casualties—might make it back down here tomorrow or maybe even later."

Brad envisioned the carnage in Mosul. *Only so much operating two docs can do in a tent on the back of a Humvee.* "Look, Cossar, unless we've got our own new stuff coming in, I'd bet you could spare me a couple of hours."

"Sorry, my dear Major. We just got word that the medical administrator has pointed a Black Hawk our way."

Brad threw his feet to the floor and reached for clean underwear and socks from the small dresser near his bed. He tossed the radio to his left hand and stepped over to the sink.

"Shit. How many casualties on board the helicopter? Can't be more than six."

He picked up his toothbrush and opened a bottle of water.

"Not sure. Guess we'll find out when it puts down."

"OK, Lieutenant Colonel, I'm headed your way."

8

He pulled the radio clear of his spit into the sink and ran the faucet, drowning a familiar *Gee, thanks, sweety!* as she clicked off.

Brad grabbed his Air Force PT gear and pitched the radio onto his desk. It landed atop Leslie's photographs of wedding cake and groom's cake designs, samples emailed a couple of days ago and waiting his approval. His reply using the base computer station would have to wait. The insurgents' attack had changed things.

Skipping a shower, he threw on the blue running shorts, gray shirt, and tennis shoes, and stepped out onto the warm asphalt of September Iraq. After the All Clear command, the warning sirens were silent. There was little traffic as he jogged around the sandbags to the Air Force Theater Hospital. Situated near the 12-foot concrete wall that surrounded the base, the hospital was shielded against direct mortar strikes. He hoped that the only misery ahead was the load arriving with the Black Hawk.

Beads of sweat slid into the corner of his mouth as Brad reached the rear hospital entrance. He pushed his ID badge in the face of the security post and then cleared the metal detector. Minor medical and clerical personnel jammed the rear hall. He slipped into the physicians' locker room, changed into surgical scrubs, and entered the main corridor. The wall-sized mural of Saddam Hussein greeted him, the deposed leader dressed in full military regalia as though still directing the Republican Guard that once trained on the premises. Al-Bakir Air Base had become Balad Air Base Theatre Hospital.

Brad pulled open the curtained entrance to Surgical ICU. He stared at the patient bays, all but one empty and separated by thin shelves stacked in disarray with supplies including vials of medication. Squeezed between two bays was a clerical work area: a six-foot folding table anchored by two computer monitors and littered with piles of papers and empty coffee cups, along with displaced boxes of surgical gloves and more syringes of narcotic pain medicine. The blue curtains serving as walls made the area appear no more high-tech than a movie set. Yet the equipment within and behind the drapes was state-of-the art for 2006, the same high standards required of the surgeons and nurses who worked there.

One of those nurses was Elizabeth Cossar, standing in starched, light-blue uniform, a below-the knee skirt finished with beige stockings and black, thick rubber-soled shoes. Even at five-four and with fading brown hair, her commanding pose rivaled that of the fallen dictator.

"Lieutenant Colonel Elizabeth Taylor Cossar, I am reporting for duty," Brad said. "And, my dear, it's only 'cause I love you and you're my favorite nurse over here."

"That's right, Major. You've learned, and you're sweating …and I like that."

"Glad you do, but I'm really too tired to sweat much more," Brad said, raising an eyebrow. "I jogged over here because you predicted disaster. But I've seen morgues more exciting than this place, Cossar."

She turned away.

Brad imagined the disapproval on her face. "How much longer 'til the helicopter sets down?" he asked. "Do you think maybe we should clean up this mess before our guests arrive?"

Cossar walked to one of the computers to chart vital signs. She glanced up to watch Brad survey the area and study the single occupant in Bay 3 of the ICU.

"Before Colonel Haynes went off duty last night," she said, "he left orders to send that gal out to the med unit once her urinary output picked up. She's just about made it. And don't look so smug about this mess. I've never seen you pick up after yourself. Civilian nurses have guys like you spoiled rotten."

"Noted, Nurse Cossar." Brad shook his head. "But it seems to me that what's left of the medical day team could've handled things here until the shit hit the fan. That's if it ever did. Then you could've called me."

"Where's the dedication, Major?" Cossar checked other metered readings for the female lieutenant in Bay 3. "You know this is all for OIF," she said. "You're being such an ass …"

Incoming Black Hawk with casualties blared from the speaker propped atop one of the computer screens. Pushing two loaded gurneys, the helicopter's Army medevac crew burst single-file into the ICU. Cossar grabbed additional IV supplies from an overhead cabinet, calling out, "Looks like we'll need your precious doctoring skills after all."

The lead flight medic spotted Brad's ID badge and rushed his gurney toward him. Brad stepped back when the gurney behind

10

nearly rammed the lead. The medic's breathing was heavy, almost labored. Brad wondered if he could speak.

"We unloaded these two patients first, Major." The medic gestured to the gurneys arranged single-file. "Looks like a 500-pound or so IED detonated, lots of flying shrapnel—nail and ball bearings everywhere. We got four more aboard the chopper."

Brad shook his head, wishing that the medical administrator had been playing some sort of sick prank. He checked the badge of the lead medic and his partner. Both looked to be about eighteen. Nevertheless, they were branded Army specialists.

"Then that confirms six total transports, correct?" Brad asked.

The first flight medic looked around the nearly empty unit and pointed to the patient loosely secured on the gurney behind him. "Yes, sir. The count includes this Iraqi local, burned pretty bad. Looks to be a college student, dressed conservative—short hair, button-down shirt, khakis—but not much is left of that stuff. Kid was walking along the road when the IED blew, then got pinned under when the Humvee flipped. It was our vehicle, our situation. We just couldn't leave him."

He thrust a Field Medical Card at Brad. "But, Major, the first one that I've got here is American military. We put him on a portable vent first off—thought he was worst hit. But on second look, just a couple of leg fractures that splinted up real good and a scalp laceration I sewed up. Hey, I'm no plastic surgeon, but not bad. Don't you think?"

The lead flight medic, the Army Specialist, lifted an edge of the blood-saturated bandages that encircled the top of the lance corporal's head.

Brad grabbed the rear of the first gurney, directing it to the ICU bay where Cossar waited with a blood pressure cuff. He glanced over at the Iraqi patient, and then scanned the injured American's medical information card: Lance Corporal Chad Giles, U.S. Marine Corps, age 21.

Damn roadside bombs Brad thought, as the nurse moved Giles to the stationary ventilator and checked his airway. Below the name were more details of treatment rendered at the blast site and en route to Balad. Superficial facial lacerations had been cleaned and closed with thin sterile strips, but the deep tears to his chest and thigh muscles from spraying shrapnel would need debridement

11

and would scar.

Fractured femur, left and right stood out on the next line. *From the belly-up, that armored Humvee was there for Giles* Brad decided. Then under his breath he said, "But, my friend, I'll bet you've got a nasty spinal compression fracture courtesy of that bomb. Not to mention what's going on in your gut."

The Marine's left leg and arm moved.

"Elizabeth, I need to see what's under those old dressings. Go ahead and get this guy's head CT-ed," he ordered. "Probably has a concussion."

The flight medic stepped up before the nurse could acknowledge the order. "Doc, I don't think you'll have much trouble from Lance Corporal Giles here. He's the lucky one."

Cossar had strapped the sedated Giles into his ICU bed, vital sign monitors reading stable. He was off the ventilator, oxygen now flowing though a face mask. With the urinary catheter still in place, dark fluid flowed in the plastic tubing from under his sheets, filling the bag on the side of the bed. Cossar began to peel the thick, crimson-soaked dressings from Giles' head.

"Whatcha mean, young man?" Cossar threw in without looking up from her work. "You sort of cut off the doctor, didn't you, Army Specialist? And right in the middle of issuing orders. Anyway, I've already called radiology for the CT."

The lead flight medic took a quick look at Brad and then back at the rank and name on the gruff nurse's uniform. Cossar, Elizabeth T. appeared three times his age with the strength to match. There was relief on the teenager's face when she stepped back to attend to Giles. He straightened his posture and seemed to gamble again with reporting to the military physician.

Cossar relished authority. Brad covered his smile with Giles' field medical card.

"Giles, here, was in the lower section of the Humvee when the blast went off in the vehicle ahead," the lead medic said. "His Humvee actually missed the bomb, sir."

"Well, he may have escaped internal injuries, but we'll just have to see," Brad said.

"Giles' driver lost situational orientation during all the commotion and rolled the vehicle into a ditch," the medic said. "It was early this morning, low-light conditions, sir." He looked over

12

at Cossar and found her still preoccupied. "Neuro, intact. No internal injuries. Biggest issue is leg fractures. That's the flight crew's assessment ... sir."

"Is that what you think?" Cossar asked from across the unit. "What's your diagnosis, Army Specialist or flight medic, or whatever we're supposed to call you?"

"Yes, Major ... or ... Lieutenant Colonel," the medic answered, again not sure whom to detail. "That's what I think ... my diagnosis. Corporal Giles' main issue is compound bone fractures. In fact, Major, Giles was starting to regain consciousness on the flight over, so we sedated and ventilated him to maintain his oxygen sats, but you might want to ..."

"Thanks, Army Specialist." Brad said. "We'll take it from here."

"Yes, sir. Of course, sir." He saluted. "But his buddy riding up top didn't fare so good. Looks like he may have been crushed during the roll-over. We'll bring him next."

"Like I said, we'll take it from here. Go finish unloading that helicopter. " Brad darted his eyes toward Cossar, who turned the unloaded gurneys and their drivers toward the exit. "We'll be right here waiting for you and the rest of your transport."

Brad kept his eye on the monitor that flashed the Marine's vital signs. He then performed a quick neuro and vascular exam and checked the splints meant to stabilize Giles' broken legs. The supports were properly placed.

"I guess we were too hard on those guys, Elizabeth," Brad said. "Somebody in the Army Medical Corps must've really trained 'em." He looked over toward his friend, unsure if she had even heard him. She was busy charting on one of the computers. "But one of these femurs probably needs a pin or two. Haynes can check him out, show-off his year of orthopedic fellowship."

Brad palpated the soldier's soft but slightly swollen abdomen. "Roll the sonogram machine in here. Belly feels a little distended to me."

"Maybe some internal bleeding?" she asked and entered more notes into the computer.

"Could be, but his blood pressure and pulse are holding steady, so maybe not."

While Cossar retrieved the portable sonogram machine, Brad

moved to the next bay and the injured Iraqi national. From the trim physique and full head of hair, Brad guessed the age as early twenties. The young man lay motionless, his stare to the ceiling. Though his breathing was unlabored, plastic oxygen prongs hung askew on a swollen nose, breaking the field of blood-stained bandages. The Iraqi's loose bed straps and absence of eye coverings meant he was not in opposition to the American and coalition forces.

Discolored dressings also hid arm and leg wounds received from burning bits of an exploding Humvee. Brad lifted the patient's left forearm. The pulse at the wrist was full, the IV flowing well. Damp, bloody surgical gauze wrapped a disfigured left hand with thumb and forefinger blown away.

Brad walked to the other side of the bed to check the splinted right arm. He touched the skin covering the fracture; it was warm.

"Good blood flow here," he said. There was still no response. *Must have quite a bit of morphine on board* he decided.

When Brad pulled back the sheet to assess the skin temperature and color of the fractured right leg, the Iraqi jerked his head toward him.

"My broken bones and cuts will heal," said the Iraqi. "I know you Americans will take care of me."

Brad moved to the nearby counter where he had laid the Iraqi's Field Medical Card. In the top left hand corner of the FMC was a name assumed lifted at the scene from an ID. "My, my, you speak such good English, Zarife Amarah," Brad said. "Such well-enunciated, educated English."

"I had English tutors before I was sent for an education in Great Britain, a boarding school in London, beginning in middle school. I am now back here, attending university in engineering."

"Regardless of where you go to school ..." Brad again read aloud the name, as though finally mastering it "... you're a lucky sonnavabitch." He looked up from the over-sized note card. "You know, our guys could have just left you in the streets and directed our resources toward our own."

"Doctor, you Americans claim that you are not like that. Maybe you should rethink what you really are."

Brad re-checked the guy's pulse. Then without looking up, he asked, "Do we need to talk politics, Mr. Amarah?"

"Doctor, your American ideals do not allow you to leave people to die in the streets. Your politics, your principles, have left you without any ... let's see ... how do you say it ... *wiggle room?*"

The Intensive Care Receiving Unit was quiet, empty except for the two of them, Lance Corporal Giles several feet away, and the female patient in the corner that Brad spotted earlier.

"My guys had no choice but to pick you up, Amarah, and dump you on me." Brad considered more morphine to shut the guy up. "I guess it's our fault that U.S. military hospitals are superior to yours. Fifty percent of the traffic through here is from you and your buddies, you know." Brad tossed the Iraqi's medical card back toward the counter. It made it. "Mr. Amarah, I was told that you were just an innocent bystander—just in the wrong place at the wrong time."

"No, my American friend." He grinned through the bandaging. "You are mistaken."

"Mistaken?" Brad heard Cossar roll in with the sonogram machine.

"Brad, I need you over here, stat!"

Cossar was hovering over Giles.

Brad reached them in several steps. "Elizabeth, what's the deal?"

"This guy's blood pressure is 50 over nothing, pulse is barely detectable." She cursed, pulling back the sheet from Giles' swollen abdomen. "For God's sake, Brad, what the hell were you doing over there, wasting your time talking to Ali Baba?"

She grabbed the digital meter controlling Giles' IV tubing and pounded the up-arrow keys until the Marine's fluids were wide-open. Then she ripped the automatic blood pressure cuff from his forearm, replacing it with a manual device. She furiously pumped it with air, searching for a better reading. "My God, Brad. Look how distended he is!"

Brad pressed against the now rock-hard abdomen.

"Spleen must be ruptured," he said. "Gotta get him to the OR!"

Cossar rushed a gurney to the bed. Brad took the head and Cossar the feet and they transferred Giles.

"I would certainly agree with that, Major Cummins." Brad turned his head in the direction of John Haynes' voice. "Obviously, massive internal bleeding."

15

"Colonel," Brad said.

Brad unlocked the wheels of the loaded gurney and pushed it forward. "OK, Haynes, do you think you can lower yourself to help me lap this guy?"

Haynes pushed past Cossar for the foot. "This guy's dying under your watch, Major Cummins." He smirked as he led the way to the OR. "I'm not sure what I can do to pull your ass out of this mess, but we'll see."

Brad unhooked the hemorrhaging Giles from the stationary life support systems, converted the equipment to portable, and pushed the gurney at John Haynes.

"I thought you were all cozy in your bunk with flu, Haynes. Looks like the toxins cleared your system faster than expected."

"Cut the BS, Cummins," Haynes said. "Guess my vaccine rebounded. Besides, some of us are made of better stuff than others."

Brad shouted, "Elizabeth, call the blood bank ... need four—no, make that eight—units of blood. Just get O negative." His look at Haynes dared interruption. "You better get some fresh frozen plasma to go with it!"

"Come on, Cummins, you ass. Let's go."

As Haynes guided, Brad pushed the soldier's gurney the hundred yards or so to the old shipping container that served as an operating room, clipping the Colonel's heels the entire way.

2

The Boeing C-17's lift-off from Balad was steep enough to make airspace beyond the reach of insurgent missiles. Brad groaned as the pilot of the bulky jet followed with an erratic 70-degree bank. Scoring one of the four window seats in the cargo and passenger compartment would have helped his nausea, although in pitch-black Iraq there would have been nothing to see. He felt like he was strapped in the belly of a whale.

Brad had yet to lose a critical patient during any of these eight-hour air evacuation missions. Tonight was number fourteen, and he had no plans to spoil that record with this soldier nor lose anything else in that plane. But onboard the C-17, there was no support team to match that at Balad—no Haynes to arrive first and call a CODE, no IV tech to start a new line, no respiratory therapist to assist with CPR, no one but him and Cossar. Again, the blame of an unexpected patient death would fall on him.

His final image of Lance Corporal Chad Giles—a handsome young man bound in surgical bandages, blood-soaked from the pounding of a doomed resuscitation, a lifeless body surrounded by empty packages of medical supplies and medications—brought another wave of nausea to challenge the scopolamine patches behind his ears. Brad reached for an airsickness bag when the warning light atop the struggling ventilator distracted him. *Should have stayed out of the Indian DFAC for breakfast* Brad thought, his swallow hard.

Once the pilot leveled the C-17, he felt better, unbuckled, and steadied himself to attend to his patient.

"Major, sit your tight ass down!" said the air evacuation nurse. The AE Nurse serving tonight was Lieutenant Colonel Elizabeth Cossar.

"Relax, Elizabeth!" Brad yelled. "I need to check on this cranky thing's power pack."

He fought the urge to call Cossar the same. "You're just doing your job, I know, but I need to assess this soldier. He's not gonna survive the blast under his Humvee, get stabilized in our little hospital, then die on me now."

The tension of Cossar's drawn facial muscles swept the fuselage of the jet, but Brad resisted. With the roar of the engines, he was uncertain if she had heard all the argument, but was sure she expected it. She would fill in the blanks. Brad maneuvered around the equipment and storage crates to the navy lieutenant. Despite his best efforts, the fellow would remain paraplegic, and even the long-term care facility at Landstuhl, Germany, might lose him.

"Getting knocked across this bird is not the answer, Major!" Cossar shouted back across the noisy plane. "A concussion or a broken shoulder from this potholed ride won't help this new guy, much less his ventilator, and it sure as hell won't bring back your Corporal Giles."

For the moment, the C-17 was in smooth flight. With steady stomach, Brad reached the sedated navy lieutenant. But Cossar wasn't finished; she never was.

"You did what you could for that corporal—found the ruptured spleen, fixed his kidney, stopped him from bleeding," she said. "He didn't die on the table, Major. Instead, he had a post-op cardiac arrest, and nobody could save him. Of course, you wasted precious time on that national."

Brad remembered his glance toward Amarah as he and Haynes rushed Giles from the ICU to surgery. The Iraqi waved his mutilated hand at them. Brad was certain there was a smile, too.

The plane banked sharply to the left and right and then leveled.

"I said, sit down, Major Cummins! You're really not the hot mess you think you are. Besides, that blonde fiancée of yours back in Mississippi won't jump a bag of bruises."

Brad flashed his own sarcastic smile at Elizabeth's admonishment. "Look, AE Nurse, this guy here doesn't deserve to tank from Uncle Sam's surplus equipment. Let me do my job."

Before the nurse could issue another command, Brad reached the sedated naval lieutenant. The serviceman's oxygen supply was connected properly. Everything was in order, even the ventilator's power connections. This patient was stable.

"Major, you CCATT doctors are all the same," Cossar's loud voice failing to soften with the reduced aircraft noise.

"No, we're not, Cossar," Brad said. "Of the Critical Care Air Transport Team, I'm your favorite doc, and you know it."

"You guys pick the most difficult patient to monitor on these flights, when an air 'vac nurse can do the job, maybe better."

"Yeah, you've said it before. In the air, without the smokescreen of that OR, we docs are on a level playing field with the nurses."

In the middle of her second tour in Iraq, Lieutenant Colonel Elizabeth Cossar had found her niche as an air evacuation nurse. Taking orders from physicians like Brad Cummins while working in trauma triage and in the intensive care unit back at Balad Airbase, she was only killing time until she could fly.

"Nurses, not doctors, are the real muscle of the CCATT," she said.

Cossar watched Brad navigate around the jeep, the small trailer, and other cargo to buckle back in along the sidewall of the jet. As though the pilot had looked out through his cockpit Heads Up Display and decided to play video fighter games, renewed engine thunder reverberated through the rear belly of the C-17. She raised her voice in battle.

"The difference between us AE nurses and docs is that when my shift's over, I'm through. But back at the base you'll be on your feet 'til you drop." Cossar smiled as she turned away. She suspected that Brad was faking deafness. "We'll see how dedicated you are to those patients after you've been on your feet for over 24 hours." She laughed, shaking her head, "Even if you don't have but a few days left with me, Major."

"Let it go, nurse!" Brad yelled in her direction.

" Damn, I almost forgot to order a cake from the cafeteria for the boy's surprise going away," she said under the engine noise. "The Navy sluts over in medical triage and post-op will want to get in on the action, too."

She looked back toward Brad, "Most of them, that is."

3

Each day spent in the American hospital was another day Zarife Amarah felt his skin crawl, unsure if he sensed the healing of his wounds or mounting anger. She came to him the first day of his transfer to the general medical unit, the same older female working where the helicopter first dumped him, where that doctor stood waiting. Staring up from his bed, the Iraqi read the badge: *Cossar, Elizabeth T.* Yes, the name matched the face.

Zarife fought tears during the burn treatments, more like torture than nursing care. Even when changed slowly, the bandages seemed to rip away his body, the pain much worse than that after the surgery to set his broken bones. This *Cossar, Elizabeth T.*, whom some addressed as Lieutenant Colonel, made clear she was only following doctor's orders.

"Your wounds will heal, Mr. Amarah, as long as you do as told. Major Cummins, your doctor from the ICU, left strict nursing instructions," she said. "But now, I am leaving you. I have some American soldiers to tend to."

She tightened the sheets around his bed.

"I want you to feel nice and safe with us, Amarah. You've been through such tragedy."

Zarife remembered her wink.

"Once we've finished with you here, you'll be transferred to a city hospital for long-term rehab. Your own country can pick up that tab."

She lifted his head and fluffed the pillow, then dropped it back in place.

"After I'm gone, you better do as told, Amarah. I know you're tired of all this."

No wink that time, only a penetrating stare. The nurse again checked the sheets covering him. There was no way to tighten them further.

"By the way," she said just before leaving, "Stacy Lane is the enlisted Navy nurse who will take charge until you're transferred. Some of the others will help her out. You'll be in good hands."

* * *

20

The next dozen days in Balad Military Hospital dragged for the Iraqi. Even under the haze of morphine and despite the missing fingers, the sleek feel of his cell phone remained vivid. The second he detonated the roadside bomb, the phone vaporized with much of the left hand, leaving the rest of him behind. He cursed himself for not standing close enough to the street and the line of U.S. military vehicles. But if not for Dr. Cummins, Allah would have been pleased.

Zarife's disdain for Cummins and the American ideals overcame the smelly creams and painful bandage changes. He buried his cries during physical therapy sessions with each bend and stretch to the arms and legs. He presented a good-natured, soft-spoken, and upbeat demeanor, basking in the smiles and encouragement of the nursing staff. The façade, a grateful Iraqi engineering student, tragically caught in the crossfire of war, sometimes even duped himself.

Unlike the austere Elizabeth T., the other nurses and medical volunteers were friendly, some giddy at times, often gossiping about their adored one they called *Major Cummins*. Their jabber about the doctor's engagement and upcoming nuptials represented the epitome of Western decadence for Zarife: the striking blonde waiting for Cummins back home in Jackson, Mississippi, no doubt planning a lavish, alcohol-ridden wedding—an orgy. The Major had even shared pictures with the nurses of his fiancée. Zarife assumed them provocative. The frankness of the female hospital staff in divulging their own sexual attraction to the "hot" Major and doctor only heightened his hatred for American scum.

His plans were justified.

And alone with Allah he stewed, reciting phrases and passages from the Qur'an while paraphrasing others. His message to remain vigilant came in Surah number *8,* The *Spoils of War*, his favorite: "Throw terror into the hearts of the unbelievers … an invisible soldier of God, to be a victor."

Each time Zarife repeated the lines, Allah lifted his cloud of guilt, blessing him with a second chance as long as he stayed true to his heart. Yet there was one condition: Zarife Amarah must choose a different path to paradise, a course that would expunge past failure and reunite him with other martyrs. The Iraqi smiled at the irony of his new mission against the United States of America.

21

He would inflict his own element of terror against the greatest enemy of the Muslim state and at the hand of that enemy itself.

"Ah, there are so many wonderful freedoms that come with your Western ways," he lied to Stacy Lane and the other nurses. "After I complete university and become an engineer, I will assist in rebuilding my country."

Zarife thought about the Turkish Airlines ticket from Bagdad to Atlanta, Georgia. It waited unused at his apartment, compliments of the Traveling Scholars Initiative sponsored by the U.S. government and awarded to bright Iraqi engineering students. He did not mention the prize.

Stacy was not the only one who attended him, but she was unlike the others—withdrawn and detached as she changed his bandages or discussed medication. There was purpose behind every question he asked and a target for each statement, seeing below the surface intense grief mixed with seething anger. He noticed a tear more than once.

Except for my patients, I don't like to be around anyone, at least not anymore," she had said. And unlike the other nurses, she never mentioned Dr. Cummins.

However, Zarife was relentless. He sensed a great asset in Stacy Lane.

"Like your Major Cummins, I might find love and raise a family in a democratic land like yours," he said to her more than once.

"Stop talking about family," Stacy said one afternoon. "I'll never have a family. This war has taken everything from me. It took the guy I wanted to marry."

Like the strike of a snake, she lifted Zarife's gown and plunged a needle into the top of his left buttock.

"And Major Cummins didn't save him," Stacy said.

Her hand shook as she injected the pain medication. "You'll need this before that dressing change. I doubled your dose."

"No, no, I am fine. I do not need ..."

The injection of morphine was quick. It burned.

"There, there. That will help. I noticed how much it hurt last time." She walked away, and then turned to him. "You sure do mumble a lot to yourself, Mr. Amarah. Anyway, I'll be back in a minute to take care of you."

A narcotic haze slowly surrounded him. Zarife saw his former Al-Qaeda officer and instructor, a member of the foreign jihad, as he pulled the young recruit aside during an early training session in the desert. *Zarife, you are a worthy pupil, a fast learner. You are a jewel among the other Nationalists. You will rid our land of many stinking infidels, not only the Americans, but all coalition forces. You will learn our skills, our finer secrets. I will teach you.*

Zarife breathed deeply as he fought sleep.

The next images were the faces of his aunt and cousin, shortly before they were torn apart in a Baghdad vegetable market, torched by a suicide bomber trained by the same Al-Qaeda instructors. By then, the foreign jihad had rethought its agenda and sought to control and impose fear over Iraqi citizens as well. When Zarife's family fell victim to this revised philosophy, the Al-Qaeda lost a prized pupil, and Zarife Amarah became one with Allah.

Once that morphine stupor cleared, Zarife refused care from all American staff except Stacy Lane. He spoke quietly to her, attempting to shield their conversations from others. Later, while immersing himself in silent prayer to his god and begging Allah for a second chance at paradise, his wounds were covered with new, healthy flesh and his bones healed. He cursed the infidels, the Americans, for saving his life after the bomb did not blow him to bits.

When the Traveling Scholars Initiative award had been announced, Zarife had no intention of using it. His path of terror as an insurgent in his native land was laid. However, everything changed when Major Brad Cummins and his people thwarted his plans to enter heaven as a martyr. He would now make Cummins pay for ruining glory in Allah's eyes, and Stacy Lane, RN, would help.

There was a new command, and Allah's doubts must be erased. The Iraqi now sought only one target. He could hear the military doctor's last words, smell his final breath, see his blood spilled. He knew Allah would be pleased.

The TSI had opened a window through which Amarah could strike again.

4

"This is your last day with us, Mr. Amarah. You're being transferred to a city hospital for the rest of your rehabilitation. I've even packed a little go bag for you."

"Where is Stacy?" Zarife asked.

"Nurse Lane grabbed an empty seat on a plane out of here last night," she said. "Stacy was due some R&R back home and left a few days after Major Cummins."

Like Stacy, this nurse was young, but blonde and more talkative, almost annoying. "I hope to be following her back to the States soon."

"But she was to come by this morning. We were supposed to discuss …"

"Discuss what, Mr. Amarah?"

"What is that that you have for me, nurse?" Zarife sat erect on his bed, legs stiffly extended to the floor. He yanked the bag from her hand, nearly spilling the contents.

"I've put together some supplies for you, some sterile dressings and skin tape along with a packet or two of antibiotic ointment," she said, drawing away, "just in case you're delayed getting over to your new hospital today."

He regretted his outburst. "Thank you, nurse. You are kind."

She smiled. "No problem. And if there's a long wait before the new nurses can get to you, you might want to change the bandage on that left hand."

She moved closer and gently patted his shoulder.

"I know you can do it 'cause I've seen you watch Nurse Lane change the dressings. You've watched here really close."

A groaning American serviceman in the next bay grabbed the new nurse's attention. Zarife seized the diversion, raised himself to the supply cabinet on the wall next to his bed, and shoved more gauze and ointment into the package. Just as he stuffed the bag full, a thin older man rolled a wheelchair into the room. Zarife slid back into his bed and pulled the sheets around him.

"OK, fella. I found you this pair of khakis and a shirt that ought to fit. They saved your old shoes. When you're dressed, hop on

24

into my limo."

Every bump or turn brought another jolt of pain, but he rode the corridors in silence to the exit, sitting erect in the wheelchair as though the agonizing ride were another Al-Qaeda training exercise, a reminder of the pain he would soon inflict. The Iraqi foot soldier looked forward to getting out from underneath the nose of the Americans, although the alternative was transfer to his countrymen's hospital where the groping and torture would continue.

They reached the curb outside the hospital. The attendant remained behind the wheelchair. "Sorry, looks like your taxi's not here," he said. "Nurse must've told me wrong. Guess it'll be here in a minute."

"A minute will be all right. I can wait," Zarife Amarah said. He thought again about the plane ticket in his apartment, a way out of Baghdad and to the United States. He would be on the heels of Major Brad Cummins' own departure from the Air Force Theater unit—both tabs gratis of the U.S. government.

*   *   *

"Ignore those transportation instructions, my friend," Zarife told the cab driver in their native tongue. The driver was a poorly shaven Shiite who looked about his age. "The destination has changed. I am sure that the Americans have already paid you well."

The Shiite looked over his shoulder, catching another glimpse of his fare. Then after getting a better look at him in the rearview mirror, he shrugged.

"What are you looking at, driver? Again, I will call you *my friend.* The Americans' money will more than cover where you are to take me now."

The driver stared ahead. "I am not looking at anything, man, except maybe a crazy person? When I was told to take you to City Hospital, my question was *Why would anyone want to go there?*" He laughed. "My brother, you might as well go to an Iraqi prison. Better chance coming out alive."

"Ah, you are much smarter than you look, my friend. But I do not need your opinions. What I do need is quiet."

The cabbie shrugged again. He had been paid. What did he care?

Several blocks later Zarife said, "Turn at that next corner and head toward the west bank of the Tigris. My apartment is in a neighborhood near there. Now do your job, and take me home. I have work to do."

5

The plan changed. Suspicious of being followed, Zarife Amarah stopped the taxi eight blocks from his apartment and walked along the Tigris, darting between buildings and checking over his shoulder every few steps. He carried only the sack of supplies pilfered from the hospital so he moved briskly and unhindered. The strength in his legs surprised him.

That old man was a fool to have me in a wheelchair.

Two blocks from his apartment he spotted a heavy-set man close behind, but the figure stopped at a market and lost interest. A woman who looked American smiled at him at the next corner; he slid into an alley to escape her. Zarife never saw the woman again.

Once inside the stale air of his apartment, he slept for 12 hours and awoke to the disgusting stench of his soiled bandage. Remembering the nurse's instructions, he peeled away the gauze. With even the slightest movement, sparks of pain shot from his wrist to what remained of his left hand. The new, red flesh covering the area was nearly healed, but still exquisitely sensitive. Zarife was surprised that his body still begged for narcotic relief.

"I should have persuaded that new nurse to give me, as they say, 'one or two for the road,'" he said to himself. "If I was American the military doctors would have replaced my fingers with some appliance."

Zarife redressed the wound, applying a thinner dressing, not as taut. The effort left him hungry. A few dusty cans of meat and vegetables were on a shelf in the kitchen. He ate, then packed a suitcase. The travel papers for the flight to Atlanta remained on the table by the door, just where he had dropped them before surprising the American convoy with his bomb. Now he needed the documents. Whatever weapon he used to strike vengeance against America and its military doctor he would obtain in the United States. It was simple to buy guns there, even materials for explosives.

He left the door unlocked and most of the lights on. The landlord would realize soon enough that there was a vacancy. Zarife walked to the bus stop, bought a ticket to the Bagdad airport, and melted into the throng of noisy passengers.

Clearing airport security was uneventful: visa and passport in order, his belongings passing a thorough search—nothing but toothbrush, toothpaste, and simple clothing. An American military officer approached at the departure gate and asked, "Why are you traveling to the U.S.?"

"I am going there to study engineering. Plan to come back and rebuild my country. Once the war is over, demand will be great for new schools, factories, roads, and bridges."

"That sounds good, young man," he said. "We need more of that attitude."

Zarife caught the uniformed man staring at his injured hand and smiled. "Thank you, officer, for all that you Americans are doing for our cause."

"Have a safe trip to Atlanta."

The man walked away. Zarife looked over his shoulder as he presented his ticket. The military officer was talking to another male passenger, another Iraqi.

"Welcome aboard Turkish Airlines Flight 36 to Frankfort, with continuing service to Atlanta, Georgia. Total flight time is ... just under 30 hours." The male flight attendant announced overhead in Arabic and then in English to low groans as Zarife entered the tourist cabin of the airbus, his head low as he moved down the aisle.

Other American military dotted the cabin: reading magazines, talking on cell phones and among themselves; two were already trying to doze. Several rows down, a couple tried to calm their screaming infant. Then he saw the woman in an aisle seat ahead, her face buried in a book. Zarife forced himself forward, holding his ticket to his face while studying the opposite side of the jet. He was certain she had not seen him. Another quick survey of the surrounding rows revealed no one else familiar.

Zarife had nothing to store overhead so he slid into his window seat and managed to fasten the seat beat without hurting his hand. If he stretched his neck and leaned to the left, the Iraqi could just see the top of Elizabeth Cossar's head just two rows up, probably still reading. He could still hear the older military nurse say *After I'm gone, you better do as told, Amarah.*

He decided that there would be no need to pass by her again and hoped that she would exit the plane in Frankfort. If she left her seat for the rear restrooms, he would pretend to sleep. *Maybe she will use the toilet just behind first class. That will be closer for her.*

Zarife grabbed the in-flight magazine from the seat pocket in front of him, flipped it open and hid his face. *She will never know that I am headed to the U.S.*

"Sir, would you care for a blanket? Compliments of Turkish Airlines," the attendant said in Arabic.

"Yes," he answered in the same language, but just above a whisper. "May I have a pillow as well?"

"I'm sorry, but I did not hear you," the attendant said.

"I think he wants one of these pillows to go with that blanket," her crewmate, following behind, said in English, the same attendant who announced the welcome. "Poor guy needs some shut eye. Here you go, sir, but it isn't much." He handed Zarife a small, scratchy-looking pillow. "Hope your hand heals up real quick."

The two moved over to the passengers in the next row as Zarife covered himself with the dark blue blanket and leaned against the window. The grumpy nurse had not left her seat. Zarife wished for one of the sleeping pills she used to give him but soon did not need it.

* * *

The refueling in Germany woke him.

"If you are continuing on to our final destination in Atlanta, you may deplane for the restrooms and snack bars on the concourse," the male attendant announced. "If you do so, please take the *seat-occupied* card from the pocket in front of you and place it on your seat. We will begin re-boarding in 45 minutes. Thank you."

Zarife watched Elizabeth Cossar stand and retrieve a cloth bag from the overhead bin. She was carrying a purse as well. *Good. She is visiting in Frankfurt. I will not have to put up with the bitch all the way across the Atlantic.* She placed the card in her seat. *Shit.*

He folded the blanket and dropped it onto his seat. The dressing on his hand looked fresh enough, but probably could use changing. He remembered the supplies packed in his checked suitcase. *Hand will have to wait, but I need to piss.*

There were already three passengers waiting in line for the

29

restrooms in the tourist cabin. The OCCUPIED sign above one of the two doors was lit. By the time Zarife reached the rear, the line was down to two. The other door still had not opened.

"Sorry, gentlemen, but one of our restrooms is out-of-order."

The same attendant pointed to the sign and then lowered to a whisper, "Don't think it's anything serious. Stopped up, it seems. Mechanics are fixing it from the outside. Should be working by the time we take off."

Walking away toward the service area, the attendant said, "You still have time to deplane for the facilities at the gate."

Zarife stood still, except for glancing back toward the front of the plane. There was some milling about, but no Cossar. The restroom door popped open and closed. A male Arabic voice startled him.

"It's all yours."

Before Zarife could step forward into the restroom, he spotted Cossar in the aisle and threw himself into the nearest seat. He grabbed another copy of the in-flight magazine and spread it across his face.

"Sir, my father is sitting there." The girl was American. He guessed New England. "He went to get something to eat. Didn't you see the card?"

She stared down at his hand and then looked away, embarrassed.

"Miss, I must have made a mistake," Zarife said hurriedly, his accent thick. He saw Cossar return her bag to the overhead compartment and stuff her purse under the seat, then seem busy with buckling the seatbelt.

"No problem, I'll move," he said, this time in flawless English.

Zarife's short naps en route to Atlanta were interrupted by his study of Cossar. The woman accepted offerings of meals and snacks. She read, watched the in-flight videos. There were three trips to the restroom, one to the front facility, the rest at rear. She never saw him. The blanket screened well.

*   *   *

"Welcome to Atlanta. I hope your hand gets better," the attendant said.

Zarife remained one of the few passengers onboard. He nodded, his head down, waiting for Cossar to deplane and clear the arrival

30

gate inside the terminal. The young woman ahead had struggled with repacking her books, magazines, and laptop into a carry-on suitcase and entered the aisle just as he approached. He slowed so to distance himself from her as she pulled the carry-on up the aisle, the wheels bumping the metal seat supports that lined the passageway. The young woman stumbled near the exit, losing her grip on the suitcase. As it fell back toward him, Zarife braced, managing to protect his hand.

"I'm so sorry," she said. The feminine southern drawl was pleasant. It was familiar. The woman turned away from him. She was wearing a baseball cap imprinted with the capital letter *A*, a blonde ponytail swinging from the back, and makeup still heavy despite hours on the airbus. She was the one, the nurse who packed his bag of supplies just before he left the military hospital.

Zarife's first thought was to ignore her, that maybe she would not recognize him, but then he lowered his head and shook *No problem*.

The young woman turned back around, nearly tripping again as she entered the docking terminal. "Sir, weren't you the engineering student I took care of back in Balad, the one that had been talking to Stacy? And didn't we transfer you to Balad City Hospital?"

"Miss, are you OK?" the male attendant asked.

"Yes, sir, I just tripped. I'm such a klutz."

Zarife pushed past into the docking terminal. His objective was to get away from her. But she had recognized him from Balad, and he was supposed to be in the city hospital, not en route to America. The gate was at the end of the docking terminal. Signs directed passengers toward baggage claim and ground transportation. There was an emergency stair to the right. Of the two airport personnel standing near, one was helping an elderly woman with a wheelchair, the other busy on a computer keyboard. Just around the corner from the gate a banner obscured a dimly-lit, abandoned vendor unit. Oversized lettering on the banner announced: *Coming Soon ... Another Taffy Town.*

Zarife walked back to the gate. Alone there, the diminutive young woman still struggled with the rolling suitcase. "Nurse, yes, it is me," he said. "I am your patient."

"Hey, yeah. I thought so," the young nurse said, still puzzled. She reached behind her to steady the roll-on.

31

"But why are you in the U.S? Does Dr. Cummins or maybe Nurse Cossar know?"

"I received an educational grant to study in Atlanta," Zarife said. "*Use it or lose it* I think you people say."

"Congratulations! Good luck with that. But your hand needs more treatment."

"But there was no time. Will you look at my hand? It really hurts." He thrust his left hand forward, the bandage yellowed. "There is a quiet spot over this way." He gestured to the area with the banner.

"Sure, I've got a minute," she said. "No one's meeting me at the airport."

Zarife led her past the roped-off areas and trash receptacles to the front of the future Taffy Town. She continued to grapple with her carry-on, one of the wheels dropping off as she lost the handle grip.

"Does Stacy know about this?" she asked. "I don't understand why you didn't tell us you weren't going to the other hospital."

Before the carry-on toppled to the floor, Zarife grabbed it with his good hand and threw it against her. He pushed both behind the banner, his arm cradling her waist, the mangled hand covering her scream to a whimper. He kicked the suitcase to the side and twisted the nurse's head. The body went limp, her red lip stick streaking his bandage. He felt dampness against his leg, soaking upward into his dark jeans, and knew that her bladder had emptied just as the Al-Qaeda instructor had warned. Zarife lowered the body to the floor and left it beside the carry-on. The next day's construction crew would find everything.

Peeking outside the banner, he found the transporter and wheelchair gone. The only person remaining at the gate was the Turkish Airlines employee still immersed in computer work. He thought about killing her, too, but security cameras would be focused there. She had seen and heard nothing. Zarife left the area for baggage claim and ground transportation.

He needed to get out of the airport before security spotted the body but knew that he could not abandon his suitcase. His fingerprints were all over it, just like on the blonde nurse's neck. Zarife followed the signs and was surprised that the wait at baggage claim was not long.

"Mr. Amarah?" A teenager holding a makeshift white cardboard sign imprinted AMARAH stepped from the crowd near the exit to ground transportation.

As the guy followed, Zarife continued toward the exit with his suitcase.

"Mr. Amarah, I'm here to pick you up. I'm from Georgia Tech. My work study job is transporting bigwig guests like you to the University."

He smiled.

"I don't need anything from you."

"Sure you do. I'm your ground transportation to the dorm. I volunteered. My car is parked out in short term.

"How did you identify me?" Zarife asked.

"You were the only one who looked ..."

"Foreign? Like a terrorist? I said I don't need your help." Zarife spotted the signs to rentals. He would need to present an ID, a driver's license. He needed a map. "Forgive me. I'm very tired. Your name?"

"*Blake*. Name's Blake."

"Blake. My friend. I am so tired. Very long trip. And my hand, it is hurting."

"Man! Gosh, what happened?" Blake asked.

"My country's a mess. This shit happens."

"Sorry about that, man," Blake said. "You might want to check with student health tomorrow."

"Maybe so," Zarife said. "Can you show me where that is?"

"Count on it, man. Need help with that suitcase?"

"No, I've got it." Zarife saw no police, no airport security. No one was following. Time was wasted with this infidel, the kid shorter and of lighter build. Spiked hair made him look even weaker.

"The plane ride was very long, Blake, and I am really tired. Can we go to your car?"

"I better give the school a call first and tell them that you made it, that we're on the way," Blake said.

"But my hand is in such great pain." Zarife raised it to his face. "I need to get to my room now, lie down."

"Sure thing. You're in McDonald Hall. At least that's where administration told me to take you."

Blake led them through the exit to Ground Transportation. The line for a taxi was long, an impatient crowd was lengthening.

"Are you too tired to walk to my car?" Blake asked. "There's a shuttle we can take to short-term parking, if you want."

"My legs are fine. I can make it."

Zarife spotted security cameras at the entrance to hourly parking as he and Blake walked to the teenager's car. They reached the center of the lot where the 1998 Camry was sandwiched between a suburban and a passenger van, the area quiet, not even a plane overhead. Security lighting was ample but there were no security cameras.

"You know, Mr. Amarah, it's amazing," Blake said. "You speak pretty good English."

"That's what everybody says, and it's OK to call me Zarife."

Blake walked to the driver's door, pulling keys from his jeans pocket. Zarife lagged behind, near the rear of the vehicle. "Zarife, I'll unlock the door for you. Come on around."

"Aughh… my stomach."

Blake ran to Zarife, who was cradling his mid-section with the good arm and bending. "Hey, you didn't say anything about your stomach."

Zarife tore the keys from the teenager and pushed him to the pavement behind the Camry.

"Hey, man, what's this shit?" Blake looked up.

Zarife popped open the trunk. He grabbed the lug wrench inside and plunged the sharp end into Blake's left eye. The eye exploded. Yanking the wrench free, he swung the end with the metal socket into the boy's face, crushing the forehead, then lifted the lug wrench and swung again at the throat and lower face. There was a gurgling sound. He threw the body into the trunk, leaving bloody handprints on the hood.

Zarife surveyed the parking lot—quiet, still no one around. A crumpled newspaper topping a nearby trash receptacle served to wipe the hood and his hands clean. But there was still the problem of the blood splattered on the asphalt. The more he stared, the more it seemed to blend into the black surface. He searched the trash, finding a couple of fast-food sacks, empty except for a wad of napkins that he used to mop most of the remaining blood. Zarife then reopened the trunk and tossed in the bloody newspaper and

McDonald's bags, but not before removing Blake's wallet from the back jeans pocket. The $46 would help the $200 sent by Georgia Tech for travel emergencies and incidentals.

Zarife placed his suitcase on the backseat and headed toward the exit.

"I need your parking time card."

"Here, take it." Zarife found the parking receipt in Blake's wallet and handed it to the attendant at the exit. He wondered if the attendant might have seen Blake in the Camry earlier.

"That'll be eight dollars."

Amarah slid a ten from the wallet. "Keep the change."

"Thanks, sir, and you have a nice night."

The gate lifted.

"No." Amarah did not budge. His MapQuest instructions were packed in the luggage. "First, I need directions to Interstate 20."

"Sure. Out of here turn right and follow the access road to Airport Boulevard, then the signs to the interstate. That'll be I-85 to 20. Here's a little map. It's kinda sketchy."

"I'll take that."

"Hey, where ya from?"

Ignoring him, Zarife checked the rearview mirror. There were several cars in line behind. No white suburban, no passenger van, no police. He considered pleasing Allah with another explosion, maybe near the Atlanta airport, but somehow that method of death no longer seemed satisfying. And Allah had not asked for it.

Zarife pulled onto the access road. He imagined the eyes of the American doctor, the major, seven hours away in Jackson, Mississippi—fear replacing disdain for the Iraqi people. Once the doctor was dead, Allah would no longer see Zarife Amarah as a failure.

Obtaining a gun would be the next objective, then locating Stacy Lane. But first he needed to stop somewhere along the way and empty the trunk.

6

The volunteer collected his last ticket at the entrance gate. The bulk of the crowd had already passed through as fatigue overcame the grandfather of Chad Giles. Nevertheless, he decided to remain for the rest of the Blue Angels air show. He missed his days as a navy pilot. Walking the tarmac on the outskirts of Memphis, wearing a University of Tennessee baseball cap, Chadwick Giles was certain this was to be his final show, the decision reached even before he recognized Brad Cummins.

The last surviving Giles pushed down the peak of his cap to shield his eyes, fighting tears as he relived the government's explanation of his grandson's death: *Lance Corporal Chadwick Giles III survived a roadside bomb blast set by insurgents but later died at Balad Air Base Hospital of surgical complications.* Military officials assured him that everything possible had been done to save Chad. The attending surgeon was the best, a Major Brad Cummins.

He had googled an Internet post of a newly-ranked Major Brad Cummins, pictured with other military officers at an Air Force ceremony before his tour in Iraq, their kudos for Cummins screaming from the computer screen. The image of the major was tagged with a brief bio of the handsome recipient, including his plans to settle in Mississippi. Giles could not argue that under different circumstances, he would have shared in the admiration.

As the Canadian Force's Snowbirds entertained overhead, Grandfather Giles hid behind a group of spectators and watched Cummins and the pretty girl enjoy life: relaxing on a blanket spread out in the green space, downing hot dogs and beer, the major throwing a Frisbee for their black lab to retrieve between fly-overs. Several weeks before his death, his grandson wrote of meeting someone in Iraq, a nurse, whom he planned to bring home once they lined up concurrent furloughs. Giles wondered if Chad's new girlfriend had been as pretty as the one with Major Cummins.

Suddenly more planes joined the star team Diamond Formation, transforming into the six-jet Deltas. The major's girlfriend joined in the applause of the crowd, her face beaming in the late afternoon sun. Cummins moved even closer to her, embracing her.

Realizing he had stepped out of his camouflage, Giles slid back into the group of people standing not far from Cummins and the girl. He was certain that as they fondled each other the beautiful couple never noticed his stares. They would still have no reason to recognize his face, nor guess his name.

It would be easy to follow them. All Giles had to do was wait.

7

Leslie reached back between the seats and stroked the lab's sleeping head. The dog did not move. "Brad, you sort of blew me off yesterday at the air show," she said, still looking at Bullet in the backseat.

Brad had driven onto the entrance ramp to Interstate 55 South, the gasoline gauge to his SUV now reading *Full*.

"What are you talking about?"He merged into the thick and unforgiving traffic coming out of Memphis as pine and hardwood trees flew by.

"You ignored me when I asked you about Iraq. You haven't mentioned it since you've been back."

She continued to pet the dog; he was too exhausted from the trip to look up.

The three had spent the night in a private suites hotel on the outskirts of Memphis, one with a first-floor vacancy and drive-up access. Brad had smuggled Bullet inside, where the dog remained quiet as commanded, lounging on one of the queen-sized beds while Brad and Leslie had sex in the other. A slip with his master into a patch of woods between the hotel and the interstate accomplished two bathroom breaks. Brad left no spilled dog food or black hairs as evidence for housekeeping.

"You realize that it was hard being away from you for that long—physically away from you," Leslie said. "It would have helped it I could have called you more."

"Personal cell phones were contraband," he said.

Brad thought back to the day he left Iraq, when he was given access to his cell phone and first read the anonymous text: *I will give you a little wiggle room.* There had been several since, the most recent that morning, and all from a number that he did not recognize.

"I tried to email you as much as I could," Brad said, "hoping to keep up with all this wedding stuff—praying you wouldn't totally bankrupt me over it."

"I'll ignore that," she said, rolling her eyes. "In all fairness to you and President Bush, I did feel like I had my thumb on you while you were over there, even with the government's censors."

He watched her. She was rubbing Bullet's ears. Leslie was difficult to read sometimes, but he loved her. She was gorgeous.

"Les, while I was in Iraq, I told you everything you needed to know—that I missed you and that I had made it one more day."

Brad looked out his window. A driver on the northbound side was victim to the highway patrol and a pad of speeding tickets. Instead of braking, he released the accelerator to slow to the speed limit. There was no reason to argue about the physical stress of their separation. They had more than made up for lost time.

"I just threw myself into my new shop while you were gone," she said. "I know a downtown stationery and book store was a gamble, but after all you agreed to it ... said I needed to be busy while you were in Iraq and stay busy after we married."

Leslie stroked Bullet's head again. "Not only will I be the wife of an important doctor, I'm saddled with competing with the military, too."

The dog looked up, as though bothered, then eyed Brad before resuming the snooze.

"I'm sure you don't even remember looking at the print design, but you should be happy that all of our wedding invitations will be wholesale through my shop."

"You emailed it over to me right before you sent the wedding cake photos. Everything looks nice, really fancy. And I hope the wedding cake is edible for what that caterer is charging me ... us." Brad had inched back up to 78. There was no highway patrol car in sight.

"It's Irish crème, my favorite," she said. "And the invitations are Crane, engraved. And you can't appreciate that in an email."

The silence that followed was broken by Bullet's snoring, the surface of Interstate 55 flying beneath them. Brad wished the distance between Memphis and Jackson was shorter.

Leslie spoke. "You've done nothing but avoid serious conversations with me since you got back."

She crossed her arms.

Brad fought the urge to depress the accelerator as his pulse quickened. Having escaped a speeding ticket for over three years, he had finally earned a lower car insurance premium.

"That's not true," he said.

"You know what's funny, Brad? From your emails, I knew more about what was in your head than I do now."

"Leslie, that's ridiculous."

"But I guess if your deployment had been after the wedding, then things would have been a whole lot worse for me."

Leslie returned her attention to the dog. Bullet lifted one ear before deciding to ignore her.

"I guess this fellow will get his own bed in our house," she said. "Bullet seemed to like all that stretching-out room back at the Marriott. It's a wonder we didn't get thrown out!"

As they passed the 80-mile marker to Jackson, Brad hoped for a change of subject: no more wedding plans, no criticism of his behavior, no probing into his time overseas. They were approaching the next interstate exit, and he planned to feign need for a bathroom break if necessary, but for now he would just sit and take it.

"I guess guys just love their dogs," Leslie went on. "Last week while Caroline and I were unpacking some new book releases, she told me that her husband's lab sleeps between the two of them. Maybe I should have a talk with my matron-of-honor. She should have gotten some things ironed-out in the pre-nup."

Brad let the Vaiden exit and a pit stop pass by and reached behind for the dog. "Might be a good idea, but odds are that Caroline can take care of herself. As for my boy, here, I believe he knows his place in our relationship."

As though tired of being disturbed, Bullet jumped for the rear seat.

"Maybe so," Leslie said, "but he sure missed you while you were gone—though Brian and I took turns with dog sitting. Your brother is better at dog-stuff than I am."

"Bro's always been good with dogs. There was this golden retriever he got when we were growing up. The dog died of kidney failure right before Brian entered med school. Really tore him up."

Brad reached again for his own dog and then remembered Bullet was in the back of the vehicle.

"Broke me up, too. Same for Mom and Dad."

"I guess I can play along and talk instead about my pets, too… like when I was in elementary school and our cat ate my goldfish. But I'm not going to fall for that, Brad."

40

Leslie grabbed her purse and removed the wedding planner bound in white suede with gold monogramming of her future nitials, *LCC*. She tossed the bag back to the floor and glanced at the roadside. Several deer grazed at the tree line.

"We've got at least an hour before we get home. Plenty of time to iron out some stuff about the wedding—like maybe coming up with your list of groomsmen."

"OK, then. Number one ..."

"But I still want a full rundown about your time in Iraq. Like, did you get sick on the way back in the C-17 like you did on the way over? See any interesting stuff? Who'd you work with ... you know?" Leslie flipped through the pages of the white notebook.

Brad twisted his neck from side-to-side, stretching it, and took a deep breath, unsure if he could stomach another hour. "That time is not something I want to discuss, Leslie. I went over there and did what I was sent to do and came back. That's it. You ought to be satisfied that I came back in one piece."

"It's that Giles guy, isn't it?" she asked.

"Of course not," he said.

Hard silence followed, with only the sound of wheels grinding over the edge of the shoulder, raised bumps designed to keep drivers on the road. Brad pulled the vehicle back in line.

"Anyway, what are you talking about?"

"You didn't think I knew anything about that, did you?" she answered, bracing herself against the dashboard and with the hand loop mounted on the ceiling.

"Why would you know anything about the servicemen or women over there, unless they were from Jackson?"

"For gosh sake, Brad. We're getting married in a few months. I'm practically already your wife. Men tell their wives stuff, particularly if they're messed up about it."

"Come on, Leslie. Cut the crap. What do you mean 'what happened to Giles'?"

Before Brad were flashes of the yelling episode with Haynes, the Marine's internal hemorrhage and the subsequent surgery, the failed resuscitation afterwards, the grueling medical inquest that followed.

She answered with a long, deep breath and arms more tightly wrapped around her chest. "Keep your eyes on the road," she said,

41

staring at the pavement.

For a few moments there was only the droning of the wheels. Both thought they heard Bullet snoring.

For Brad, the scuttlebutt around the military base remained fresh. *Cummins waited too long to decide to operate on that kid ... Too bad that Colonel Haynes wasn't there from the beginning ... The Major was wasting his time on that Iraqi local and let one of our own bleed to death ... What was he thinking?*

Leslie said, "I guess you could say I sort of found out by accident, so I'm not letting you off the hook. Whatever happened with that patient, that Giles guy, can't be all that top secret."

"What do you mean you found out by accident? Something on the Internet?" He stared across at her, his knuckles blanching against the steering wheel. "I don't think so."

"I found out Friday afternoon right before leaving the shop to go home to pack. A woman came in, said she was a nurse from Atlanta, home on furlough from Iraq and driving through Jackson to visit a relative."

"Elizabeth Cossar?"

Brad remembered something about her living in Atlanta.

"She recognized my name from the business cards at the register, and then seemed to recognize my face. The woman looked mid-fifties. Said she served with you over there, and she knew that we were engaged."

Brad forced a smile. "Cossar was the head nurse in the Air Force Theatre Hospital. We worked together pretty closely. I showed her your picture a couple of times, so she'd know the competition."

Leslie shook her head. "You're trying to make light of this."

Brad shook his head. "Ok, then. What did Cossar tell you, Leslie?"

His fingers dug deeper into the leather of the steering wheel. Leslie remained fixed, staring through the windshield.

"She asked me how you were doing, had you gotten over the death of ... that corporal, lance corporal, somebody named Chad Giles, so I asked what she was talking about.Then the woman, this nurse, said you were pretty torn up over losing that guy. That there had been an investigation, an inquest, and that some officers— maybe they weren't officers—just people, military people—

claimed that you cared more about some Iraqi in the hospital than you did the American who died."

"Dammit, Leslie, you know me better than that."

Brad raised his hand and pounded the steering wheel. The SUV swerved onto the shoulder. Leslie screamed and Bullet started barking, jumping back to the second seat. Brad eased the car back onto the pavement, losing little speed. Traffic was light, the dark gray pickup truck behind them barely slowing.

"Good God, Brad! What the hell's wrong with you?"

Leslie groped again for the loop above the passenger door, bracing herself against the dashboard with her left hand.

Brad forced a deep breath.

"Your tone, your questions … make me feel like I'm back at the medical inquest. You seem to be taking the side of the quick-to-judge."

He looked into the rearview mirror. No blue lights. Nothing but the gray pickup.

"I'm sure you did nothing wrong over there—that you did everything right as a doctor. Totally right, in fact. Of course. But please, please don't kill us on the way home. Keep this freaking thing on the road."

Bullet sat back down and resumed his snooze. Several miles passed. Brad relaxed his grip on the wheel.

"I've thought about that soldier nearly every day since I came back," Brad said. "I promise you that I did everything for Giles and when I was supposed to do it. It's just that when the kid crashed, I was doing the preliminary on a local brought in at the same time by our medevac team. The Iraqi looked to be in pretty bad shape, but policy is to treat all patients the same."

"I'm sure that it is."

Leslie relaxed her grip and let out a deep breath, then reached again for the day planner.

"But this Cossar woman said that when she got back from getting some piece of medical equipment for you—a sonogram machine, I think—the American's condition had gone down the tubes, and that you weren't even watching him."

"I can't believe she would say that kind of …"

"*Down the tubes* is not exactly how she put it, but that's what she meant."

Brad watched the road as they neared Jackson, keeping it at 70. He missed the pick-up pulling up beside him for a few seconds as though to pass, but instead falling back into traffic. He thought of nothing but that dismal morning in Iraq. Cossar's detailed testimony before the Mortuary Affairs Team had cleared Major Brad Cummins of medical negligence in the death of Lance Corporal Chad Giles, and Brad had loved her for it.

"Are you sure that's what that nurse said? She and I are … were … friends."

Leslie opened the book to the section labeled *G*.

"Change of subject. I shouldn't have told you what that woman said. Let's nail down some of the wedding details, like your groomsmen. Need six. I'll write them down and turn in the names to the tux shop tomorrow."

No one came to mind except his twin brother Brian as best man. Brad managed a smile and a wink.

"Les, let's talk about a bunch of hard-legs later. For now, why don't we skip to the honeymoon?"

"Whatever. *Honeymoon* it is." Leslie flipped to the *H* section. "The travel agent called last week and asked if you had looked over the brochures she left for you in the doctors' lounge."

"I think I may have found one on the Internet that I like better. That resort in the Caymans is overrated. Maybe we should talk to her again or maybe look around for someone else to book the trip."

"Fine, I'll leave that up to you." She shut the notebook. "It's going to be tough enough for me to deal with flowers, bartenders, and my bridesmaids as well as your procrastination. I think we should hire an event planner, a professional wedding planner."

They passed through Madison and then Ridgeland as Jackson approached. The lighting above the string of automobile dealerships along Interstate 55 North masked nightfall. Brad had missed his headlights flip on. He was exhausted.

"Let's talk about this some more before you haul off and hire somebody like that. That just means more money."

"OK, then. Let's talk."

"Whatever," he said.

"Caroline told me about this guy from Montclair named Minor Leblanc," Leslie said as she slid the book back into her purse. "He's really good. He can help us with the pictures, the food, the clothes, the ceremony ... all the details."

"What a surprise," Brad said. "There must be hundreds of people in that service venue, a dime a dozen."

"No, I think this guy's different," she said. "Caroline says he networks with all these people who can do the flowers and the food, too. Just like what you see in New York or California."

"What's the guy's name?"

"I told you it's *Minor Leblanc*." Leslie crossed her arms. "You're not listening to me, Brad. It's like you aren't even interested in getting married."

"Come on, Les. Do we have to go through this again? You know I'm interested, real interested."

Brad put his right hand on her thigh and inched it upward.

She pushed away. "I've decided there'll be no more of that for awhile ..." Her voice trailed off as she looked out the window.

"Leslie, what's the deal? We're in love and can't live without each other. So let's make it simple and just get married."

She didn't move. There was no answer.

"Look, I really do have a lot on my mind," Brad said. "Brian's been fussing about how much money the practice lost while I was in Iraq. Plus I've been worrying about that guy who died, and then you throw it in my face."

Brad stopped himself from slamming the steering wheel a second time.

"Your damn story about the nurse and her surprise visit and then all of your questions about Giles and his death ..."

"Believe me. I wouldn't have told you if I had known how mad you would get."

Brad shook his head. "Since I've been home from Iraq, I've done everything to forget . . . tried to plan some fun stuff for us to do, like taking Bullet to that air show."

"I could think of some other 'fun' things." Leslie reached back to stroke Bullet's head. "Maybe leave this fella at home next time."

The SUV passed under a street light as the dog lifted his face, parted his lips, and seemed to smile. He kept his eyes closed.

"I like to forget unpleasant things," Brad said. "Working helps with that, too"

He reached again toward Leslie. When she didn't respond, he hesitated for a few seconds before lifting the turn signal.

"But when I'm really alone with you, I don't think about anything else. Then I'm OK," Brad said.

He turned onto Lakeland Drive, heading east.

"So if a big wedding with this Leblanc guy is on go, then we'd better stop by the clinic instead of going straight home. I need to check my patient list for this week, for the next several months. It better be full, really full."

Leslie smiled as they passed the Mississippi Agricultural Museum and the old Smith-Wills Stadium on the left. Five-o'clock traffic had long cleared. "Glad you're finally on board, Brad. I'll call Leblanc tomorrow and schedule a fitting for my wedding dress."

"Let's still be practical about this thing, Les. Maybe come up with a budget for this gala that we can stick to?"

"Your brother got into medical school and surgery residency before you did," she said. "He built a gorgeous, four-story building for y'all to practice in. The place has got to be a cash cow."

The new building boasted in-house surgical suites with private anesthesia staff, a state-of-the-art medical record system for 2006, and covered parking for physicians and employees. Leslie grabbed her purse from the floorboard and rummaged through the contents.

"As long as you and your brother keep churning it, and you stay in town to work in that palace, I'm sure you can afford the wedding that I . . . that we . . . want. And if Brian's giving you your share of the profits, then why so much worry about expense?"

"A human being can only work so hard, do so much . . . even a doctor, Leslie."

Leslie pulled out her lipstick and stroked it first across the upper lip and then the lower. Brad watched her work the color in.

"From day one, the deal has been everything down the middle, 50–50, even the profit on Diana's work."

Brad remembered his last paycheck, same number of zeros, but down somewhat from the pre-Iraq deployment figure. He had not questioned the amount. He thought again about the slow-down of the practice while he was away.

"If I were you, I'd keep an eye on Brian and the books," Leslie said without looking toward her fiancé. "And I'm going to keep my eye on that Diana Bratton. No woman doctor working with you should look that great."

8

Dr. Bratton strolled up to the receptionist behind the ornate counter and looked up from the chart of her last patient. The day had been long.

"Well, which bad boy won this month?" she asked.

"I can barely keep my britches on! Looks like it's Dr. Brian."

The middle-aged woman pulled the last ballot from the *Dr. Cummins-of-the Month* ballot box, a cardboard receptacle kept stashed under the ledge. The head laboratory technician would soon be twenty dollars richer.

"I'm sure both dudes are sweating it out," Diana said. "But since the guys are identical twins, don't you think the contest is sort of silly?"

"That didn't keep you from betting this month. Did it, Dr. Bratton?"

"I guess you caught me on that one," Diana answered. "Another buck, another lost bet."

"Maybe you'll come out on top next month. By the way, I can stay late any time and lock things up, even after dark. Besides, I'm due some overtime."

"Overtime pay. That's an idea, but I'm just a hired hand to those Cummins boys and always the last one to finish-up."

"Overtime or not," the receptionist laughed, swinging her sweater around her shoulders, "they don't pay me like they do you."

"You'd be surprised," Diana said. "My daughter and I are on a pretty-tight budget."

"Doctors …," the receptionist said, "always singing the blues."

"Don't get me wrong," Diana said. "I'm grateful to have a job. Fixed salary for now will have to do, along with an iron-clad contract. That's what brother Brian wanted."

She walked away from the reception area through the lobby to secure the front door.

"Maybe she's just sore that we don't have a beauty contest for female doctors around this swanky place," the receptionist mumbled. "But then she'd win every time."

She dumped the ballots into the trash receptacle under the desk and removed her purse from the drawer. "Wait a sec, Dr. Bratton. I leave out the front."

The contest would start again next month, the box ready for a poll of clinic patients, pharmaceutical reps, janitorial staff, and new secretarial hires, as well as anyone else interested. Then would come the betting on the winner.

Diana stopped at the water cooler and placed a Styrofoam cup under the dispenser. She smiled at the thought of the ridiculous monthly pool and her lost one-dollar wager, the contest certainly a novelty, and just one more example of her learning to tolerate the attention commanded by the handsome, athletic Cummins brothers. As the most recent physician to join the three-person group, she expected the hotty-of-the-month pot to become history with the announcement of Brad's engagement. However, the contest lived on.

And it was Brad's love life that had landed her this additional night on call. *I'm such a push-over*, she thought, after agreeing to sub for his long weekend get-away. His plans with the girlfriend were to head up to Memphis, or maybe it was down to New Orleans—she could not remember which.

I need to hear more of the secretaries' gossip she decided.

In Brad Cummins' absence her workload always doubled. Today her lunch break and two hours of afternoon clinic had been cancelled by an emergency appendectomy and removal of a stone-filled gallbladder. One man's trip to the intensive care unit meant further delays. When Diana was finally able to return to soothe the ruffled feathers of her own waiting patients, she hurried through the clinic appointments without appearing rushed. She finished up about eight-thirty after helping an elderly couple to their car.

She and her daughter had needed the job, needed the money. Besides, a position at the new Surgical Center of the South with Brian and Brad Cummins sounded prestigious, even though it was her first offer.

Maybe I should take Haynes up on his deal she thought. "See you tomorrow," Diana said to the receptionist as she locked the front door behind her.

Diana then walked toward the rear of the building, back through the large, now empty waiting room framed with dual fireplaces and custom wallpaper. The cocktail-party music no longer squeezed through hidden speakers. There was no clicking or buzzing of fax machines or printers. No phones ringing. No appointments being scheduled. No more buzz of employee gossip. Brian had long finished his clinic patients. Everyone had left, and the nightly janitorial staff was not to arrive until much later.

Diana rounded the corner to her office, the door kept unlocked so that secretaries could drop off mail and nurses seat patients for private consultations. Her desk and credenza were hidden by unsigned stacks of patient charts waiting for her review. In the top desk drawer were her laptop and the study session files. The general surgery recertification test was in two months.

But exhaustion trumped the memorization of research articles and practice exams. She still had the two months. Besides, Kelsey would want a bedtime story, a long one.

Diana felt for keys and cell phone in the lower right pocket of her white lab coat and unlocked the bottom desk drawer for her purse. She checked for texts. The college-aged babysitter usually complained when Diana was late getting home, and the message was never happy. There was one unread text.

"Good gosh! I hope this time she isn't quitting and didn't just leave Kelsey there by herself," Diana shook her head and followed the prompt on the screen to bring up the message. To her surprise, it was not from the babysitter.

Diana stared at her cell phone. Haynes' text was only a few minutes old. She wished her number was not listed in the hospital physician directory.

Saw you had rough day at hospital. Boys not paying u enough?

John Haynes had called last week, but she declined the lunch invitation to talk about her future, something she envisioned as no better with his clinic than with the Cummins boys. Then the next morning he tracked her down in the hospital corridor.

"Still too busy to have lunch with me?" he had said. "We could just run up to Primos."

"Dr. Haynes, my patient schedule is just too packed. I catch up with my paperwork at lunch. Sorry."

"Stop the B.S., Bratton," he said as the two surgeons maneuvered through the hall. "We've got a better spot for you. Hell, you'll make twice as much with us." He spoke almost loud

49

enough for a passing nurse and a several patients to hear.

"Sorry, Dr. Haynes. I need to stop by the lab and check on some test results for my next case." She ducked into the side entrance of the laboratory. He followed.

"We were glad when Brian left our group to go out on his own, and we would never have hired his little brother," he said as Diana stopped at the first computer screen.

She scrolled through several pages of results, pretending to study values of sodium, potassium, and other electrolytes. Diana reached for the note pad beside the monitor. The busy lab tech looked annoyed, picked up a tray of blood specimens near Diana, and moved out of the way.

"My practice has wanted to take in a female surgeon for some time, and I think you would be a good fit."

Diana felt for a pen in her top pocket. Haynes handed her one from his scrub shirt. She took it, scribbled on the note pad, and stuffed the unneeded information in the front pocket of her white coat. She hurried back into the hall. She could think of no other diversion.

She looked behind as he followed, his long legs easily overtaking her. She guessed Haynes to be in his early forties. His broad shoulders, firm posture, and classic facial features were topped with wavy, dark hair (that, if colored, Diana wanted the name of his stylist).

"Brad and Brian don't keep current with their surgical skills," he said. "I've seen them both in action, particularly Brad."

The few dignified wrinkles across Haynes' forehead and at the corners of his mouth seemed to deepen. They had reached the entrance to the surgical suite. "Dr. Haynes, I'm ..."

"*John*," he said.

"*John*, then." Diana said. "Look, I'm nicely situated where I am. Besides, you and your partners really couldn't afford me or the legal fees it would take to break my contract with those Cummins boys."

"I've just worked with Brad, Diana. Our tours in Iraq overlapped. You'd be better off with me," he said. "You think about it."

Several missed calls from John Haynes followed during the ensuing days, and then a reprieve. Then there were the glances exchanged earlier that afternoon in the ER. Texting was now his method. *Maybe I do need to check out what Haynes has to offer* she thought.

No, maybe I need to get a new cell number instead she decided, closing her office door and walking down the hall toward the rear exit. Fatigue overcame her desire to burn a few calories so she abandoned the stairs to the underground garage for the physicians' rear elevator.

Diana felt the still air and the lingering mugginess of a Mississippi fall creep into the building as she turned the corner to the elevator. The energy-savings timer had cut the air conditioning and overhead lighting to after-hours level, but still tolerable for the housekeeping crew. A yellow light from the elevator controls emanated through the surrounding dimness, reflecting from the polished brass plate around the buttons. Diana pushed the down arrow to no response. She depressed the control again, again no response.

Diana glanced around. She was alone—too early for house-keeping.

"Hey, anybody else trying to use this thing?"

The chill she felt from the dead silence surprised her. Her thirteen years of night-time work through college, medical school, and surgical residency had long-since erased the fear of being alone.

Diana called out again. No answer. She flattened her hand against the down control and tried to pry open the elevator doors. Her next thought was to kick the elevator, but aching feet nixed the idea.

"For what this Taj Mahal had to cost, you'd think the architect would have put in a fucking decent elevator," she said, again hitting the frozen elevator control before rechecking her cell phone. No other text, no missed call from an angry sitter. "I guess this time she's writing a resignation letter."

She dropped the phone back into her pocket and turned in the direction of the rear stairwell.

"At least somebody could have reported this piece of crap broken."

Diana's growing anger over her late day was directed more at herself than anyone else. She took this job. She was working too

51

hard. Something had to change. Suddenly, adrenaline overpowered the day's fatigue, and she rushed for the corridor to the stairs on the opposite side of the building.

From the large windows lining the passageway, Diana spotted a car turning into the physicians' parking garage. It was Brad's. "Pretty Boy, back home from his long weekend." She threw open the door leading to the stairs, the after-hours lighting barely illuminating the steps. Her footsteps echoed behind as she hurried down the stairs.

"Well, if you and the chosen one are planning to take the elevator up to your office, P.B.," Diana said as she neared the second floor, "you'll be out o' luck."

9

The patient parking area of the Surgical Center of the South was bare except for several empty fast-food bags scattered on the asphalt and a used diaper tossed in a corner near the entrance. The trash radiated under the fluorescent lights pouring from story-high metal poles. Brad whirled his SUV into the parking lot, flattening the diaper. He pulled up to the underground garage entrance and reached across to the glove compartment for his ID badge. He thought about trying Leslie's thigh again. He found the thin plastic card atop a package of Kleenex and an extra cell phone charger. The badge slid smoothly through the entrance terminal, lighting the four-inch display with *Brian Cummins, MD*.

"That's funny," Brad said, waiting for the barrier gate to the underground parking to lift. "I guess Brian and I must have switched badges by mistake in the lounge."

"I think that darker shade would be better," Leslie said, digging deeper into her purse for another tube of lipstick. "And where the hell is my phone? Found it." She flipped open the case to a dark screen and pressed the power control several times. "Damn. Battery's dead."

"I was in a hurry, changing out of my scrubs after a short case," Brad said. "Must've grabbed his badge instead of mine. I was late to pick you up."

"Hurry, Brad. The thing's going to close and hit us."

Brad released the brake and the vehicle descended the ramp into the garage. The gate barely cleared the rear bumper.

"Brian had been on call. He probably never noticed the switch."

"I need to run up to your office and use the phone to call Minor Leblanc," Leslie said. "Caroline says he books up really fast."

Brad shook his head. "Sure, Leslie, go ahead. Whatever."

"Anyway, I need the ladies' room."

Brad pulled into his parking space and tossed Brian's ID badge back into the glove compartment. He watched while Leslie changed her lipstick, admiring herself in the vanity light and mirror of the windshield visor. No matter what the shade, and even with bare lips, she was magnificent.

"Aren't you wasting your time?" he asked. "There's nobody up there to fix up for, not even a janitor. Housekeeping doesn't come in till around ten."

"I'm going to be Mrs. Dr. Brad Cummins in a few months. A lot is expected of me." She winked.

Brad leaned back against the car door and watched her apply fresh mascara and have second thoughts about the hair, then tie it back after a brush through.

"I'll be right up behind you," he said. "But first, Bullet needs a potty break." He reached for the dog's leash.

"Boy, let's walk up the ramp to those flowerbeds. Hope your uncle's not anywhere around to see you take a dump in this overdone landscaping."

The young oak trees, magnolias, and azaleas had survived the blistering summer, but the blooming annuals had not. There would be little left for Bullet to damage.

Leslie dropped the two lipsticks, mascara, and hair brush into her purse and popped open the door. She stepped out of the SUV and walked toward the elevator.

"Won't I need your key or badge or something to get in?" she asked before disappearing around the corner.

Bullet jumped out of the rear seat and pulled against the leash. Brad fought hard.

"Wait a sec, Les. Let me give you the key before you go up."

Leslie screamed and Bullet bolted toward her. The handle to the leash flew from Brad's hand, nearly striking the dog in the rear, the animal's high-pitched growl drowned by Leslie's shrieking.

"God, Leslie, what the fuck's wrong?"

Brad found her outside the elevator shaft, the doors blocked open by a man's legs. The right leg was bent unnaturally at the knee and overlapped the left. Brad looked inside the small elevator. His brother's head was thrown back against the rear wall, green eyes fixed blankly on him.

"I was still trying to get my phone to work and stumbled over him," Leslie cried. "He didn't move when I stepped on his leg."

Bullet jumped back and forth over Brian Cummins, wanting to lick his face but somehow knowing that he should not. Brad retrieved the leash and struggled against the animal's force. The handle again flew from his hand, ricocheting against the walls of the elevator. Brad managed to retrieve it and wrestled Bullet from the elevator.

"Leslie, Call *911*," he yelled, tying his dog to a pillar supporting the building. Above Bullet's yelps, he again yelled, "Call *911*."

"I told you my cell phone's dead!" Leslie said.

Brad reached into the pocket of his pants and tossed her his cell. He then cupped both hands against the inside edge of the elevator doors, braced his legs against the pavement, and pushed against them until the doors gave way.

"Brian, come on man!"

Brian's face and eyes remained frozen, lifeless. Brad knelt to the mouth and nose and listened: no breathing. He supported his brother's head and neck with his left hand as he worked the torso and legs flat with the right. He felt the left side of the neck and then the right: no carotid pulse, nothing. The only movement was his own trembling fingers.

The Cummins family was gone. All that he had left was Leslie.

"Oh, God, Brad! What happened here?" she screamed again. "Do something, CPR, or something!"

"Shit, Leslie. You're making this worse."

Brad started pumping Brian's chest, counting the compressions. Sweat dripped from his face onto his brother's body. He stopped CPR to recheck for a carotid pulse. Still nothing.

Leslie repeated the clinic address to the *911* operator and then screamed, "Oh, my God, Brad! Look at your hands!" She pointed and screamed even louder.

Shrill barking answered.

Brad stared at his hands. Dark red blood traced the lines of his palms. He ripped open his brother's white coat and spotted the *Brad Cummins, MD* identification badge clipped askew to the lapel. Just as the coat, the scrub suit top was clean – no blood except for that left by his chest compressions. He felt foolish for not having done a more thorough physical exam and checked his brother's face, his head. He pushed away the thick dark hair covering Brian's forehead. Blood oozed from a neat hole above the right eye, pooling underneath the body.

*   *   *

Diana ran from the stairs toward her car, thinking of the babysitter, her soon-to-quit babysitter. She pushed the remote and the interior lights brightened just as she heard screams from the other end of the garage. She ran to the noise.

"Hey, what's wrong? What's wrong over here?" Diana called again, pushing past Leslie and her cell phone. Her eyes met Brad's. "Brad?"

"It's Brian," he answered.

"Let me help."

"It's no use, Diana. He's dead."

An ambulance siren burst in the distance.

"It think it was supposed to be me," Brad cried, and sank into the corner of the elevator car, his hands covering his face, his brother's blood streaking his cheeks, his brother lying next to him.

"It was supposed to be me."

10

Diana found Brad at breakfast in the doctors' lounge. He was sitting at the small dining table, squeezed between two healthy potted plants sent in remembrance of Dr. Brian Cummins. Other arrangements remaining from the funeral service lined the bookshelves and counter tops, many wilted. The lobby receptionist had slipped on watering duty. Rumpled magazines, short piles of old newspapers, and dirty coffee cups added to the clutter, but Diana decided not to clean up the mess. She was already overworked.

"Brad, we need to talk," she said.

"I don't want to talk anymore," he said. "Every time I call that Detective Key Martin about finding the shooter, he's unavailable. Assistant says he's out in the field, working on several criminal cases, but I think he's just screening calls."

He tossed the wrapper from his sausage and biscuit toward the trash. He missed.

Brad said, "Brian's death was more than just a robbery gone bad. The police are wrong."

"What about the damaged lock on the medical supply cabinet in the clinic?"

"Nothing was stolen, Diana. Brian's car wasn't even touched. His keys and wallet were still in his coat pocket."

Diana had heard nothing that evening until Leslie's screams; however, she had been on an upper floor.

"Any reason the building doesn't have security cameras?" she asked.

"My brother spent tons on marble counter tops for the patient check-in areas and bathrooms and on landscaping the place." Brad paused, feeling guilty about his plans to let his dog relieve himself in that expensive landscaping. "But Brian scrimped on security, and I don't blame him because our area of town has always been pretty quiet."

Brad had seemed so distant since the murder, so distracted, cancelling one appointment after the other. His dead brother's patients remained loyal to the practice, more than doubling her load over the past few weeks, and the referrals and consults never slowed. Despite her exhaustion, her own misery, Diana felt sorry for Brad.

"Martin hasn't mentioned anything about fingerprints?" she asked.

"No other prints, just the three of us: you, me, and Brad. No employees use that elevator."

"I'm sure the police will come up with something. It was just an unfortunate, random thing."

"It first popped up when I was leaving Iraq, when I was allowed to reactivate my satellite phone."

"What popped up?" Diana thought about Kelsey, at home with the babysitter.

"There were a lot of old voice mails and texts from people who didn't know I was out-of-pocket for four months. There was one text I got the day before I left for home: *I will give you a little wiggle room.*

"You think a text message has something to do with what happed to Brian?"

"That's the same thing that an Iraqi student, this Zarife Amarah guy, said to me when I was examining him over in Balad. We thought he was just a bystander when the IED detonated. When I told him that we would try to fix him up, he said in well-spoken English, 'OK, Doctor, I will give you a little wiggle room.' "

"You said that night in the elevator that you were the one that was supposed to die. You think that someone is after you—this Iraqi guy?"

Brad flipped the TV channel.

"I guess you think I'm just paranoid, maybe delusional." Another flip. "I promise I'll start carrying my load around here."

Diana glanced at the screen. *How many channels carried sports?* She thought again about Kelsey. "I know you have a lot on your mind, Brad, but that's what we need to talk about."

She sank into the sofa across from the breakfast table.

"I can't keep up this pace much longer," she said.

Brad didn't move from the television.

"Running late in the office everyday and on call every-other-night is not what I bargained for," Diana said.

"My brother did a good thing when he hired you." Brad pushed more buttons on the remote. Donald Trump was being interviewed on *Fox and Friends*.

"Gee, thanks. I'm sure Brian cleared my employment with you."

"He did," Brad lied. "But this place, this practice, was Brian's baby. If I hadn't liked you, hadn't thought you were tough enough, it wouldn't have mattered."

"I'll take that as a compliment. But tough or not, I'm never at home. My house is a mess. I'm afraid my daughter won't know me soon. She's furious that I copped out on the trip to Disney World."

Brad found some replays of a football game on ESPN. Two attractive women were making commentary.

"I've had to hire another babysitter—an older lady who could move in and work full time," Diana said. "Kelsey doesn't like her as much as the Holmes Junior College student who quit on me."

"Sorry. I saw that co-ed dropping Kelsey by your office a few days after Brian died. The girl was cute."

Diana stepped to the under-the-counter refrigerator for a low-fat yogurt. "The problem is this new lady gets two nights off a week, so that ..."

"Leaves you without help some nights. I'm getting the picture: sometimes Kelsey has to tag along with you while you're on call," Brad said.

"I keep a sleeping bag stuffed under the couch in my office for her, just in case. She's even slept with me in the hospital doctors' lounge. So far no one has complained. At least not to my face."

"And I don't think they will. She seems to be a well-behaved little girl."

"You're missing the point. This can't go on, Brad. Something's got to give."

There was another replay of a long drive for a winning touchdown. She felt him watch her pitch the empty yogurt container into the trash can. A drop shot.

"Here's the revised hospital patient list," she said. "I admitted four from the ER last night on call; one is still in the ICU. You might get a page from the floor about a wound evisceration and an abscess that needs to be drained. Have fun."

Diana yanked her white coat from the hanger and left, lifting her cell from the side pocket. Brad would assume a call to her daughter. She had never mentioned an ex-husband or a boyfriend or any social life.

What Diana did not recognize was Brad's growing attraction for her, not just because she looked good in a wrinkled, slept-in scrub suit, but because she commanded control even in difficulty. Her surgical talent and intelligence added to her beauty.

The cell number went through. Diana looked over her shoulder. She was alone.

"Haynes here." The voice was unfriendly, gruff.

"Dr. Haynes, this is Diana Bratton. I can see why some of your patients have left you. It's too early for a bad day."

"It's *John.*"

"Dr. Haynes, I'd like to meet with you again to talk about my surgical practice."

"I can take the time to talk with you. I'm not surprised that you called."

"But I don't want to meet again at the deli … too many people at Primos. Plus I'm short on baby sitters. Can you come by my house tonight?"

"Your house?"

"My daughter will be there. I live in Belhaven."

"Yes, I know. Checked your address. St. Ann."

Diana hated the physicians' directory.

"Time to meet?" Haynes asked.

"I'll have to get Kelsey some supper and put her to bed." Diana checked behind her. Still no Brad. "Let's say 8:30."

" See you then," Haynes said. "We can work something out."

*   *   *

Haynes walked back to the master bedroom from the study, still wrapped in a bath towel. He placed his cell on the antique chest near the bed and eyed himself in the mirror above. His hair had dried while he talked with Diana Bratton. He liked the way he looked.

"So you decided to hop back in bed after our shower?"

"You wore me out," the girl said, laughing.

"I won't be able to go out to dinner tonight after all," Haynes said, another glance in the mirror. "Maybe tomorrow."

"But, John, remember? I'll be leaving soon."

"That's right. Your furlough's almost over."

"You don't sound disappointed," she said.

He had wondered how long it would take for Diana Bratton to follow-up with him.

"John? An answer? Or do you still want me to call you *Dr. Haynes* ?"

The girl had raised her voice, but there was no one else around to hear it.

"Of course not," he said.

Haynes walked back to the bed and leaned down to her. He kissed the young nurse deeply and ran his hand under the sheets. "Am I disappointed that you're leaving, Sugar?" He massaged each of her breasts. "I'm crushed."

She arched her back as he moved his hands lower.

"But Fincher just called and asked me to take calls for him today and tonight. His new wife has gone into labor. Ron's always last minute, you know."

"If there're a lot of sick ones tonight, I can come up to the hospital and help you," she said.

"Nope, the nurses at Jackson Metro might feel slighted." Haynes touched her again and she moaned. "Besides, Sugar, you'd find the stuff here child's play. There'll be plenty of grief waiting for you when you get back to Iraq."

She pulled herself up in the bed and fluffed her pillow. "I'm sorry you won't be coming back with me, John."

Haynes reached for the shirt left tossed on the lounge chair the night before. He held it up to inspect. *Still presentable* he decided. He found his Zegna trousers behind the chair. They were wrinkled.

"Where are my boxers?" Haynes asked.

"I threw 'em over in the corner," she answered and pushed the hair out of her face.

Haynes checked his watch. He would be late for his first patient.

"Why don't you order take-out from Bravo tonight. Get a pizza, the Margherita, but ask the waiter to add grilled chicken. I'll drive over and pick it up, then run it to you between pages."

"Sounds yummy, but what if you stay for a few minutes for a slice or two?" The sheets moved as she crossed her legs. "I saw a couple of bottles of wine left in your cooler. Maybe we could open a bottle of that Kendall Jackson."

"No way." He looked again at his watch. "I just told you. Gotta

61

take calls tonight. Fincher, remember? His wife? The baby?"

She watched him find his underwear from behind the chair and get a new pair from the dresser. He removed a fresh starched shirt, silk tie, and another pair of Zegna trousers from the master closet, dropped the towel from his waist, and dressed. After setting the tie in the mirror above the antique chest, Haynes fastened the alligator belt.

"We used to drink a lot of wine, John. Work never stopped you before," she said.

"I'll be sure you get the pizza tonight." Haynes walked toward the door leading to the hall. "I don't know what you do around here all day, but call the restaurant about seven and place the order. I'll pick it up at the take-out window."

He left the bedroom, his steps heavy against the heart-of-pine wood flooring.

"John, if you're going to be so busy taking Dr. Fincher's call, then why didn't you just put on scrubs instead of getting so dressed up?" she called from the bed.

"New hospital policy. Can't wear scrubs in," he yelled back from the hall.

Stacy threw off the sheets and dressed in one of John's starched button-downs from the closet. She had eaten little the day before and the idea of pizza weighed heavily on her, even in the morning. She walked into the study and out onto the small back porch that overlooked the manicured croquet court. A private, fifteen-acre lake stocked with bream and bass glistened just beyond, bordered by a dense stand of pine, dogwood, and oak trees. The smooth surface of the water oozed tranquility. Stacy did not want to leave.

"I need to see what I can find around here to eat," she said, rubbing her taut belly. "Then I'll need to hit the gym afterward."

Suddenly, there was a voice.

"You did not come by my hospital bed to say good-bye."

Stacy put her hand to her throat and caught the scream.

"What are you doing here?"

The Iraqi student she remembered from Balad stood a few feet outside the screen partition. His dark hair was now neatly combed, and there were no bandages. She had never seen him stand. He was taller than she had thought.

"I have a visa to study in the United States," Zarife answered. "I have thought many times about the sad nurse, crying over losing the man she loved."

Stacy smoothed the shirt tail and wished it were longer. She wondered if the door from the back steps into the porch was locked.

"But how did you find me at this house? I'm only visiting."

"For many days I lay in my hospital bed. There was talk from the other nurses, names. It is easy to locate someone's address. I was looking for Dr. John Haynes. It is a wonderful surprise to find you here."

Zarife seemed to survey the grounds and enormity of the house. "Dr. Haynes is your older relative?" he asked.

"No, just a friend."

Stacy again ran her hand down the front of the shirt. She thought about how she jumped to sleep with John after first meeting him in Iraq, drawn to the financial security. Then she found hot Chad during a meal on the base. Sex came even quicker. They continued in dark corners, behind curtains, anywhere a security camera was absent. He became her true love. She would steal off base to see him whenever she could get away from John Haynes. Stacy still ached for Chad's touch and the way he felt inside her.

She was certain that John never suspected.

"Like I said, you seemed so distraught over the death of your young companion in Iraq, that he survived the killing of war but died at the hands of one of your doctors," Zarife said.

"I lost everything when Chad died," Stacy said. She moved closer to Zarife, a screened wall still separating them. He walked along the stone path leading to the door and ascended a few steps.

"You mean you lost everything when Chad was killed," he said.

"I've thought a lot about what happened over there. I was trying to be a good nurse when we talked—changing your bandages, keeping you as comfortable as I could. But I had been hurt, disappointed."

Zarife moved further up the steps.

"I realize now that Chad was injured in combat," Stacy said. "A coward with a bomb ultimately killed him."

"A coward, you say? Wasn't the coward the doctor who killed the love of your life?"

"No, Chad and his squadron came across a roadside bomb, that's how he died. Complications of surgery."

Her hands shook.

"I can see that you have much anger boiling inside you, Stacy. You can resolve that anger."

He walked up the last few steps and stood facing the closed door.

"I need to move on with my life. That's why I'm here in this house."

Stacy felt her pulse quicken. Her heart began to pound in her chest.

"Your hands are trembling, Stacy. Sort out your anger and learn where to direct it. That way, you will be able to resolve your rage."

"I wonder if John has some Valium stashed in the bathroom someplace."

She flexed her fingers. Her palms felt moist, sticky.

"I was beginning to accept what happened to Chad, but now I'm not so sure," she said.

"You seem even more anxious, more fragile than when I knew you in Iraq. Then you were only sad over the loss of your boyfriend. Remember, you said it would be hard to live without the true love of your life."

Stacy eased back into a wicker chair and sank into the cushion. Zarife tried the knob, and the door opened. He stepped into the porch and stood above her. She tried to avoid staring at the disfigured left hand.

"Stacy, you don't want to resort to pills," he said. "You need to find a better way to eliminate that anxiety, a way to flush out the cause and get rid of it."

Stacy dug her fingers into the upholstery, partially covering the arms of the chair.

"I saw a lot of wounded people over there. Sometimes I have nightmares, flashbacks. But it's different with my boyfriend's death. I've kept a lot of guilt inside."

Zarife laughed. "Why would you be guilty?"

"My boyfriend Chad was dead before I got to talk to him or even see him alive up close."

"Your boyfriend was injured and died after surgery, you told me. That shouldn't have happened."

Stacy wished for a box of tissue. She wiped her eyes with the back of a hand.

"I didn't even get to touch him before he died."

More tears.

"So the American doctors, the military physicians, they were there to take care of your boyfriend."

"But he died anyway."

Another wipe with the back of her hand.

"I am truly sorry for your loss," Zarife said.

He surveyed the porch and looked through into the study. The area was quiet. He shook his head slowly.

"Such a tragedy. Even with the finest medical care available in the world, the U.S. military doctors couldn't save your Chad."

Stacy continued to sob quietly.

She said, "From the very beginning, I didn't do anything to help him. Our nursing unit over in Balad was a pretty tight group, but I kept our relationship secret. I was afraid to get close; someone might suspect. There was lots of yelling when they called Chad's CODE. Supplies flew everywhere. But I still didn't help."

"Try to keep going, Stacy. You must dry those tears." Zarife placed his good hand on her shoulder. "Crying hasn't helped you so far."

She stared through him, and the weeping slowed, but her loss felt even greater.

"To relive what happened cuts very deep, tears apart your soul, but venting your anger at this time is best for you," Zarife said, "particularly at this stage of your grief, your loss."

He rubbed his hand down to Stacy's arm and back to the shoulder. There was a gentle pressure of reassurance.

"Release that anger: that is what they taught me when my family was killed by a bomb."

Stacy shook her head and stiffened. Her eyes felt wet. She looked up at Zarife; her vision was cloudy.

"I wanted to scream when the head nurse briefed us on the medical tribunal's findings. But I couldn't show any emotion at all," she said. "Chad was just another soldier to them ... just an unexpected death on the base."

"The report said there was no one to blame, none of the doctors or nurses on duty?" Zarife asked.

"I realized then that the war was to blame. The Iraqis, the militants."

"Could you have saved him, Stacy?"

"No! No! Of course not!" Stacy sprang from her chair, pushing him away. "The physicians, the surgeons were in charge of taking care of Chad." She turned back to face Zarife. "The doctors, they were the ones who could have saved him, not me!"

"That's much better, Stacy. Express that rage."

"I didn't mean to scream, Mr. Amarah, and I wasn't screaming at you."

"Who then, Stacy? Who were you screaming at?"

"Myself. I was screaming at myself."

"Yourself? Why were you screaming at yourself?"

Stacy admired Zarife Amarah; she felt she could confide in him. Even though the Iraqi student had lost family in the war, he was still trying to make something of himself. He seemed determined despite physical deformity. Besides, without a release of her emotions, she was going to explode.

"I was pregnant, she said. "I slipped Chad into my quarters a couple of times when he was on leave from his base. Sometimes he surprised me, and we were careless. We once had sex in a restroom and behind some curtains with patients not far from us. We played a game to see how quiet we could do it. I loved him, everything about him."

Zarife took a quick look down toward her waist. "You were pregnant?"

"I got an abortion. Right after I got back to the States."

"Do you regret that? Is that why you feel you should scream at yourself?"

"I could have had a piece of Chad to hold now. But I was afraid I'd lose some military benefits if I returned from my deployment pregnant. "I didn't know what to do, didn't know who to turn to. I didn't want to be labeled as a one of those single moms. I had considered more training, maybe becoming a nurse practitioner and letting the feds pay for it. Like I said, I didn't know who to turn to."

"You should have asked someone like me."

"You?"

"By someone like me, I mean a friend, Stacy."

66

Stacy's eyes sank to the painted wooden floor. She cupped her face in her trembling hands and ran her fingertips to her throbbing temples, then to her scalp, mussing her hair. She shook her head, and dropped her hands to let the thick brunette hair fall back into place. Anyone like Zarife could see and feel the pain.

"Just as we cannot change the fact that you aborted that poor child . . ."

Stacy raised her head, her blank stare meant defeat.

". . . aborted that child that you and Chad made together, we cannot change the fact that you have lost Chad . . . lost him forever," Zarife said.

"I've lost Chad . . . forever."

"And you didn't have to. It wasn't your fault."

"No, no." Another rub of the temples. "Chad's death was not my fault."

"Then whose fault was it, Stacy?"

"Chad's fault. He was the one who enlisted. Chad told me that his grandfather didn't want him to. But he had always dreamed of a military career."

"You're wrong, Stacy. It wasn't Chad's fault. He was just serving his country."

"He could have stayed in Tennessee, finished college."

"Could have, but like you said, he pursued his dream," Zarife said. "And I want to pursue my dream."

Stacy sat limply on the chair cushion, her hands lowered.

"You're right. Of course, it wasn't Chad's fault that he died. And it wasn't my fault either. I couldn't have done anything."

"Think back to what you said earlier," Zarife said.

"You need to go now. I'm not dressed. And John could come back at any minute. This doesn't look right."

"Forget that. You were a registered nurse over there in Iraq, not a specialized trauma or ICU nurse. Your boyfriend did not die because of you."

"I know. I realize that. I said that already."

"He died tragically. And you aborted your baby, his baby. A part of him could still be with you."

Stacy's cries were hysterical. "Why are you saying that now?"

Stacy pressed her fingers again to her temples and rubbed them.

"Stay focused, Stacy. I'm only trying to help you. Look at me.

Why did Chad die?" Zarife bent down to her.

"He just died. Sergeant Cossar, the head nurse, reported that he didn't make it after surgery. That Major Cummins did everything he could. I saw him in the CODE. John was there, too."

"Did he, Stacy? Did Cummins do everything he could to save your Chad?"

Stacy gripped the arm of the chair. Her voice became weak, unsteady. "That was the report, I told you. There was a review. There was an operation and he died."

"Listen to me." Zarife's eyes did not leave her. "You lost Chad, the love of your life, and Cummins was in charge. Is he hiding something, Stacy?"

"Hiding something?"

"See, you solved the mystery all by yourself," Zarife said.

"Now," he stood and opened the door from the porch to leave, "what are you going to do about it?"

11

Built just after World War II, Diana's house was a nondescript, compact two-bedroom with a shallow front porch. The dim street light at the end of the short driveway cast a faint shadow on the red-brick exterior. The porch light popped on as Haynes pulled his Mercedes toward the one-car garage, which was more of a carport, nearly touching the rear of Diana's Nissan.

He decided on the front door.

"Dr. Haynes, perfect timing. I just finished reading Kelsey her nightly fix of Harry Potter."

"Much too formal. *John,* remember?"

"I appreciate your coming by. Glad you weren't tied up late at Metro."

"Can I come in?"

Diana blushed. "I'm sorry. Please come into the living room."

Haynes followed.

"Have a seat on the couch, Doctor ... I mean, John."

Haynes studied the small fireplace and the large houseplant struggling on the hearth. The light brown carpet and the drapes hanging at the front window had both outlived fashion.

"Your house seems cozy, Diana," he said, feeling claustrophobic.

"Plenty of room for Kelsey and me. I rent this place from a couple over in Eastover. Their son used to live here while he was in med school."

"Damn, you ought to own your own place."

"I'm still paying off school loans, even a few leftover from college ... made the mistake of helping my ex-husband pay his off before mine. When we split, he didn't feel obligated to do the same."

Haynes stood and moved to the fireplace. He touched one of the plant's dead leaves.

"Why did you call me over here tonight, Diana?"

She seemed surprised.

He liked that.

"You said you wanted to discuss your career," he said.

69

"Yes, I did."

Diana stood, arms crossed. She walked back toward the entrance.

"You need to end these games you've been playing with me, John."

"What's up, Diana? Before Brian Cummins was shot and his brother was left high and dry, you seemed perfectly content with your surgical career."

"It was obvious when you first called me. All you wanted was to take the 'wonderful female surgeon from the Cummins boys'."

"Please sit back down, Diana—you've misunderstood me," he said, a forced look of concern. "The day after Brian Cummins' funeral, I saw your name all over the hospital surgical schedule."

"I had to take over Brian's entire surgery schedule. The patients couldn't be put off, and his brother was in no shape to step in ... not at first."

"But that means you're making more money," Haynes said.

"Wrong. I'm still under the same physician employee contract. No provision for more money if one partner gets murdered." Diana fell back into the couch, hands covering her face. "I'm sorry, that sounded cold."

"No problem. Sounds like shitty professional business to me. Brad Cummins must be an idiot not to pay you more now."

"Brad's not an idiot. He's ..."

"I told you the other day in the hall over at Metro that the older brother was the brains of the practice, or at least he was."

Diana looked around the tight room, even behind her, as though someone could have overheard them. "I was wrong to call you tonight, Dr. Haynes." She fought tears. "Brad, the clinic, needs me."

"Sure he needs you. But so does that daughter asleep in the next room, in a tiny bedroom, I would guess. Kelly ..."

"It's Kelsey."

"Kelsey is going to want things. You're going to want to send her to a private school and a nice university. Then there's a wedding. Unless you remarry or hook-up with someone, get someone to foot some of the bills, you'll be just another overworked surgeon, an underpaid one at that. You'll never have a moment to yourself."

70

"Brad and I just need to talk. Make some plans for the future of the practice."

"That guy's only interested in coming out on top. I know him. He's just riding your coattails since big brother's not around anymore."

"Dr. Haynes, that's enough. I know there's a lot of rivalry between the two surgical groups. But I owe something to the memory of Brian Cummins. He was the one to step up when I needed a job."

Diana wiped her eyes with the back of her right hand.

"I was wrong to let you tempt me to leave my practice just to ..."

"Just to get a better deal? It's OK to say it, Diana. You want, you're gonna need, more money."

"I feel really bad about calling."

"Haynes Healthcare will double your present salary with room for an even split of the profits in two years. As long as you stay busy, that is, and perform well."

A five-year-old version of Diana appeared in the doorway. She clutched an American Girl doll and a white, furry, toy dog.

"Mommy, I heard a lot of talking."

"Kelsey." Diana knelt to her. "You're supposed to be in bed. Dr. Haynes and I were just talking about hospital stuff."

"Are some people sick?" Kelsey asked, rubbing her eyes.

"Yes, but they're going to get better. In fact, Dr. Haynes is on call tonight. I'm sure he needs to go back up to the hospital to take care of them." Diana picked up her daughter, squeezing her.

"Actually I left things in pretty good shape at Metro, and my pager or phone hasn't gone off, so I'm good."

"Kelsey, let's help Dr. Haynes to the door, then you need to get back in that bed. Big day tomorrow at pre-school."

"Don't worry about me, Diana. I know the way," he said.

Diana gave Kelsey a kiss on the cheek.

Haynes opened the front door to the porch and called back into the room. "Kelly, we need to find a way to help your mommy not work so hard, or at least find a way to get you a nicer house."

A moth flew in from the light.

"Think about what we discussed, Diana. You're going to need me," he said, clearing the porch and front steps in seconds. He

71

clicked open the Mercedes and jerked it back down the driveway.

Turning into the street, Haynes noticed the small car parked on the other side with headlights lit. He grabbed the flashlight from his center console, rolled down his window, and directed it across to the driver.

"Hey, buddy, don't park across from somebody's driveway. I almost hit you."

"Don't be so loud, Doctor. Your friend inside might hear us," the voice familiar, the interior of the small vehicle dark.

Haynes' flashlight at first missed the driver's face.

"I got a look at her," the voice said. "Pretty. Very pretty."

Haynes checked Diana's house. Only the porch light remained lit. Diana was inside, curtains drawn.

"What are you doing here, Amarah?" Haynes asked.

"I have followed you. I have seen your home. We all know that you Americans live in decadence, but your place … over the top."

"You have no concern about me. That's not what I'm paying you for."

Haynes checked the house. The porch light was off, no Diana.

"Back at your house, your mansion, I watched the two of you through the window, you and the young slut living with you. Are you paying her, too?"

"Stay away from me, Amarah. One call from me and the Feds will be all over you."

"Your 'Feds' brought me here, Doctor, to do your work. I have already done you a favor, I believe. But I am running low on funds."

"You haven't done anything for me," Haynes said. He noticed the drawn curtains move in Diana's living room window. The porch light lit.

"Dr. Haynes?" Diana's voice pushed through the opened door.

"This guy's just lost. I'm giving him directions. See you in the hospital tomorrow."

The front door closed.

"Another object for you, Dr. Haynes? More gratification?"

"Let's call it off, Amarah."

"Not an option, Doctor Haynes. This isn't about you."

12

Leslie Coachys stood on an upholstered stool in the floor-length window of Brad's twelfth-floor apartment. The glass-lined walls of the main living area afforded panorama considered spectacular by urban Mississippi standards. To the east was the one-hundred-year-old "new" state capitol building and farther to the right its antebellum predecessor, topping Capitol Street and the streaking headlights of advancing traffic.

Other lighting peaked through the tops of live oaks that lined the side streets below the renovated, art deco-style Plaza Building. The trees hid the few homeless scattered in the doorways of lawyers' offices and other downtown businesses. She saw none of it. Leslie saw only her reflection in the window.

"This gown is exquisite, just exquisite," Minor Leblanc announced, his head shaking from side to side with excitement as he stretched to measure for an adjustment at the shoulders. "Barely needs a thing from my seamstress."

He clapped his hands in approval.

"Miss Leslie Coachys, you look gorgeous, from forever!"

"Are you sure it doesn't make me look heavy?" she asked.

"Nothing could ever, ever make someone as fabulous as you look heavy. When I saw this gown in New York and thought about your body, I had to scream—just brought me to tears."

He smacked his palms together again, this clap louder than the first.

"What makes you so certain about my body?" She turned first to one side and then the other, her hands to her hips. The reflection agreed.

"Jesus! That doctor fiancé of yours wouldn't put up with anything heavy." He checked the bodice and spread the train to its fullest. "This wonderful thing is fabulous, just fabulous," he said. "And you will become even more fabulous as you live on."

"I hope Caroline can keep the train fanned out when Brad and I walk up the church steps. I just hate weddings when it gets all bunched up … ruins the photos and video."

"Don't worry one bit." Minor Leblanc's head shook more

rapidly, almost vibrating. "We'll get all of that worked out in rehearsal. Besides, your doctor will be there. You can ask him later if your matron of honor was paying attention to my instructions."

Minor lifted the train to expose her flip-flops. "Where are your pumps?" he asked. "You need to wear your pumps to these things!"

Leslie waved off the reprimand. She lifted her hands to her breasts, then ran them down the ivory silk of the $9500 Vera Wang gown, stopping at the hand-sewn bead work at the waist. The diamond solitaire caught the beam of the concealed overhead lighting and glistened.

"Water that exquisite thing, and it might grow into something bigger than three carats," Minor said.

"I don't think Brad would've sprung for even this," she said, continuing to study her ring finger in the light, "if he had known the price of this dress."

"Child, please! When your doctor sees you in this gown, he won't care what it costs. You will be the most fabulous bride that anyone in this town has ever seen. Forever!"

Leslie dropped her hand and again studied the Vera Wang. "I'm not so sure, Minor. I expect that we … that he … stumbled into a little windfall of cash when his brother Brian died. Their parents are dead and there were just the two boys. Don't you suppose there's a money market account or some stocks?"

She held up the ring once more and smiled. "But I bet that clinic building has a really big ass mortgage," she said.

"Let your doctor worry about that mortgage, you fabulous thing." He made another adjustment to the gown. "You said something about a windfall? You and I should have just flown to New York, gotten an appointment with Miss Wang herself. This body screams for Wang Couture."

He smoothed an area over her left hip. "With your figure, we could have gone with a sheath or mermaid style instead."

"I'm glad you didn't bring anything like that down. This traditional look is what I want. What Brad wants, too."

She thought again about the $9,500 price tag, plus Minor's commission. The cost as well as the look would be a surprise for her future husband on their wedding day. At least she had cut the stylist out of a commission by selecting the ring herself.

"Whatever," Minor said. He returned with a straight pin from his leather accessory bag and pushed it through the future hem line.

"Once you're in this exquisite piece, all you'll need is a little lip gloss, a taste of good eyeliner, and a hint of concealer. Then let the nuptials begin."

Another clap, the loudest yet, brought barking from down the hall.

"I hope you've got that thing locked up!" Minor's head trembled, now for another reason. Sweat glistened on his brow.

"That's Brad's lab. I've got him shut up in the guest room. He'll settle down in a minute."

"Jesus," Minor said.

Leslie fanned the train of the gown then let it fall.

"Our wedding will be bigger than most around here, Minor. But this ring is what really sets the tone." She pushed the stone into his face and tossed her head again in the reflection. "But I can only squeeze Brad so far."

Minor left again for the living room sofa and returned with an oversized Louis Vuitton garment bag. "Too bad your Dr. Cummins doesn't do plastics, seems that's where all the money is. I could him send lots of clients ... might even consult with him myself."

He unzipped the bag.

"But you'll never need any work; you're too fabulous."

"Didn't I read in your newspaper column that spanx and lipstick were all a woman needed?" she asked.

"What I said was *Between spanx and expensive lipstick, the world is yours.*"

"Go ahead and slip out of that thing, and I'll hang it in here for the seamstress," Minor said.

He walked back to the living room sofa to his over-sized gold lame jacket. As he put his right arm through the sleeve, a tone from a speaker inside the apartment door announced a visitor.

"Miss Leslie, what time was the doctor coming home?"

There was no answer from the closed bedroom.

More beads of sweat erupted on Minor's forehead. He wanted his selections a surprise; for now the bill would be enough of a shock for Dr. Cummins. He entered the foyer and pulled his left arm through the expensive jacket, then buttoned the middle button. The doctor would not push a door bell at his own entrance. Minor peered into the six-inch video monitor mounted flush with the wall, below the even smaller speaker. There was a young man standing on the sidewalk, looking down as he spoke into the call box.

"Janitorial service. Can you help me into the building?" His voice was clear, good diction.

Minor checked around the corner to the hall that led to the master bedroom. The door remained closed. *I guess they don't have an extra security screen in the bedroom* he decided. *I don't need to bother Miss Leslie with this.*

Minor pushed the talk button. "Are you here to clean the Cummins apartment?"

"No, I am here to clean the common areas of the lobby and the elevators. My supervisor is always here to let me in, but so far he's a no-show. Really shorthanded tonight. Other guy called in sick."

"I'm just a guest here. The lady of the house will have to be the one to buzz you in, but she's," Minor bent toward the bedroom hall, no sign of Leslie, "still indisposed."

"I don't need to get into your … her … apartment, sir, just into the lobby. I'll lose my job if this place does not get cleaned."

The sweat ran as a thin stream onto Minor's checks. "Sorry, but I don't think I can …"

"Please do help me out, sir. My wife and I have a small baby at home, a newborn, and I can't get home late again tonight. Nobody else will answer."

Minor remembered pulling into guest parking an hour earlier and noting that most of the owners' parking spaces were empty.

"OK, I'll help you out this time. You need to get back to that little baby. And I don't want you to lose your job."

Leblanc pushed the button marked *Authorize Entrance.* A buzzing noise followed as the young man disappeared from the screen.

"Could have at least said *thank you,*" Minor said. He turned to Leslie's voice coming from just outside the bedroom.

"Here's the dress. Minor, where are you?"

"Here, fabulous. Let me take that from you and put it in the Louis Vuitton."

Leslie met him in the living room. "Someone at the door?" she asked.

76

Minor held the gown gently, sliding it on a hanger before draping the designer bag around it. "It was one of the Plaza's cleaning crew, needed to get in to clean the lobby. Something about his supervisor not showing up."

Leslie reached for her purse and a hair brush. Three strokes and a slight twist of her neck put the blonde hair in place.

"That must have been Jeremiah. Brad said he's been around for a long time, used to clean up lawyers' offices downtown before this building was renovated."

Minor ran the zipper up to the insignia clasp and stretched the bag along the sofa. He reached for his chinchilla coat.

"Don't think so. This was a young man."

"A young man? And isn't it a little warm for that, particularly with your jacket?"

"Yes, young man. Never looked into the camera, but he spoke with a young voice … seemed educated … hair was dark, thick, cut short. Complexion also a little dark, too, from what I could see on that tiny screen."

Leblanc donned the matching fur hat.

"And, no, it's never too warm for style."

"I guess management hired someone new in housekeeping." Leslie tossed the hairbrush into her purse. "Hope they didn't let nice Jeremiah go. He's like family … so nice, so calming. Always makes me feel warm and safe and welcomed around here," she said, walking back into the master bedroom for a tube of lipstick.

"I'm sure your Jeremiah fellow will find something else," Minor said, placing the garment bag over his shoulder. He opened the door to leave the apartment for the final time.

"I'll call when the alterations are done."

"Did you say something else, Minor?" Leslie returned to the living room as the door to the apartment snapped shut. "OK, then. Guess he'll call me next week for a final fitting."

She found her purse and rummaged for car keys.

"Bullet!" She looked toward the hall to the guest room. "Better take him out before I go," she said just before the buzzer.

Instead of walking down the hall to the guest room, she followed the sound to the foyer.

Opening the door, she asked, "Minor did you forget something?"

13

Brad was greeted with a smile from the young woman at the reception desk.

"May I help you?" she asked.

"I'm Dr. Brad Cummins. Detective Key Martin asked me to meet him here."

"Yes, Detective Martin is in the back with the ME. You'll need to sign in, and I'll need your ID."

The glass doors opened behind Brad. The young woman said, "And, ma'am, you'll need to sign in, too."

Brad reached for his wallet and turned to the female figure. "Diana?" he said.

"I couldn't let you come down here by yourself. I know you haven't slept since the police came to the hospital yesterday."

"You're right. I haven't. But I did manage a shower."

"I'm sorry the system is putting you through this," Diana said. "Seems so unnecessary." She leaned against the reception desk.

"They needed positive identification of … her body. Leslie had no ID on her. Her purse was the only thing missing from my apartment."

"Dr. Cummins, if you prefer, the ME can show you a photo; that is, if you don't want to see the body," the receptionist said.

Detective Martin walked into the office. He smiled at Diana.

"Dr. Cummins, they've got everything ready for you. Just follow me," Martin said. The receptionist returned to her computer.

The hall behind the reception area was cold and bare, the gray, tiled floor a sharp contrast to the carpeted offices in the front of the building. Brad expected a scene similar to a detective drama, something from *CSI* or *Law & Order*: a stack of body bins arranged like deep drawers or maybe a glass-paneled viewing area. Instead, they approached a simple metal gurney, a body covered with a sheet.

Detective Martin motioned to the medical examiner, and she exposed the face.

"Yes, that's Leslie," Brad said, his own face pale, expressionless—a match for the body on the gurney. "That's Leslie

Coachys, my fiancée."

Diana stepped closer. She put her arm around Brad's shoulder and steadied him. Before she could put a tissue to his eye, Brad wiped away the tear with his hand.

"Maybe I needed to see this," he said, "to accept that she's really gone."

Diana gave a slight squeeze to his shoulder. He didn't move.

"I loved her," Brad said. "Leslie was a good person, harmless."

"Thank you, sir. That's all we need," the medical examiner said. "Detective Martin, will you show them back to the front?"

"Sure. There should be some paperwork to complete."

* * *

Caroline had hoped to slip in and out of the clinic to meet with the administrator without running into anyone, particularly Dr. Bratton. She wondered if she looked as green to Bratton as she felt.

"You're the one who told him about Leslie?" Caroline asked.

"Yes, he had been on call the night before and never made it back to his apartment."

Caroline had never met Dr. Bratton, and from Leslie's description she had hated her.

"The police showed up at Jackson Metro with the news just as Brad was knee-deep in an emergency appendectomy," Dr. Bratton said. "They showed their badges to the OR Director, and she called me in to relieve Brad. Pus was everywhere when I scrubbed in."

The green drained from the face of Leslie's former business partner.

"I made up some reason for him to scrub out and report to the front desk, something about another patient in the ER, but he wouldn't leave until I told him that something had happened to Leslie."

Dr. Bratton patted her eyes with the sleeve of her white doctor's coat, smearing mascara. "Lucky me," she said.

Caroline held her tears. Bratton was tall, attractive—her makeup modest, but applied correctly and in a flattering shade. She seemed genuine. No wonder Leslie had been jealous. Caroline thought of her as *Diana*.

Diana said, "Those of us left to finish the case thought we heard Brad's cries coming from the nursing station."

Caroline scanned the file of financial records she was holding

79

while Diana checked her text messages. Each thought about the upcoming funeral and shed another tear or two. Caroline spoke first. "I'm sure you're busy, Dr. Bratton. I just came by to touch base with your clinic administrator. She's been moonlighting as our bookkeeper."

"Bookkeeper?" Diana asked.

"I wasn't just Leslie's best friend, I was her business partner, too."

"That's right. Brad mentioned something about a new bookstore or gift store or stationery store downtown. I'm sorry I haven't had the time to check it out."

"Yes, ma'am. It's all those things. The business was Leslie's idea, and she was good at that short of thing. So I'm suddenly at a loss."

"Please drop the *ma'am*. It's *Diana*."

"Sure. Thanks. *Diana*."

Diana led Caroline in the direction of the administration area. "I'll bet you were to be in the wedding."

"Matron of honor."

Diana nodded. "You must miss her."

"I do."

"And I guess you're having to work kind of hard, Dr. Bratton… Diana. First Brian, now Brad is not working."

"You're right. I joined a practice to make it three surgeons. Now it's just me … but only for two more days. Brad told me he would be back to work the day after the funeral."

Caroline said, "The guy's lost two people he loved. Maybe if he throws himself back into his practice, it will help."

"These two murder investigations aren't making it any easier," Diana said.

She left Caroline at the administrator's office and went back to her waiting patients.

14

"Naw, surr. I wasn't there to clean that morning. Miss Leslie had asked me da day before to check a leaky faucet in the powder room."

Detective Key Martin referred to his notes.

"I thought you worked in the janitorial department of the Plaza Building?" Martin asked.

"I do. Yes, surr. I do. I does odd jobs around the Plaza, too. Odd jobs. Like fix leaky faucets on ma days off."

"And how did you get into the Dr. Cummins' apartment that morning?"

"Dr. Cummins, he gave me a key. Here it is, in my pocket."

"So you have a key to the apartment that Dr. Cummins shared with the deceased?" the detective asked.

"I don't pay no attention to nobody's business. Dr. Cummins' name was what's on the mail slot."

The audio system in the interrogation room picked up a snicker from the deputy detective sitting beside Jeremiah Willis. Brad and the others standing on the other side of the glass wall heard it.

"Sometimes Dr. Cummins would be caught up at the hospital and his dog needed to be walked. So he would call me sometimes to walk his dog, 'specially if Miss Leslie wasn't there."

"So you were friendly with the dog."

"Yes, suh."

"That's why the dog didn't jump you when you entered the Cummins apartment?"

"I didn't see no dog; I didn't see Bullet when I walked in an' found ..."

Brad could see his friend Jeremiah's tears.

"Where was the dog when you opened the apartment with the key that Dr. Cummins had given you?" Martin's deputy asked.

"I ran to Miss Leslie. Called her name. I heard Bullet bark from the extra bedroom."

"You seem to know a lot about Dr. Cummins' apartment," Detective Martin said.

"Yes, suh. I told you. I been up there before. Lots of times. To fix things."

"I believe that Dr. Cummins had recently acquired the apartment, that it had been newly renovated." He looked back up from the note pad. "Do you know what *renovated* means?"

"That it was a new," Willis answered.

"So you would go up lots of times to fix things in a new place?" the detective asked.

"I helped Dr. Cummins move in there when he got back from the service, and then helped Miss Leslie move in. I helped hang pitchurs. She wanted to move some towel racks to a different place. The paint needed touchin' up."

From the deputy: "Mr. Willis, you knew all about Dr. Cummins and Miss Coachys. Did you think of them as well-off, as rich?"

"Naw, suh. They was nice, real nice. S'posed to be getting married."

"Look, Mr. Willis," Martin said. "I don't think you meant to hurt Leslie Coachys. You thought no one was at home."

"You're right. Didn't think nobody was home. Just s'posed to fix a leaky faucet. Didn't want to bother nobody."

"I think you used your key, Mr. Willis, to break into that apartment," the detective said. "Miss Coachys was in the master bedroom and didn't hear you come in. The dog was there, maybe napping on the couch. He knew you and didn't put up a fuss ... was probably glad to see you. You shut him up in the guest room to make sure he didn't get in the way."

More tears. "Naw, suh. That ain't right."

"You started going through the place," the deputy said. "You knew where the valuables were. She walked in from the bedroom, surprised you, and you killed her."

"Naw, suh. I didn't. I would never hurt nobody."

"We won't need you anymore today, Mr. Willis," Detective Martin said.

The deputy lead Jeremiah from the room as Brad and Diana continued to watch and listen from the observation room.

"Jeremiah Willis isn't capable of something like that. Just look at him, Diana, an old man with arthritic hands," Brad said.

"Maybe what the detective just said is correct—that Leslie surprised Mr. Willis. Maybe he carried a knife with him for his own protection, you know, working odd hours downtown. Maybe

82

he just panicked."

"Adrenaline is a powerful thing, but I just don't see it," Brad said. "And about Bullet being shut up in the guest bedroom? I told Leslie to put him there while she had that Leblanc guy over to the apartment."

Diana caught the quiver in Brad's voice and put her hand to his shoulder. He wiped a tear but continued to stare into the interrogation room.

"Most women would carry a purse with Kleenex," she said. "Sorry."

There was quiet laughter.

"I thought I was all cried out," Brad said, as the deputy brought the next person in for questioning.

"The newspaper article said the cause of death was stabbing. Have the police mentioned anything about fingerprints?"

Brad stiffened and turned his head away.

"I'm sorry, Brad. You didn't bring me down here to pry."

"I brought you down here, Diana, because I don't know whom to trust anymore."

Diana nodded. This time she almost reached for Brad's hand.

"Other than Leslie's fingerprints and mine, the only ones the detective told me they lifted were Jeremiah's and Leblanc's."

They both looked through the window as Minor Leblanc adjusted himself to the metal chair after wiping the seat and back with a handkerchief.

"Minor Leblanc," Diana said, shaking her head. "From what I've heard, he would be less likely to hurt someone than poor old Jeremiah."

"Has Leblanc ever worked with you, Diana, or should I say, on you?" Brad smiled.

"Do you think he needs to?"

"No, I think you're holding your own just fine."

"State your full name," the detective said on the other side of the window.

"Minor Charles Leblanc."

"Address?"

"And your name, sir?"

"Mr. Leblanc, my deputy has already told you my name. In fact, we met when we located you in a women's dress store yesterday.

83

But if you have forgotten, it's Detective Key Martin of the Jackson Police Department."

"Well then, Detective Martin, my address is Number 6 Vontage Drive; Montclair, Mississippi." Leblanc's smile was full, seemed exaggerated. "What can I do for you here?"

He pulled another handkerchief from his jacket and mopped his forehead.

"Let's start with your occupation."

"I am a personal stylist. I have a lot of clients in the metro-Jackson area. I also plan weddings and parties and fashion shows."

"What is a personal stylist, Mr. Leblanc?"

"Detective Martin, a personal stylist is someone who helps his or her clients to achieve their full potential."

"Is that what you were doing with Miss Coachys last week— helping her to achieve her *full potential?*"

Leblanc's head shook rapidly side to side, vibrated, as he stuttered to answer.

"Miss Leslie Coachys asked me to design her wedding from start to finish. Her potential was to be fabulous, beyond fabulous."

"How long were you there in the apartment with Miss Coachys?"

"Less than an hour. We were fitting her Vera Wang that looked simply . . ."

"And the deceased was paying you by the hour for your services and for the dress, I assume."

"Oh, do we have to refer to that lovely, exquisite thing as the deceased? That sounds so severe."

Diana turned Brad toward her. She left her hand on his shoulder. His complexion was nearly ashen.

"Brad, do you really want to watch? First the trip to the morgue and now this," she said.

"Detective Martin thought I might pick-up on some discrepancy, something that he and his assistant might miss, I suppose." He returned her questioning look. "I'm OK, really. And thanks for coming down here with me."

"No problem. Mr. Kruger's hernia got cancelled, so suddenly I was free at lunch."

They both turned to the detective's next question.

"Mr. Leblanc, what was Miss Coachys paying you to achieve

her full potential?"

"Fifty dollars an hour for wedding design and personal shopping plus 20 percent commission on the price of that fabulous Vera Wang and her other accessories."

"Perhaps you were concerned that the deceased ... Miss Coachys ... might not pay you for those services and the expensive dress and maybe even the accessories?"

"I would never think such a thing." His head continued to tremble; his hands followed. Sweat poured from his forehead.

"Miss Leslie made it clear that her fiancé, Dr. Cummins, was paying for everything. She wanted to look spectacular for him. But beyond that, I wanted her to look spectacular for herself."

"Where did you go when you left the apartment?"

"Immediately drove the dress to my most trusted seamstress to be altered. She works quickly and is so very precise."

"Is this seamstress located in Jackson?"

"No, her place of business is in her house just south of Yazoo City. The piece was already marked, so I dropped it off on my way home."

"And her name? Address?"

The deputy detective noted the responses on a yellow legal pad.

"Did you speak to this seamstress?" he asked.

"No, she was in a back room with another client, so, as I said, I just dropped off the Vera Wang. Took it out of the Louis Vuitton garment bag and hung it ever so carefully on a rack in her living room. She was expecting it."

Leblanc blotted his eye with his handkerchief. "And my seamstress had the alterations completed well before anyone even heard about what happened to that poor, poor precious thing."

"You said the seamstress was expecting it, the dress?"

"Yes, I called her from my cell phone as I was driving up the road to her house."

Martin pulled a list of cellular calls from a separate file.

"Is that the call here?" He turned the page to Leblanc, quickly gesturing with his pen and not waiting for confirmation before flipping the page away.

"About how far a drive is it between this 'trusted' seamstress' house and the downtown Jackson apartment shared by Miss Coachys and Dr. Cummins?"

85

"The way I drive …. 40 minutes, maybe 45 in heavy traffic."

"Maybe we should pick you up for speeding, too, Leblanc," the deputy detective said.

Minor unfolded a clean embroidered handkerchief. He missed some sweat and wiped the table surface dry as he straightened in his chair.

"Exactly why have I been brought down to police headquarters, Detective Martin?"

"You seem to be the last person to see Leslie Coachys alive. Your fingerprints are all over that apartment."

"Fingerprints? Oh, Jesus! I've been over there many other times with other things."

"All paid for by Miss Coachys?"

"She would sometimes give me cash, mostly write checks."

"Were those checks on her personal account or …"

"No, usually written on Dr. Cummins' account."

Leblanc seemed satisfied with his answer. Brad nodded in agreement. Diana rolled her eyes.

Martin asked, "Mr. Leblanc, was Dr. Cummins' dog in the apartment while you were there with Miss Coachys?"

"I don't do well with dogs, particularly large ones. Miss Leslie had him locked up in the guest room. I heard him bark once, but *thank you, Jesus* he got quiet—guess the poor tired thing went right back to sleep."

"Was there anyone else in the apartment with you and Miss Coachys?"

"The fitting was private. She told me that Dr. Cummins would not be coming home that night … something 'bout being really busy at the hospital. Besides, she did not want to spoil his fabulous wedding day surprise."

"Was the deceased with you the entire time you were in the apartment?

"Certainly not. She went into the master bedroom to change, the last time to remove the gown when the fitting was completed. I certainly wouldn't have followed her in there."

Key Martin fought a grin. "Minor Charles Leblanc, I think you killed Leslie Coachys."

"Oh, my Jesus. I would never hurt that precious thing!" Minor said. "Miss Leslie was so dazzling in the Vera Wang."

15

Brad shook the ice in his Belvedere laced with soda and a splash of lime. His sad, stone-faced expression had not changed much since Diana left him earlier that day at police headquarters, although his skin had a rosier color.

Another text appeared on her cell phone.

"It's the ICU this time," she said. "Emergency colon resection from last night just spiked another temp. But I'll take care of it."

"Diana, I don't see that guy killing anybody, much less Leslie. By the way, thanks for having a drink with me. That stuff at the police department was harder than I thought."

They were seated in a cozy area off the lobby of the newly reopened and renovated King Edward, a 1920's hotel located in downtown and only a few blocks from his apartment.

"Less crowded in here, don't you think? And it's away from all those windows in the lobby," Brad said.

"Glad I could slip away. Besides I haven't seen this place since they swept out the pigeons and the homeless—Jackson chic," she said. "About the 'that guy killing someone'—I take it that you weren't referring to the poor fellow in the ICU with the ruptured abscess."

Diana held the cell screen up to Brad.

"His nurse has called me about six times in the last hour."

"I'm sorry, partner. I've let everything drop in your lap."

"Oh, it's *partner* now." Diana tapped the call-back number on the screen.

"Surgical ICU. Fortenberry." Brad sat close enough to hear. He took a longer sip of his vodka.

"Betty, what's going on now with the gentleman in nine?"

"Hi, Dr. Bratton. Sats are up and staying there. BP's stable. Thought you might want to lower the vent settings."

Brad listened as Diana issued orders to the ICU nurse. Not only was she a great surgeon, she also knew her internal medicine. "I guess that's Mr. Walsh," he said.

She nodded, cell phone still pressed tightly against her face.

"He's been shuffled from Brian first to me and now to you."

87

Another swallow of vodka. "Diverticulitis has had him for years."

Their waitress reappeared. "Sir, would you care for another Belvedere?" Brad admired her long dark hair and long legs. She was a pretty, light-skinned African American.

"Why not? I'm not on call." Brad tilted his head toward Diana and sank back into the chair. "She is," he said.

"I'll be back in a sec with your drink. And the lady?"

Diana ended the call and said, "Another Diet Coke but hold some of the ice cubes."

"And a little less soda and lime for me this time," Brad said.

"Mr. Walsh will be waiting for you when you get back to work. Day after tomorrow, I believe you said?"

"Right, but try to get the ol' guy out of intensive care by then please, Dr. Bratton. Nurse Fortenberry will help you."

"I'm sure she will." Diana finished the first Diet Coke and laid her cell face-up on the table's smooth surface. She kept her eyes down and bobbed the phone between her thumb and middle finger.

"Brad, we need to talk."

He placed his empty glass next to the cell phone and looked in the direction of the waitress and the bar. "I know we need to talk. You've carried the practice for weeks, what with Brian's death and now this."

"The *this* is that you just lost the girl you were getting ready to marry. With all that's happened, no one would question your being away from the practice. You're only human, Brad."

Her cell phone vibrated.

"Damn," he said.

She retrieved the phone.

"This one's personal. I can get it later."

"Personal?"

"Not what you think. I'm not that lucky." Diana said.

The waitress brought the second round. "Maybe y'all need a bowl of nuts or some cocktail crackers? Be back in a sec."

Brad downed a third of the vodka. It was stronger than the first.

"You underestimate yourself, Diana."

"I'm not worried about anything but making a living for Kelsey and me. I can handle myself."

"No doubt about it." Brad took another swallow.

"And you seem to be handling things pretty well for yourself, at least for the moment," she said, watching him. "That is, with a little help."

"Like I said – not on call."

Diana thought about Kelsey at home alone with the babysitter. "I didn't come here to talk business, Brad. I came to cheer you up. But I think you're already there."

Another swallow, over half his new vodka was gone.

"I signed on to make a three-person practice," she said. "Suddenly it's down to two surgeons. Now for two more days, it's solo."

"Diana, I know this whole situation sucks. I wasn't pulling my weight even before Brian died, and now this thing with Leslie."

Brad's eyes seemed to moisten again.

"Look, I was wrong," she said. "You're still dealing with all that stuff back at the police station. This discussion can wait."

"I owe you, Diana. I know I do. Brian was always the leader, always made the decisions, business-wise."

Diana glanced again at the phone number highlighted in the new text.

"I was a slouch when I got back from Iraq, trying to make up lost time with Leslie, and when I was working, I had that soldier from Tennessee on my mind, the one I let …"

"Good God, Brad. I'm the one who should be sorry. You must think I'm a real bitch."

"You've got a right to complain about the hours you've been putting in. You've got a family." Another third went down. "Your little girl at home … I know she misses you."

Brad looked down into the cocktail glass and swirled the few ice cubes.

Diana cupped her palm around the phone. She lifted her glass of Diet Coke and took a long swig.

"Go ahead and answer the text. Maybe you can salvage the practice and hang on to our patients."

"It's getting noisier in here. I'll step outside and get it," Diana said.

"Sure. Make yourself at home. You're the one working."

Brad continued to jiggle the remaining ice of his cocktail as he watched Diana walk across the marble floor through the hotel lobby. Gone were the tennis shoes or black clogs. She had worn heels that accentuated her thin calves. He finished the drink as her rear disappeared though the glass doors.

"Dr. Cummins?"

The hotel insignia was at eye level, embroidered on the front of a dark blazer. Brad sat up in his chair and leaned forward, felt lightheaded, then wedged the thick cushion behind his back.

"Yes?"

"I'm Morris, the manager of the hotel's upper floor apartments." He motioned to the gold-colored name plate pinned to the lapel of his dark blazer. He had blond hair, styled upright with gel.

"Dr. Cummins, I believe you had called about renting one of our luxury units?" Morris held a thin, black leather folder in his right hand, the left tucked inside his pants pocket.

"Oh, yes." Brad stood too quickly, shaking his head in an effort to clear it. He managed not to wobble. "I checked into one of your rooms when my place at The Plaza became, you might say, *off limits*."

"I read in the newspaper about your fiancée and the police investigation. I am so, so sorry for your loss."

"The police investigation is on-going, so they pretty-much have our … have my … place cordoned off. Still searching for evidence, they say. Anyway, I wouldn't have wanted to stay there, at least for awhile."

"The good news is that we recently had a one bedroom unit become available on the top floor. There's a waiting list, but if you act fast, I think we can accommodate you, particularly considering the circumstances. I would be happy to show it to you. Preferably now, if you have time?"

"But I'm waiting for my friend. She stepped out to make a call."

"As I said there is a long waiting list, Doctor, and I go off duty in a few minutes."

Brad did not see Diana through the glass doors out onto Capitol Street.

He asked, "How'd you know I was in here, in the bar area, I mean?"

"You professionals are busy people, so hard to track down. The girl at the front desk said she saw you go into the lounge."

The manager seemed to refer to the contents of his leather

90

folder.

"Maybe I am disturbing you at this time? I would hate for you to miss out," he said.

Brad rechecked the doors, "I understand that, but you see, Mr. …."

"It's Morris, Doctor. "You see, the vacancy is really good news for you. The King Edward is very sought after." He gestured to the folder. "And remember, the waiting list?"

There was still no Diana. "My friend stepped away to make some calls, but I guess it's going to take a while."

"Dr. Cummins, the offer is time-limited and you already know the quality of our accommodations. But you will need to approve your new home. Shall we take the elevator?"

"OK. Sure. Why not? I don't need a big place, but I'm curious about the view of downtown."

" Great. Then let's head on up and take a look."

As Brad reached into his pants pocket for his cell, he set the cocktail glass on the mahogany end table. The glass slid to the edge, nearly off.

"Do you need to take a call as well, Doctor? Remember, my shift is over in a few minutes."

"Just need to send my friend a message in case she beats me back here."

He felt the effects of the second strong vodka as he punched in: *Headed up with apt mgr Morris need to see vacant apt before gone.* "Texting not that bad, considering," he said, sliding the cell back into his pants pocket.

"Did you say something, Dr. Cummins?"

"Nothing important."

Brad tossed a 20 and a 10 on the table.

* * *

"Dr. Haynes, this is Diana Bratton. You called."

She looked back at the entrance to the King Edward.

"Like I said, call me John."

Another non-urgent text—she could answer it later.

"Dr. Haynes, if you're calling about our meeting the other night, this is no time for me to consider another practice offer. I'm surprised that you don't see that."

"What I see, Diana Bratton, is that you're not looking after

91

yourself and that cute little girl of yours: Kelly."

Diana bit her lip. *Kelly* it was.

"I guess I need to increase the ante a bit."

Another text popped up: the surgical ICU again. Brad's text followed.

"You young women physicians drive hard bargains. My partners have authorized another 50,000 annually; that's on top of what I promised last week."

"Fifty thousand?"

"Plus we'll take six months off the probationary period. You'll make partner in no time. And then there's more vacation."

"John, thank you, but …"

She stepped back from behind the column of the façade and studied the entrance. Through the large glass doors she could just catch where she and Brad were seated. The waitress was gathering what was left of her Diet Coke and the silver metal cup still brimming with mixed nuts.

"I've got to return some calls. And the SICU just texted again."

"Diana, you can't put this off much longer. Private school, nice clothes for Kelly. We can get you out of that dumpy neighborhood and into Eastover or maybe up to Bridgewater."

She looked down at the text. "Gotta go, John." She ended the call and tapped the number for the surgical ICU. "Dr. Bratton here."

Fortenberry rattled off more vital signs and fluid measurements, this time for another patient.

"Increase her IV fluids. Go ahead and get another set of blood cultures," Diana said. "We'll leave the antibiotics as is for now."

"Yes, ma'am. I'll call you back in an hour if her temp's not down or if I need anything else."

"Fine," Diana said, ending the call. "I bet you will."

She had walked back into the seating area lined with shelves of books, surrounding a large, flat-screen television. She and Brad had been replaced with another couple. She reread his text and then called to the waitress.

"Miss?"

"Sure, Honey."

The young woman walked toward her, the dish of nuts still on her tray. She placed a fresh napkin on a table at the other side of

92

the fireplace.

"Can I get you another Diet Coke, or maybe a glass of wine this time? Your friend closed out your old tab."

"My friend sent me a message that he was going upstairs to look an apartment with a Mister ...," She again brought up Brad's text. " ... Morris, the apartment manager."

"So do you want to start a new tab, Hon? I probably should get a credit card this time."

"No tab. But do you know exactly where I can find Mr. Morris and my friend? Maybe they went to the leasing office first?"

"I'm new here, Honey. Unless they work in the bar or kitchen, I don't know 'em." She was tapping her ink pen softly on her serving tray. "Why don't you try over at the front desk, Hon."

"Sure, thanks." Diana walked away, then turned to the waitress. "And nothing else for me."

Hey back at the bar. Should I wait for u? As she walked across the central lobby toward the registration desk, Diana hit send and her text to Brad disappeared.

16

A guest stood waiting to check-in, monopolizing the clerk's attention. Diana stepped back to study the lobby. An ornate iron railing bordered the circular walkway of the second floor, giving the area the feel of a rotunda. Her cell phone chimed again, this time a call.

"Brad?" she answered without checking caller ID.

"Dr. Bratton, it's Fortenberry again. Sorry to keep bothering you, but you might want to come in to check on Mr. Walsh. I'm having trouble keeping his blood pressure up. His temp shot to 103, and his color's not good. I sent some blood gases and another CBC. No results yet."

"Worried about ARDS?" Diana asked.

"Maybe so." the nurse answered.

"Then consult pulmonary, get a fresh set of blood cultures, and increase his oxygen concentration. I'll be there in a minute. And go ahead and start some Dopamine for his blood pressure. Use the protocol."

"Yes, ma'am. Thanks."

Diana stood in the center of the marble floor and searched the railing above for Brad. She checked her phone again for a response to her text. Nothing. She ended the call from the ICU and turned to the registration counter. The new hotel guest was wheeling his luggage toward the elevator, registration folder clutched in the other hand. The hotel clerk was typing on a computer keyboard. Diana returned to read the name on her blazer.

"Excuse me, Angela, but I'm looking for my friend. He's meeting with a Mister …"

A man about Diana's height pushed through a concealed door behind registration.

"Angela," he said, "the new lease for that vacancy on the top floor is here to inspect the unit before she moves in tomorrow, and I can't find her set of keys. They were right on the top of my desk. Did you get them?"

"No, Mr. Morris, I haven't seen them."

"Maybe they're inside my blazer. I can't find that either.

Thought I left it on my chair when I went out for a smoke."

Diana asked, "You're Mr. Morris?"

Morris turned to her, almost startled. "Angela, please help this nice lady with her check-in."

"So, are you Morris?"

"Well, yes. I'm Charles Morris. Can I help you with something?"

"Diana Bratton, Dr. Diana Bratton. I was having a drink here with a friend a few moments ago and understood that he was meeting with you right now to look at an apartment."

"I would love to show your friend something, Dr. Bratton, but our last available unit has been leased. We do have a waiting list, though."

"So you weren't meeting with Brad Cummins, Dr. Brad Cummins."

"No, ma'am. You're the only doctor I've met today. But if you'll excuse me, I have this client waiting to see her new apartment."

"Sure. Thanks for your time."

Diana scrolled through her cell contacts and tapped *Brad*. The call went directly to voice mail.

"Angela, hurry and look through your drawer for the extra key to that unit. The tenant's waiting in my office," Morris said. "I'll have another set made tomorrow."

"Pardon me, Mr. Morris, but what is the number of the unit you were planning to show?"

"12-B, but why?" The clerk handed Morris the key. "I just explained that the unit is leased—and for a full year."

"Thank you." Diana reached across the counter and grabbed the key from Morris. "Sorry, but I need to find out what's going on."

Diana ran across the lobby to the nearest elevator and pushed the call button. The doors opened.

"Miss, I need that key." Morris called out. "I'm sorry but the unit is already taken."

"Don't worry, you'll get your key back."

As the elevator doors closed on the perplexed manager of the King Edward, Diana heard him say, "Call security. The woman's nuts."

Diana paced the car as the elevator panel lit its way to the twelfth floor. She spun the key in her fingers and tossed it between her hands. She should be with Mr. Walsh in the ICU, but his nurse was a good one and the pulmonary consult would take care of things.

Maybe Brad found somebody to hook up with. An old girlfriend? Somebody new? The Mr. Morris thing was a ruse? she wondered. Brad had downed two vodkas in thirty minutes. So much for dealing with grief over a murdered fiancée.

The doors opened at twelve. There was a directional sign on the opposite wall. Unit 12-B was to the right.

She thought about the manager calling security.

The illuminated exit sign was at the end of the hall, also to the right.

"I've lost my mind," she said. "But I've got to see what's going on."

Her plan was to check out the apartment, leave the key in the lock, take the stairs down to the lobby, and slip out a side door. The security guard or the manager would never see her again.

* * *

Zarife Amarah had unlocked the apartment and held the door open for Brad.

"Step right in, Dr. Cummins," he said. "You'll want to see all of the amenities your new home in our lovely hotel has to offer."

"Don't mind if I do, Mr. Morris." Brad held his empty glass to the light. "Any concierge bar service on this floor?" he asked as he sauntered into the freshly painted apartment. A granite-topped island jutted from the wall, separating the living room from the kitchen.

A blow to his back crashed Brad into the wooden base, his head hitting the granite. The thick cocktail glass and one remaining ice cube flew from his hand. The glass smashed through a window and flew out to the street.

"Turn over and look at me, infidel," Zarife growled. He bent to shove the barrel of his pistol into the rear of Brad's head.

"Something tells me that your name's not *Morris*." He turned slowly to stare into Amarah's weapon. "If it's my wallet you want, take it."

Brad winced reaching for his rear pants pocket.

"Don't move again, Doctor." Zarife tossed his blond wig toward

96

the window. It flopped against the remaining panes and fell to the carpet.

Brad rubbed the back of his head as he peered through the bruising haze. He was nauseated. "You're that Iraqi, the student that got caught in the blast."

"That's right, Dr. Cummins, the student ... *the poor student*. I heard some of your friends, your criminals, call me that. *The poor student ... at the wrong place ... at the wrong time.*"

"What in the hell are you doing here?"

"You should know that, Doctor."

"Look, if its money you need ... like I said, you can take my wallet. I think there's a couple of hundred in there."

He reached again toward his back pocket.

"I said don't move, Doctor, you ass."

"If you need more cash than that, we can go to an ATM. There's one up Capitol Street."

Brad pushed himself up against the kitchen island.

"I told you not to move! You are a miserable serpent!"

The Iraqi screamed. He lunged toward Brad, pressing the tip of the gun into Brad's forehead.

"Hey, man! Slow down. I'm not sure what your problem is, but we saved your life over there."

"That is right. You did save my life. You left me to live disgraced in Allah's eyes. And I must also live a cripple!"

Zarife slapped Brad's face with his disfigured left hand.

"Our guys in physical therapy were going to help you with that. At least they were supposed to. They were to get you a hand prosthesis and all that. I'm not an orthopod, but ..."

"Shut up, you fucking infidel!"

Another slap, harder, still with the disfigured hand.

The gun slipped from Brad's forehead and scraped his check. He smelled the metal and the faint scent of gun powder. He managed a glance at the door from the hallway.

"Doctor, you are a fool. I am the one who set that blast."

Amarah repositioned the end of the barrel firmly against the middle of Brad's forehead.

"No way to wiggle your way out this time," Amarah said. "By the way, I sent you those texts."

"How did you get my cell number?" Brad squinted past the gun

97

toward the door. He estimated the distance at 40 feet.

"I was to die, Doctor, wanted to die. You and the murdering invaders stopped me from meeting Allah. You disgraced me."

Zarife lifted his left arm to strike again, the barrel of the gun slipping off Brad's forehead.

Brad braced his hands behind him, pushing against the base of the island. He lunged into the Iraqi's chest, a sharp, shooting pain flooding his own. He threw his arm at Amarah, dislodging the gun from his grip. The pistol flew to Amarah's right as it fired. The globe over the kitchen island exploded while the gun followed the cocktail glass ten feet to the window and down to Mill Street.

Just as the gun fired and the glass exploded, Diana popped the key into the lock and opened the door to Unit 12-B.

"Brad, my God!" she screamed.

*　　*　　*

Detective Key Martin drove up Mill Street along the west side of the King Edward Hotel. He had stayed late at police headquarters to review the findings from the Leslie Coachys murder investigation and gone over the interrogations word for word. He didn't have enough to hold either suspect. Before he could reach for his radio to check in with his deputy, a blur plunged from above to shatter on the hood of his patrol car, spraying tiny shards of glass onto the sidewalk that bordered the hotel. Martin pulled into the adjacent parking space and grabbed the microphone.

"Somebody's tossing stuff out of a hotel downtown," he told the police dispatcher.

"Like what?" the dispatcher asked.

"A highball glass, that's what it looked like."

"What kind of guests are they booking into that place?" the dispatcher asked.

"Paying ones, I hope," Martin answered.

They both laughed as a revolver shattered his windshield before it settled in the crater on the hood. Broken glass peppered the detective's head and shoulders.

"What the hell is goin' on up there?"

"Sir?" the dispatcher said.

Martin jumped from the cruiser. He counted about 12 floors from the street as he removed a handkerchief from his pocket and slid the revolver into an evidence bag. He locked the weapon inside the trunk.

"I'm going inside the King Edward," he told the dispatcher. "We don't have guns tossed outside of hotels everyday in Jackson."

A man and a young woman were behind the front desk.

"Do you have guests on 12?" Martin asked.

"Only condo and apartment units on that floor," Morris answered. "Some woman grabbed my pass key to the only empty unit. I've called security."

"Looks like someone from that floor threw a gun out the window. What unit are you talking about?"

"12-B. It's near the elevator."

"And the stairs?"

"Around the corner. But it's a long way up to 12," Morris said.

"You talked me into it. Elevator it is," the detective said.

* * *

Zarife Amarah had recovered from Brad's blows and had him in a head lock. Neither man noticed Diana. Things changed with her second scream. When Amarah turned to the noise, Brad broke free and twisted Amarah's elbow out of joint in one motion.

"Brad?"

With the diversion, Brad knocked the Iraqi across the room toward the bank of windows. Amarah pulled a large shard of glass and threw it in Brad's direction, piercing his left thigh.

Brad groaned, yanking the glass dagger from his leg. The artery beneath answered with a bloody spray across the wooden floor. Clutching the wound, Brad rolled to the wool carpet, a dark red pool collecting beneath him.

With a third scream, Diana flew at Amarah, the shrill sound hanging in the air behind her. Amarah pulled at another section of the broken panes, accidentally slicing his wrist. His blood splattered Diana's face as he hurled the ragged glass at her. Dodging the projectile, she plunged head first toward him, propelling Amarah through the bank of windows. He landed atop the detective's squad car still parked below on Mill Street.

Martin ran to the noise pouring through the doorway of Unit 12-B. Despite taking the elevator, he was short of breath. He recognized Dr. Cummins, pale, hands covered in blood, more

99

blood on the floor and carpet, but the man was moving, groaning. The woman squatting at the wall of broken windows was with Cummins earlier at police headquarters. He recalled that she was a female doctor, another surgeon.

"Who threw the gun out the window?" Martin asked.

17

Hospital security gave up sometime around noon. The entrance to 442 had been a revolving door since breakfast when Dr. Brad Cummins was transferred there from the recovery room. Celebrities seldom graced the trauma ward of Jackson Metropolitan Hospital, so having a local physician as a patient was about as celebrated as it got. The vascular surgeons were successful in repairing Zarife Amarah's laceration to Brad's femoral artery, and multiple blood transfusions replaced what spilled in the King Edward apartment. Brad's body was left swollen, forcing his eyelids near closed. Still he welcomed the steady stream of visitors throughout the day.

The nurse in charge of the three-to-eleven shift was sick of the commotion. One Cummins patient after the other, one physician after the other had been in to see the young doctor, each shaking his or her head while leaving and walking by the nursing station. *"Those Cummins boys have had such tragedy. I wonder what's next."*

This last visitor of the shift approached. "Can you tell me what room Dr. Brad Cummins is in?"

The nurse looked up from her review of the updated patient vital signs. She kept her fingers in position on the computer keyboard.

Where were the nursing assistants and the ward secretary? she thought. "Sir, visitation's long been over, but no one seems to care about rules anymore."

She noted the day's newspaper folded under his arm, the front page headline visible: *Another Doctor Attacked.*

The tall man smiled. "And the room number?"

"442. Around that corner and down the hall. Five doors on the left."

She guessed upper sixties as the man smiled again, tipping the bill of his sports cap as he turned away. Thick grey hair curled out from under the rear of the cap. *Maybe early sixties.* The nurse returned to the list of numbers and the keyboard.

Around the corner, the hall was deserted, most of the patients asleep or sedated. The door to room 442 was closed; the man pushed it open. The same young man from the Memphis air show lay in the bed, oxygen tubing pinching his nose, an IV in one arm, the opposite leg propped up under the sheets—no pretty girl around this time.

"Dr. Cummins, I'm Chad Giles, the only Chad Giles left. I've driven down to Jackson several times to talk to you. Lost my nerve every other time, until now."

Brad studied the figure through the waning haze of a narcotic injection. "Giles?" he said. His muscles tightened in reflex. The sutures in his groin felt on fire.

"You doctors don't take too well to being sick, to being down, do ya?"

"No, I guess we don't."

Fighting a groan, Brad braced against the foot of the bed with the uninjured leg and folded the pillow under his back so that he could sit up. He saw Mr. Giles smile at his wincing in pain.

"Is there something I can do for you, Mr. Giles?" Brad thought about pushing the nurse call button, but did not. "You must be that serviceman's father or grandfather ... the one who died in Iraq before I came back home?"

"I am that serviceman's grandfather. His father, my son, died when Chad III was a toddler, along with my daughter-in-law."

The effect of the narcotics lingered. Brad forced himself to focus on the man's face.

"I'm sorry. What happened?" The man resembled the Chad Giles in Iraq, not from the young guy's battered, swollen face before surgery or in the recovery room afterward, but from the GI's military file photo.

"It was a house fire. My grandson was spending the weekend with us when it happened."

"Like I said, I'm sorry, Mr. Giles." Brad managed to sit up higher in bed.

"Sorry for what, Dr. Cummins?"

"I'm sorry for the fire ... the tragedy. Your loss."

"My family's been through a lot of tragedy, Dr. Cummins. Which loss are you talking about?" Giles pulled the chair from the window closer to the bed.

"Mind if I have a seat?" Giles asked.

102

Brad reached for the control to call a nurse and depressed the button.

"I think the nurse out there is really busy, Dr. Cummins, Major Cummins. Is there something I can get for you? Some water? Another pillow?"

"What are you here for, Mr. Giles?" Brad relaxed his hold on the control and moved the injured leg, more sharp pain.

"I was given some information about my grandson's death. The information wasn't clear, sort of confusing. But I got my congressman to look into it. He was happy to do it ... coming up for re-election and all. He got me your name ... let me read the official military report that said you tried to save my grandson ... that you were a good doctor."

"We did all that we could."

"I think there's more to it, Dr. Cummins."

"What do you mean?"

"My grandson's medical report said that he survived his injuries, that he made it through the surgery. But he died anyway."

"That's right. His heart stopped."

"My heart stopped, too."

The man looked more broken than angry.

Brad said, "Mr. Giles. There's nothing I can do here to help you. As you can see, I'm sort of indisposed. I'll be happy to talk to you later, maybe help you get some counseling or some other help."

Giles popped out of the straight-back chair toward Brad's bed. The chair crashed backward to the floor.

Brad fumbled for the call button. His only defense was a plastic water pitcher with cup and the TV remote.

"That's where you're wrong, Doctor. There's gotta be more to it: something else, someone else."

The nurse pushed open the door. "Dr. Cummins, I heard a noise from outside in the hall. Making one last walk through before I leave."

She stared from the overturned chair to the visitor. "Sir, you're still here?" She looked back to Brad. "Dr. Cummins, is everything OK?"

"Yes, Powers, everything's fine. Mr. Giles just stumbled."

She righted the chair. "It's very, very late. If this gentleman is

103

going to be an overnight visitor, then I'll need to call for a cot."

"No, ma'am," Giles said. "I'm not spending the night. I can go ahead and leave."

"Powers, he'll be out in a minute. Go ahead and finish your rounds."

"I will, Dr. Cummins, but you need some rest. Got to get you out of that bed and back to work. That new partner of yours needs some relief." She dimmed the lights a bit. "Security will be back around in a few minutes to check on things."

"Thanks, Powers." The door shut behind her, and Giles walked toward it.

"Mr. Giles, wait a minute," Brad said. "Did I hear you say that there must be something else, someone else?"

"Doctor, my grandson had just met someone over there in Iraq, a nurse at that hospital. A pretty young girl."

"A nurse at our hospital in Balad? Where he died?"

"That's what he said in his letter."

Brad still felt foggy from the last narcotic injection, the haze compounded by the sleeping pill Powers made him swallow earlier. Compassion for the distraught, almost-old man came over him, a man desperate for a glimpse into the final days of his grandson's life, a man grasping for answers.

"I never saw any nurse asking about your grandson, in a personal way, I mean."

"She was probably afraid to," Giles said.

"What do you mean?" Brad asked. He was suddenly having difficulty focusing on Giles' face.

"The nurse broke up with some doctor over there when she started dating my grandson."

"It certainly wasn't me."

"I'm not saying it was you, Dr. Cummins. That's not why I'm here. It was an important doctor."

"An important doctor?" Brad raised his head to attention. His tongue felt thick. "Some people think of me that way."

"Chad wrote me that the doctor was older, that he had almost caught them together, that maybe he was even stalking them."

"This is a lot to take in," Brad said, his voice slurring.

"One day the girl showed up with a bruise. Tried to hide it from Chad with makeup. Some excuse about stumbling into a door.

104

Chad suspected that the doctor got real jealous and hit her."

"I don't remember seeing any beat-up nurses," Brad said.

"I wrote him back, asked if maybe they should file a complaint against the doctor, maybe for being abusive."

"And ... did they?"

"Don't know. I didn't get anymore letters. I worried that this important doctor might come after Chad. Then a few days later, I got word that Chad was dead."

Brad wondered if he was ·hallucinating: *How do addicts function?* As he sank deeper into a medicated stupor he thought again about the nurse call button.

"Mr. Giles, are you trying ... trying ... trying to say that a military physician ... military doctor ... killed your son out of jealousy?"

"When my congressman told me that everything you did looked by the book, I just started to think about that doctor beating up Chad's girl. Something just didn't sound right."

Despite the pain medication and sedatives, the sutures started to throb again. Tensing his muscles during Giles' visit had only intensified the pain. He wished for another shot of Demerol or even just Percocet. *Addicts!*

"Can you help me, Dr. Cummins? Chad was all I had left."

Nurse Powers's replacement for the eleven-to-seven shift entered the room. "Hi, Dr. Cummins," she said. "Powers signed out that you might need something extra to help you rest and for your pain. Roll over and let me give you this little happy juice. Won't hurt a bit, Doc."

"Guess I better be going, Doctor. Thanks for talking to me."

Giles left the room.

"Wait, Mr. Giles. I need to ask you some more questions." Brad tried to lean forward and reach for the door. "Can you come back in the morning when I'm not so drugged out?"

"Now, be a good boy and let me see that butt cheek, Doc," the new nurse said.

"I'm not sure I need anything else. I'm already pretty wasted," he said.

"Dr. Cummins, just be the patient, just this once," she said.

Brad managed a wince as the needle pierced his buttock, although he felt practically nothing.

The memory of the weeks after the death of Lance Corporal Chad Giles became a blur: the inquest, the medical review, the accusations, his acquittal by the medical tribunal.

In the cloud of his own hospital bed he searched his memory for a young female nurse hovering near Chad Giles III, someone near the recovery room or in the waiting area after the futile resuscitation efforts at Balad.

He saw no one.

18

This was her second visit to police headquarters in two days.

"Thanks for coming in to talk to me, Dr. Bratton." Detective Martin stood from his desk and computer screen as the female officer escorted Diana into his office. Martin was taller than she remembered but no more handsome. His baggy jacket was wrinkled.

"I went by the hospital this morning to talk to your boyfriend about this case," he said, sitting back at his desk. Diana sat in the chair beside. "But Dr. Cummins had just been given some medication and ..."

"He has a few broken ribs and a concussion, in addition to his vascular leg injury. And besides, Brad Cummins is not my boyfriend, Detective. We practice medicine ... surgery ... together. That's all."

"Whatever you say, Doctor. And please call me Key."

"*Detective* will work fine," she said.

"I just assumed that since the two of you were at headquarters yesterday and then at the hotel together last night that ..."

"No, I just met Brad ... Dr. Cummins ... at the King Edward for a drink. He needed a friend."

"A friend?" Key asked.

"He'd lost his brother, and then his fiancée. He'd had too much to drink, and I can't say that I blame him. And he wasn't on call. I was."

"You seem to always be around when this kind of stuff happens to Brad. I mean, like you say, *Dr. Cummins*. You were there at the hotel last night and in the parking garage of the Cummins clinic when his brother was shot."

"Detective, as you know ... "

"*Key*, call me Key," he said.

"You know that I work in the Cummins medical office, Key. And I have a car that I park there under the clinic building."

"What a mess there was in that elevator that night," he said.

"And you questioned me that night, and I told you everything I knew."

"And earlier this afternoon, I went back over those notes."

"Then what exactly can I do for you here?" Diana checked her cell for any new messages, exaggerating the motion and surprised that her fingers trembled.

"I know you're busy, Doctor. Maybe we should continue this later?"

"No, go ahead. But I'm the only physician covering the practice at the moment, and I'm tired of leaving my daughter at home with a babysitter."

"I just need some answers. Can get 'em now or later."

"Ask everything you need. Just get it over with." She checked the cell again. She wished for a phone call or a new text. Nothing. "I've still got time. I guess all the patients have been scared away by the crap that's been going on."

"I expect there are plenty of patients out there still waiting for you and Dr. Cummins, especially you."

"It's amazing the number of visitors Brad … Dr. Cummins … has received while he's been hospitalized. When I see patients in the clinic, the first thing they ask me is *How's Dr. Cummins?* or a few cross the line with *How's Brad?*"

"You know, Dr. Bratton, I've worked some cases that involved female doctors: mostly medical office break-ins, a few domestic problems, a mugging, one carjacking, never any murder cases. But I've never been to a female doctor, you know for doctoring."

"You ought to give it a try," she said.

Key Martin found Dr. Diana Bratton attractive, a natural beauty: slender with thick, dark hair pulled closely against the nape of her neck. Her long fingers were well-manicured but lacked polish. He decided that she was too professional to wear much makeup. But if she was trying to hide her appeal, she was doing a poor job.

He wondered if being treated by her as his physician, if being touched by her, would feel awkward.

Dr. Bratton asked, "Will there be anything else? I thought you were going to ask me some questions about the murders."

Diana retrieved her purse from the floor beside her chair. "I need to get back to the office," she said, walking to the door. "Please call me if you come up with anything."

"Doctor, wait just a sec. Do you know much about social media?"

"Social media?" Diana stopped.

"You know police are into social media," he answered. "I checked out your clinic's website and your Facebook page. Nice photo of you and a little girl on your page," he said. "Your daughter, I suppose, the one left with the babysitter?"

"My Facebook page? What does that have to do with this?" she asked.

"Routine investigation, that's all. Too bad I wasn't your friend. Saw nothing but your employment at the Cummins boys' clinic, a list of some research projects published while you were a resident over at the med center, not much else."

"I don't spend much time with that kind of thing, Detective." She caught his frown. "OK, Key," she said.

He smiled. "I followed the link to the older Cummins, the one that was murdered. He still had a listing. There were memorials and tributes posted on his wall. Kind of creepy, if you ask me." Key noticed Diana check her cell again.

"But I couldn't find a Facebook page for your friend ... your partner, Brad."

"It seems that you would be more interested in that guy who tried to shoot Brad ... Dr. Cummins ... at the King Edward."

"You mean the guy you pushed out the hotel window?"

"I believe I had good reason."

"Yeah, self-defense all the way. Looks like you saved Brad Cummins. The Iraqi fella's doc over at Jackson Metro tells me that his patient will be on life support for quite sometime, might never come off. They might even have to pull the plug. But it's a political thing."

Key pulled up an image of Zarife Amarah borrowed from his visa. "When this guy was sprawled across the top of my squad car, I would have taken him for dead."

"Never saw the guy before that day," Diana said. She walked back into Key's office and studied the computer screen. "Yep, that's him. The guy I pushed out the window."

"I went back by the hospital after lunch and caught Dr. Cummins between pain shots. He told me that he treated this Amarah guy over in Iraq, but didn't see through the disguise at the King Edward. "

"I heard them fighting and arguing inside the apartment when I opened the door with the key I took ..."

"Yeah, the manager down at the desk isn't very happy with you. I talked him out of filing a complaint."

"That's a relief. Now I can get some sleep."

The detective grinned at the sarcasm.

"So it seems that this Amarah guy is responsible for all of this?" she asked.

"Good guess, Doctor," he grinned again. "But we need to tie up some loose ends. Re-examine the evidence." He clicked to another page displaying a copy of Zarife's travel documents.

"Homeland Security shared this with me. Didn't bother with Interpol. The young fellow was a no-show at Georgia Tech—had signed up for some sort of student-exchange program."

"How long had he been in the U.S., did you say?" Diana asked.

"Landed in Atlanta just before the Commins trouble started. University secretary over there in Georgia told me they assumed a missed flight ... figured he would show up in a day or two."

"Sounds like they weren't too worried about it," Diana said.

"A *no-show* meant less headache, I suppose," Martin said.

"Brad ... Dr. Cummins ...said the guy was yelling something about Allah and stuff like that."

"Dr. Bratton, it's OK if you call Dr. Cummins *Brad*. After all, you two work closely together—bound to be good friends."

"*Dr. Cummins*," Diana said, "must realize that over in Iraq he saved the life of this murderer, that he took the Hippocratic Oath to the next level." She walked to the only window. "Now he's got more baggage to deal with."

"Your Doctor Cummins shouldn't beat himself up so bad."

"He's already drinking too much," Diana said and then turned away. "Damn, I shouldn't have said that."

"Better keep an eye on him. Anyway, Amarah wasn't a suspected terrorist. Homeland Security thought he was on our side. Otherwise he wouldn't have set foot over here."

"Of course not," Diana said.

"Of course not," Martin said.

19

Her impulse was to start the morning with Brad.

Instead, she pulled-up the patient records in numerical order. First, Mr. Carpenter in four, then Mr. Murphree in seven, Evans in 10, Wooley in 12, and Upton in 17. Brad Cummins would follow Mrs. Upton, his room at the end of the hall away from the nurses' station.

"Your incision looks great, Mrs. Upton. What do you think about going home today?"

"Are you kidding, Dr. Bratton? Yes!"

Diana ducked into a hall cubicle and signed into the physician computer portal. She entered the order to discharge Mrs. Upton, and then she scrolled to Brad. The download of the morning's follow-up CT scan appeared in seconds, complete with the option to enlarge the image of Brad's brain, quadrant by quadrant. There was no midline shift of the hemispheres, no skull fracture, no epidural or subdural hematoma.

Studying the pictures, Diana felt odd, an uncomfortable feeling of near intimacy with Brad as though she were reading his thoughts—or at least wanted to. She peered over her shoulder and then up and down the corridor. No one was watching.

Diana signed off the computer and walked toward Brad's room.

"You didn't need to knock, Dr. Bratton," he said, hung-over from yesterday's medication.

"I always announce myself when I step into a patient's room. Don't you, Dr. Cummins?"

"Sure, I knock," Brad said. "But I don't call my patients *Doctor.*"

"Regardless of who you are, your head CT is stable. And it looks to me that your facial edema is down considerably. What've those nurses been doing for you?"

"I'm not sure. I can barely remember last night."

Diana looked past the facial bruising. Somehow Brad's narrow, perfectly proportioned noise had not been rearranged by the Iraqi's attack. Even with the swelling, it blended perfectly with the rest of his classic facial features. His thick, dark hair invited fingers even after a trip to the OR, recovery in the SICU, and no shower for nearly 48 hours. Lying supine in the hospital bed, his legs and pelvis covered in thin sheets that stopped just above his groin, he looked somewhat taller than six-two. She was drawn to his bare chest and firm abdomen and the bandages encircling his lower ribs.

"I guess the nurses are just following your orders." Brad gagged on the last sip of orange juice and with the sharp pain grabbed the elastic chest supports. "Hey, give me a little help here. Won't you, Doc?"

"Problem patients like you earn an early discharge," grinned Diana.

She noted *Concussion resolving* in Brad's chart. *Patient ready for discharge soon.* She caught another glimpse of his chest and paused a second when he pulled at the sheets. If the vascular guys who fixed that gusher in your leg agree, then you're outta here. The sooner you go home, the sooner you're back at the clinic."

"Anywhere would be better than this hospital bed," Brad said.

"You can bet that your office schedule is over-booked," Diana said. "Maybe your patients waiting on surgery won't be too mad."

"I think I'll stay another day," he said.

* * *

The guest room overlooked the rolling terrain of Madison County, green grass interrupted by century-old oaks and strands of white picket fence. John Haynes' cows grazed in the open pasture, staying clear of the fencing, no plans to go anywhere. At the west end of the room, the Mississippi sunset filled the window, framed in antique wood salvaged from a cotton warehouse in Memphis and stretching the length of the wall.

"I've got a view of the lake and croquet court from my wing of the house," Haynes said, "so I didn't want my guests to feel slighted."

"Wouldn't have expected any less of you, brother."

"You never called me *brother* in Iraq."

"That would have been disrespectful . . . a breach of the doctor - nurse relationship," Elizabeth Cossar said.

"If I had known you were working in Balad when I signed up, I would've picked someplace else," Haynes said. "It was bad enough that I was stuck over there with Cummins."

112

"Like you had any choice," Cossar said.

"I'm career military, sis. I can take it."

"You might have served a weekend or two in the reserves down in Hattiesburg, but I don't see a Purple Heart anywhere around here." Cossar turned back to the window.

Haynes set Cossar's suitcase near the bed. "So, am I the last stop on your little tour of the Southeast, your family reunion of sorts?"

"My leave will be over in just a few days. I've worn out my welcome everywhere else. Our cousins in Charlotte were the nicest." Cossar retrieved the bag and moved it to the chaise near the window. She unzipped it.

"Are you going to stand there while I unpack?

"You don't expect me to believe that you're here out of sisterly love, do you? Like I said, you pretended that you didn't know me."

"Didn't want the other guys to be jealous."

"Particularly your doctor boyfriend," Haynes said. He retrieved the television remote from the bedside mahogany chest and raised the giclée on the opposite wall. A large flat screen television that equaled the dimensions of the reproduction art appeared beneath it. "I just had this thing installed. Got one in the master, too. What do you think?"

"I didn't come here for TV, John." She withdrew a makeup and toiletry kit from her suitcase and walked toward the guest bathroom. "Are you going to watch me freshen-up, too? I thought you had enough of that growing up."

"Can't think of anything more disgusting," he said. "And if you're here to see your boyfriend Cummins, he's in the hospital."

"I knew that. All the crap that's happened to him even made news in Atlanta and Charlotte."

Haynes heard the water run in the lavatory. He called to her from just outside the bathroom door.

"Word around the hospital is that his practice could go under. His late brother hired this female surgeon before he was shot; she's all that's holding the place together."

The water stopped. Elizabeth's face appeared in the doorway. "Cute? I bet."

"You might say so. At least way above average," Haynes answered.

113

"You going to ask her out?"

"Probably," he said.

Stacy Lane slid around the hall corner that led to Elizabeth Cossar's guest room. Voices drifted through the opened door just beyond, barely muted by John's firm steps against the hardwood floor. Suddenly, the steps were coming in her direction. Yesterday he had warned Stacy of his sister's call and the uninvited visit.

During her time in Balad with Elizabeth Cossar, the elder RN never dropped her charge-nurse persona or failed to exert her higher military rank. Stacy assumed the witch exuded authority even in her personal life.

John's instructions were to be scarce during Cossar's stay, better yet, invisible. In a sprawling 12,000 square foot home, she had no problem with that. Enough was enough. Stacy had taken more than her share of orders from Elizabeth T. Cossar, RN.

Besides, Stacy would be leaving soon.

"What are you doing out here?" he whispered, although the toilet could be heard flushing inside the guestroom bath.

"Just wanted to see what brotherly-sisterly love is all about. Never had that as an only child, you know."

Haynes pulled her down the hall by the elbow.

"If you think this is foreplay, you're losing your touch, Doc."

"Shut up," he said, as he pushed her through the garden room and library.

Stacy yanked free in front of the stone fireplace, the Oriental runner twisting underfoot.

"By the way, I heard what you said about Dr. Cummins' partner. Sounds like *way above average* is all you need to screw somebody. Is that what I am? *Way above average?*"

Haynes cupped her buttocks and pulled her body against his. His kiss was deep. "You were the lucky one, Stacy. All of those nurses over in Balad wanted me. Wavy grey hair is a turn on."

"You have an *old-guy* complex." She reached to run her fingers through the hair.

"I preferred you," Stacy said. She returned the kiss.

"I told you not to talk about that guy," Haynes said. He released her, but kept a lock on her elbow as he led her further into the opposite wing of the house.

"John, we only hooked up a couple of times in Iraq, and that

114

was when you weren't around."

"You're not listening to me, my dear." Haynes turned the knob to the double doors of her bedroom. He devoured her cleavage and put his other hand under her skirt. Her back fell against the doors and parted them.

"I've listened to you plenty, John," she gasped. "I did exactly what you told me to do after Chad Giles died."

"And what was that?" Haynes lifted her blouse over her head and buried his face in her chest.

"You told me to stay clear, not to come around."

She unbuttoned his shirt. The belt was next.

"That's right, but that's not what I want you to do now," Haynes said as he locked the door and tossed Stacy Lane onto the bed.

20

The line was long for valet parking, so Cossar veered to the left where there was no waiting. It was a busy day for Jackson Metropolitan Hospital: few empty beds and lots of visitors. The parking lot appeared full, but she circled and found a space in the last row. On the other side of the thick boxwoods and tall, ivy-laced ironwork that bordered *Self Parking*, Cossar eyed the *Doctors Only* section and its BMWs. If not for the ironwork, she would have stepped over the shrubs to be nearer the hospital entrance.

"I'm here to see Dr. Brad Cummins. He's a patient here."

The hospital volunteer scrolled her computer screen. "Yes, you're right. I thought he might have been discharged already."

"The room number?" Cossar asked.

"428."

"And the elevator to 428?"

The volunteer checked her terminal. "Oh, look. Dr. Cummins' discharge work just went through." She punched a few more keys. "But if you hurry you might still catch him in the room. Remember, he's on four."

"The elevator?"

"Right down that hall, past the gift shop."

The elevator opened and Cossar stepped onto the fourth floor. The fourth-floor charge nurse was pushing Brad in a wheelchair with one hand and pulling a metal cart loaded with potted plants and flowers with the other.

Cossar read the name badge. "Powers, I'm a nurse, too. I'm qualified to push a wheel chair."

"What are you doing here, Cossar?" Brad asked. "I thought you were in Atlanta."

"I'm visiting the sick and infirmed, like all the other crazies filling up that parking lot outside. Don't people in Jackson have anything else to do?" she said.

"It's OK, Powers. I know this woman," Brad said. "She's a friend, or used to be."

"I don't care if she's Florence Nightingale, but a Jackson Metro

116

nurse is supposed to escort each discharged patient to his or her vehicle."

Brad said, "You know y'all are short-staffed up here and could use a hand. Remember, I've been a patient."

"Dr. Cummins, Sweety, even with two nurses out we answered every call light for you and gave you a shot whenever we could," Nurse Powers said.

Powers moved from the rear of the wheelchair as Elizabeth Cossar stepped up.

"Don't worry, Powers," she said. "I'm not out for your job."

"Thought never crossed my mind. But you go ahead and do the honors this time. It's not like the good doctor is going to turn me in or something." She handed Brad a long, brown envelope containing his release papers. "Y'all have a nice visit on your elevator ride down to the lobby. I'll bring the cart down in a few."

"Don't keep us waiting," Cossar said.

Powers ignored her and grinned at Brad. "Promise you won't report me to the administrator, Dr. Cummins?"

"Secret's safe," Brad said as Powers returned to the nurses' station.

The elevator reopened and Cossar rolled Brad inside. The door closed behind her. "That one gives our kind a bad name," she said.

"Powers is a sweet gal, Elizabeth. Just 'cause she butted heads doesn't make her all bad."

"Don't like her."

"You don't know her."

"Don't like her anyway."

The elevator reached the first floor and Cossar rolled them in silence for a few moments down the main corridor, passing the gift store with the lobby in sight.

"I thought you liked me once, Elizabeth."

"I adore you, Dr. Cummins."

"My late fiancée didn't seem to think so when you came by her bookshop. She said that you were critical of my surgical management in Balad with that Giles fella from Tennessee."

Elizabeth Cossar positioned the wheelchair near the end of a bank of chairs in the lobby. She sank into the one next to Brad.

"It was fate when I ran into ...now, what was her name?"

"Her name was Leslie."

117

"That's right, *Leslie*," Cossar said. "I strolled into her store and realized who she was. We started chatting. I asked her if you were doing any better about Chad Giles, but she didn't know anything about that crap."

"Did you think that maybe there was a reason I hadn't told her? Not to mention the HIPAA violation?"

"I doubt if HIPAA or any other governmental rule was your concern with your fiancée."

Brad popped open the envelope. His wallet, car keys, and a few coins were among the medical papers inside. He grabbed the keys and stood. "Damn, I'm weaker than I thought."

"Sit your ass down, Doctor, and listen to me. I told those prima donnas on the medical board over there what they needed to hear. I saved your skin."

"What in the hell are you talking about?"

"I don't know if those few minutes made a difference or not in the ICU, but I have to be honest with you. I didn't appreciate your paying attention to that sand . . ."

"That's enough, Elizabeth."

Brad stood and attempted to walk toward the exit. It was more of a wobble.

Elizabeth fought shouting, but failed. "Hold-up a minute!"

She stared down a couple of hospital volunteers carrying clipboards. Much softer: "Sit your butt back down in this wheelchair."

Brad steadied himself against the wall and complied.

"I went to Iraq to help American guys . . . and girls . . . not the assholes who were trying to kill them."

"Everyone knows our focus was on our own people, but my God, Elizabeth, we're doctors and nurses."

She rolled him down the path toward the parking lot. "Brad, everything looked OK on paper, but I saw your face when that lance corporal died, when you couldn't save him. You know you felt the same as I did, do."

"I shouldn't have lost Chad Giles. I still don't understand it."

"Protocol was followed, Brad. I testified at the tribunal." She leaned down to Brad as she pushed, then whispered. "And they believed us."

"You told it like it was. Then why did you plant that question in

118

Leslie's head?"

Elizabeth stopped the wheelchair for a few seconds. "It was obvious that you loved that girl and that's why you had kept her in the dark. She needed to know how torn up you were."

They rolled toward the visitors' parking lot. Elizabeth guided them around a speed bump, the loaded cart in tow. *Doctors' Only* was off to the side.

"What I did was lead her to her death. It was my fault she died."

"Your fault? What are you talking about?"

"Somebody murdered her in my apartment. They were after me."

"You don't know that, Brad."

"It wasn't a robbery. Somebody wanted to take me out. After what happened at the hotel, it looks to me that it was that Amarah guy."

"The morphine's still talking, Doc," Elizabeth Cossar said.

"Look, there's my rental over by the fence. Is there a wheelchair bin like they have at Wal-Mart for shopping carts?" she asked.

"Just push the wheelchair off to the side when we're finished with it. Environmental services will get it."

"Nobody invited me to the reunion? Must've missed the text," John Haynes said, sliding his ID badge through the lock that opened the gate from the physicians' side.

"Colonel," Cossar said as he walked the short brick path toward them.

"So, Brad, I see that you talked your way into being discharged early. Don't you think you might be pushing it a bit?"

"No need to worry, Haynes. I had a great doctor rounding on me post-op."

"Are you sure Diana did right by you once those vascular guys finished sewing you up? Looks like you're still moving kind of slow." Haynes waved to a couple of other physicians and a man and woman walking by.

"I'll be back in the OR in no time, eating up all those open spaces on the schedule. There won't be so much operating time left for you, Haynes."

"And, Nurse Cossar, it was good to see you again." Haynes turned to the walkway leading to the hospital entrance.

"I'm surprised he didn't mention the Giles case like usual,"

Brad said. "I read the transcript of his testimony at the medical tribunal."

"He was a saint—right?" Cossar asked.

"You guessed it: every dot, every *T*. A regular Hippocrates."

Cossar parked Brad at the passenger side of her rental car. She locked the wheelchair, found her keys, and opened the door. "If I hadn't shown up, how were you planning to get home? Drive yourself? Taxi?" she asked.

"I really hadn't thought about it," Brad answered as Cossar helped him out of the wheelchair. "Leslie's always been around to fill in the gaps, but now I need to figure out something else."

Cossar heard the sadness in his voice. "You just slide on in, Doctor, or do I need to lift you?"

"No doubt that you could do it," Brad answered. He worked his way onto the seat. His strength was returning, and his thigh did not seem to hurt as much.

"Don't worry your pretty little head. I'll unload all that stuff on the cart into the trunk and backseat," Cossar said. "And I won't break any of those flower stems."

Brad waited patiently, checking her slow progress in the rearview mirror. After she emptied the cart and pushed it and the wheelchair over to the side of the parking lot, he felt his cell phone vibrate. The text was a call for the resuscitation team to report to the surgical ICU, a cardiopulmonary arrest.

"Hey, don't they know I'm sidelined?" He slid the cell back into his pocket.

"What's that about?"

Cossar turned the key in the ignition.

"STAT call to the SICU." Brad turned his head toward the hospital entrance. "Maybe I should go back in there and see if they need any help."

"You're not going anywhere but home, Doctor," Cossar said. "Now, give me your address."

21

Haynes had opted against the stairs and took the private elevator to the SICU. Of the patients filling the unit to capacity, he was expected to round on his private patients as well as those admitted unexpectedly to him through the Emergency Department. Caring for such unreferred patients assigned in rotation to the physician staff was a condition for medical staff membership and was not dependent on the patients' ability to pay. One of these new patients assigned to John Haynes was Zarife Amarah.

"I hope you can hear me now, Zarife. The neurosurgeon says that your brain swelling is down, so you should be waking up." Haynes pushed back a big toe. The Iraqi's heart rate increased in response. "I was glad to sew up your liver for you. That sure was a nasty fall you took at the King Edward."

"Dr. Haynes, excuse me, but I have orders from pulmonary to lower the vent settings for a spontaneous breathing trial, and if this fellow passes, then I'm supposed to extubate him," Zarife's nurse said. "I was getting ready to change the abdominal dressings and check the incision unless you want to do it."

"No, Jake, you go ahead and do the honors. And I agree with Pulmonary. Go ahead and get his tube out. I bet he'll do fine on CPAP."

The nurse left to collect the sterile bandages, gauze, and adhesive tape.

"You like being a drain on society, don't you, my boy?" Haynes whispered. "I gave you a chance to redeem yourself, and you blew it."

Ten years earlier, Haynes had served on the hospital-design board that approved Metropolitan Hospital's security system. The interior security cameras were contained inside small, dark glass domes, mounted nearly flush with the ceiling. Except for a tiny, flickering red light inside each dome, the equipment appeared non-functioning. Such a camera studied the unit secretary's work area, another pointed toward the medication dispenser, and one monitored the entrance and exit to the SICU: no cameras were installed over patient beds.

121

Haynes looked around the unit. The male nurse had disappeared inside the supply closet. The other attendants were busy with their own patients. The unit secretary remained behind a counter, hovering over a computer. Haynes pressed his knuckles against Zarife's sternum, this time a twitch of his facial muscles.

"Your oxygen sats look good; you're more responsive. Time you came off some of that sedation."

"Did you say something, Dr. Haynes?" Jake stood behind him, holding the wound dressing supplies.

"This guy's definitely waking up, doing some breathing on his own. Like I said, go ahead and pull the endotracheal tube. He'll cooperate."

"Whatever you say, Dr. Haynes. You're the boss," Jake said. "And the patient seemed to be in pain a few minutes ago, so I gave him some morphine."

"Good idea," Haynes said.

Jake walked around to the other side of the bed and pulled back the sheets. His back to Haynes, the nurse loosened the adhesive and slowly pulled away the soiled abdominal dressing. A thin layer of skin came with it near the edge. Haynes noticed the Iraqi's heart rate jump again.

He found the IV site in Zarife's right forearm infusing well and scanned the rest of the unit. Everyone in the ICU remained busy. Haynes felt deep inside the right pocket of his coat, his fingers curling around the plastic syringe of Propofol. Careful not to puncture his own hand, he popped free the plastic cover from the needle and began to pull back on the syringe.

"Do you want to continue the antibiotics, Doc?" Jake looked up as he applied a lighter bandage.

Haynes dropped the syringe back into his pocket. "No, he never has spiked a temp and the wound looks good. Save the state a buck and stop them."

Jake removed the endotracheal tube and switched the patient to CPAP. The Iraqi's oxygen saturation readings and vital signs remained stable. Once Jake turned to the bedside laptop to enter Haynes' orders, the surgeon grasped the syringe, this time pricking himself.

"Shit," Haynes muttered. A speck of bright red blood oozed from his forefinger.

"Say something, Doc?"

"No, just thinking about how many patients I've got left to round on after I'm finished here."

"Relax, Doc. We've got this guy taken care of for today. Do you want me to page or text you if I need orders or if his condition changes?" Jake closed the cover of the laptop and bent near the floor to check the volume in the Foley bag hanging off the side of the bed.

Haynes slid the syringe of Propofol from his pocket and plunged the needle into the IV tubing.

With his back still to Dr. Haynes, Jake stood to remove the unused bag of antibiotics hanging from the IV stand and asked, "Can I help you with something, Doc?"

Haynes withdrew the still full syringe from the IV port and dropped it into his coat pocket. "No. Everything looks under control," he said.

Jake turned to smile at his patient. "Hey, man, you're already waking up. Doc did the right thing to get that tube out. Look how quick you're breathing on your own." The nurse adjusted the CPAP plastic tubing and gently wiped Zarife's face with a moist cloth. He removed Zarife's restraints.

"Doctor, come closer," Zarife sputtered. "I want to talk. There is unfinished business."

Haynes stared down at the Iraqi. His eyes said *Not now.*

"Nurse, make the doctor talk to me." Zarife lifted in bed, then fell back coughing. He gagged and braced his bandaged abdomen with the disfigured hand. A fresh stain of thin red fluid grew in the center of the dressing.

"Doc?" Jake questioned, reaching to uncoil the shaken IV and oxygen tubing. "I'll get more dressing while y'all talk."

"I need to make patient rounds up on four," Haynes said. "No time to chat."

With Jake gone, he shoved the needle and syringe of Propofol into the IV tubing, flushing all of the medication into Zarife Amarah's veins.

"Let me know if that joker has ripped loose his sutures, Jake," Haynes said, passing by the supply cabinet. "I'll be on four."

* * *

The extension for the Surgical ICU blared on the display of

123

Haynes' pager as he left the fourth floor elevator. A deep breath greeted the word *STAT*. Haynes walked unhurried to the nurses' station of the post-op unit. The unit secretary was bundling printouts of the charts belonging to the patients already discharged.

"Mary, how's it goin'? I've got three to let go today. Ready for some more paperwork?"

The intercom overhead announced *CODE BLUE. PHYSICIANS NEEDED. SICU. STAT*—the same message on his pager. He had hoped to be inside a patient room before the overhead call and planned to blame a malfunctioning pager.

"You got a patient over in SICU, Dr. Haynes?" Mary asked.

The intercom overhead repeated.

"Yes, I better run down there and see what's happening," he said as he gently set the printed list of hospitalized patients on the counter. He stalled for a few seconds with a double-check of the list against the one on the computer screen.

"You never know what can happen around here, do you, Mary?"

"No, sir, you don't," she answered, without looking up.

Haynes hesitated another moment or two before turning toward the elevator.

* * *

Jake hovered over Zarife, deep into chest compressions. "Dr. Bratton, I had just changed his dressings and updated Dr. Haynes. The guy was doing better," Jake said in rhythm between compressions. The Metropolitan Hospital Emergency Response team was already at Zarife's bedside.

"Has somebody called his attending?" Diana asked.

"Dr. Haynes should have gotten the same page we did," a small, frizzy-headed female answered from her position at Zarife's head where she was squeezing an Ambu bag to ventilate him. "We drew a fresh set of electrolytes, a CBC, and a tox panel. We've already given him some atropine."

Diana stared at the flat line on the cardiac monitor. "There's nothing," she said.

"Dr. Haynes and I had just pulled his tube. The guy was waking up."

"I can go ahead and reintubate him," the respiratory therapist said, now short of breath.

"The guy's young, in pretty good overall health. Has he had any other medication in the last hour or so, anything different?" Diana asked.

The cardiac monitor remained flat.

"He was starting to exhibit signs of pain, so I gave him some morphine about twenty minutes ago," Jake answered.

"How much?"

"Five milligrams IV, Doc. That's what's on Dr. Haynes' orders."

"He's had no trouble with morphine, Diana."

She managed not to flinch at the sharp voice of aggravation behind her.

"But if you think it's anaphylactic shock, then, by damn, go ahead and give him some epinephrine," Haynes said.

"You weren't here. Just trying to get the whole picture," Diana said. "Go ahead with the epinephrine," she ordered a nurse on the resuscitation team. "Your patient, John. Take over."

The epinephrine did nothing, same response as atropine. A flat line moved across the monitor: fine ventricular fibrillation or asystole.

"Let's try shocking him."

Jake grabbed the electro-conversion paddles from the resuscitation cart. Positioning them on Zarife's chest, he shouted, "Stand clear!"

The Iraqi's body twisted violently in response.

"Clear!" Jake directed again.

Zarife bolted upward from the bed, the stench of burning flesh filling the work space. Another shock brought the same.

Jake checked the placement of the defibrillators and reactivated them for a fourth time. The fully-recharged signal sounded. *Ready!*

More vicious jerking, then the patient stilled.

"Stop! That's enough!" Diana demanded. "There's no rhythm. Just stop!"

"Obviously a pulmonary embolus," Haynes said. "A big one."

"PTE is possible," Diana said. "Jake, was there an increased heart rate before this guy coded?"

"His pulse shot up when I removed the old dressing. The gauze had stuck to his skin. That was bound to have hurt." Jake resumed chest compressions, his thick forearm muscles flexed.

125

Diana felt for anti-embolic stockings in place on the patient's legs. "Has he been given all the other DVT prevention protocol?"

"Of course—stockings, leg exercises—everything we've got against clots. We held the heparin, concern about a head bleed," Haynes said. "You want to push some tPA on him?" he asked, the tone sarcastic.

"That might dissolve a clot, then he could bleed out from his surgical wounds," she answered.

"Exactly. Anymore suggestions, Diana?"

Haynes checked the electronic readings on the bedside monitors and lifted a clipboard of handwritten data as though to compare. He tossed the clipboard back to the cart. "Got any more questions about how I've handled this case?"

"Go ahead and push some more bicarb," Diana said to the nurse. "We need d-Dimer results or a pulmonary arteriogram to rule out a clot."

"God, Bratton, we need a cardiac response before wishing for the impossible. Nothing's working."

Haynes threw his white lab coat to the floor. It landed at Diana's feet. "OK, you got another idea?"

Haynes snatched gloves and a scalpel from the resuscitation cart and pierced Amarah's chest, running the knife along the top edge of the ribs, missing the major blood vessels. He cracked open the chest and held Amarah's heart, rhythmically compressing the muscle. There was movement on the monitor with each internal compression, but nothing in between. No normal cardiac activity, no spontaneous heart beat.

Haynes threw his bloody surgical gloves to the cart.

"We might as well call it," he said.

Jake typed another entry into the medical record. "Time of death 12:33 pm. Is that right, Dr. Haynes?"

"If Dr. Bratton doesn't have anything else to add, then I guess so." Haynes reached for his white coat.

"There'll be an autopsy—hospital protocol," Diana said.

She handed him the coat and smoothed the collar. Haynes' Montblanc pen had rolled a few inches away, and she picked that up, too.

"Thank you," he said. "For that, I'll take care of completing the report even though you were the first one here."

22

Eight years with the Jackson Police Department for Key Martin: one blue-collar crime case after the other – intertwined with lots of penniless no-collars. The rarity of the white collar variety shown in the Cummins and Coachys murders was a welcomed change. Any new development in the stories headlined the front page of the *Clarion-Ledger* and opened every local television news program. Detective Martin's arrival on the scene after the attempted King Edward murder of Dr. Cummins sealed his involvement in solving the trio of crimes. His notoriety as a police detective exploded with the publicity. Pressure was mounting from all sides to close the cases: the mayor, the city council, as well as the public.

Martin was not sure that he had solved either murder case. There was a link between the two that eluded him. Entering the lobby of the surgical clinic building, he remembered the first time he met Dr. Diana Bratton—at the elevator with Brian Cummins' body—and then there she was later at the King Edward when his brother was attacked.

"Dr. Bratton, I tried checking in at the front desk this time," Martin said.

"I've got a minute. My two-thirty was a no-show."

Diana entered the remainder of the last patient's entry into the new electronic medical records system, then checked her cell. No text from her daughter or the babysitter meant good news.

"What can I do for you, Key?"

"Just trying to organize my thoughts," he answered.

"Thoughts?"

"Yes, Doctor, my thoughts. Trying to ID the key players in all of this."

"*Players*?"

"Quite a scenario we've got here: a doctor's brother and girlfriend are both murdered, and within a few days of each other. Then we turn around and see him fall victim to attempted murder. Have you ever heard of anything like that?"

"No, Key, I haven't." She focused on another patient chart. "But then I don't have much time to read murder mysteries, much less watch TV or go to movies."

"You were here when we responded to the call about Dr. Brian Cummins—the night he was shot."

"Yes, since I work here, that shouldn't seem too surprising."

Diana checked her watch. The next patient should be checking in. "Like I told you that night, I didn't hear or see anything until I met up with Brad and Leslie at the elevator. They had just found him . . . found Brian. This place is a big building."

"Did you know Brad Cummins' late fiancée? Was she a friend?"

"Leslie Coachys and I ran in different circles. I've got a child. Not only that, I'm a single mom." Diana felt her phone vibrate. The text read: *Patient ready. Mr. Wiggs. Guy's in a real hurry."*

"I'm sorry, Key, but I've got to get back to work."

Martin stepped into the door. "Look, Doctor, I'm under a lot of pressure to solve these murders."

"And I'm under a lot of pressure to take care of these patients. They need me."

"I'm sure they do. But, I need you for a few minutes more."

"OK, but don't you think that the Iraqi guy did it? He was obviously after Brad."

"That's possible. But unfortunately the kid is dead. You know that. You were there at the hospital. Seems you're always around."

"Right. I was called to the CODE."

"I never got to question Amarah," he said.

"My patients are out there waiting, Key."

"Everybody's game is important."

"Game?"

"Forget fingerprints, forget DNA. Investigation is all about talking, interviewing the players."

"And I guess I'm one of the players?"

Diana's medical assistant appeared in the hall behind the detective. "Sorry, Dr. Bratton. Now we've got three patients ready. Need to step it up."

Diana brushed past Martin. "Detective, I'm afraid I can't play today. With Brad . . . Dr. Cummins . . . at home recuperating, I'm the only physician here."

"But that means a better bottom line for you. Doesn't it, Doctor? Couldn't you use more money in the bank?"

128

Diana twisted around to face him, her eyes just above his. "Keep your voice down. These patients need me; the employees need me, and you're getting in the way."

She walked a few steps down the hall as Martin followed. She stopped outside the nearest exam room and popped open a small laptop resting at the work station.

Diana said, "And, besides, when Brian Cummins died, he left a big mortgage on this place, and Brad hasn't been much help."

"The thing about money ... that seemed to strike a raw nerve with you, Doctor."

Diana continued to study the information on the laptop. "You think I'm responsible for Brian's murder, don't you, Key? Or is it Leslie's?"

"Should I, Dr. Bratton?"

She studied the patient's medical record. *Diverticulitis* she decided. "Well, like it or not, criminal or not, I don't have any more time to talk to you ... at least not today."

Diana's assistant stepped forward, motioning Detective Martin to the rear exit. "Like I said, just trying to put together the key players in these cases, and I would say you're a key player, Doctor. Get it? *Key* player?"

She ignored the pun and punched several keys on the laptop.

"Doctor, do you have any romantic interest in Dr. Brad Cummins, or maybe you were interested in the late Brian Cummins, or both?"

"That's enough, Detective," Diana's assistant responded with a frown and hands on her hips. "You'd better leave."

"And, Doctor, I just found out about Dr. Cummins' trouble with the military over his treatment of a kid in Iraq. How come nobody bothered to tell me about that?"

"Goodbye, Detective Martin," Diana said, opening the exam room door.

"Hi, Mr. Wiggs. So, that belly pain is getting pretty bad, huh?" she asked as the door shut behind her.

The medical assistant closed in on the detective; she was a half-head taller.

"Don't get me wrong, Miss," Martin said. "Your doc's OK. Very cool, in fact."

The assistant moved even closer, the frown more severe.

129

"Look, Miss, don't bother. I can find my way out."

As she led him toward the rear exit, the detective surveyed the expensive wallpaper lining the hall, original artwork interrupting the repetitive design.

"You know, this really is a nice place," he said before Diana's assistant opened the door onto the stairs and shut it behind him.

23

Diana walked through the lobby of the King Edward. The same receptionist stood behind the desk. This time Diana noticed the nose ring.

"Hey, you're that doctor who grabbed the key from Mr. Morris. Wow, that was some shit. The police have been all around this place."

"I'm not here to steal any keys today," Diana said. "I'm here to see Dr. Brad Cummins. He's got an apartment here."

"No problem. If you know a resident here, you don't have to stop at the desk, not until Mr. Morris hires a doorman."

The receptionist returned to her magazine.

"Just go on up and knock."

"Thank you," Diana said. "I hope the police won't be bothering you today." After pushing the elevator button, Diana sent a text that she was on the way up.

Greeting her at the door, Brad said, "My old place at the Plaza is up for sale. Too much history."

"This building runs a close second," Diana said and entered the marbled foyer.

The new two-bedroom apartment seemed more spacious than the one upstairs. The walls of the study to the right were lined in antiqued wood. She guessed walnut. Leather books interspersed with expensive-looking decorative boxes and bronze figures filled the shelves. To the left was the living area. She could get a glimpse of the kitchen beyond with its stainless-steel appliances and granite countertops finished with a bank of windows.

"I thought this building was all booked up."

"Funny. Someone gave this place up after the little tussle on the floor above. Seems they were offended by the gun shot and a body flying out a window." He walked toward the kitchen. "Make yourself at home, Diana."

She walked into the living room and chose the couch near the gas-log fireplace. Brad returned from the kitchen.

"You look pretty good—rested," she said.

"Guess my discharge from the hospital was right on time."

Brad opened a three-year-old bottle of *pinot noir* from the wine cabinet.

Diana sank deeper into the leather sofa. "This place come furnished?"

"No way. It's amazing how quick the sales lady at Batte's could accommodate. One call and the place is full of furniture and rugs." He held up the bottle of wine.

"I hope you like red," he said.

"Remember, I'm on call again. Tonight marks two weeks in a row."

"Then you need a little stress reliever. One glass won't hurt." Brad stopped half-way through Diana's pour. "On second thought, maybe you should be careful." He sat next to her.

"I forgot to ask you about your dog?" Diana sipped the wine. Brad's choice was good.

"I pick up Bullet at the Dog Club tomorrow; he's been boarding there during my convalescence. I'll have to do a couple of gallbladders just to cover the bill." Brad propped his feet on the coffee table and took more than a sip from his glass.

Diana admired his boots as they rested on the coffee table, a nice contrast against the textured stone surface: leather, Cole Haan or Fry, she wasn't sure. The degree of wear amplified Brad's masculinity, his jean leg pulled up over the boot just enough to spot the side zipper. Her ex-husband had worn a similar pair. He also wore the same style jeans.

Diana was exhausted. She could not repress the memory:

Peeling away her scrub suit, Diana entered the master bedroom. The bedside phone was ringing. The caller ID read: Irene Pritchett.

She hung up and found Alex getting out of the shower. He toweled himself dry, his thick head of hair springing back into place, perfectly.

"That was Mrs. Pritchett on the phone," she said. "She has flu and is cancelling for tonight."

"Can't you find someone else?"

"No, Alex, of course not. Not this late. And especially not for a ten-month old."

"Hate that. Guess I'll just have to go by myself."

He dropped his towel to the floor and walked into the closet.

Diana's pager vibrated. It was the number for the hospital obstetrics department. She stepped back into their bedroom for her cell phone and called labor and delivery.

Alex walked out in a crisp, tailored, white cotton shirt and boxers. A silk tie hung loosely at the collar. "I can't find my silver cufflinks, the ones with the black trim."

"I have to go back on duty, Alex."

Diana tossed her cell phone back to the bedspread.

"Whattayamean you have to go back on duty? You're not on call. We've had this dinner on the calendar for weeks."

"The other junior resident just went into premature labor. She's been hospitalized at strict bed rest."

"Melinda?"

"Yes, Melinda."

"Can't those OBs just give her a shot or something?"

"That's insensitive, Alex. She's already four centimeters and only 28 weeks. If the baby delivers now, then . . . "

"Don't bother with the whole sad story." Alex pushed the full Windsor up against his buttoned collar. He admired the tie in the mirror.

"Like you doctors say, what would I know? I'm just a lawyer."

"There's no way out of it. I have to take her call tonight. There was a big wreck on I-20, an 18-wheeler overturned. The ER's full."

"It's always something to do with an 18-wheeler. Those guys never watch where they're going."

Alex walked back toward the closet.

"I need you to stay home with the baby," she said.

"Bull shit, Diana! I'm not missing this dinner! You don't know what it's like to have to compete. Our managing partner holds it against sorry-ass, junior partner no-shows."

Diana approached the bathroom and closet area. She heard him open a drawer for the cufflinks and then slam it shut. She met him in the bathroom as he fastened the cufflinks, urinated, and pushed past her into the bedroom.

"Alex, this is an annual dinner. We went last year, so you can miss this time."

"Lucky me. Somehow you squeezed a couple of hours out of your precious medical career and went somewhere with me.

Wow." He picked up the pants and jacket to his expensive suit and finished dressing.

That suit always looked good on him.

"I still don't understand why you don't just call another babysitter or tell Melinda that she has to find someone else to relieve her."

"I am obligated to cover her call. She would do the same for me, Alex."

He left again for the closet and returned with a black, alligator leather belt. "Well, I guess you're just stuck. Aren't you? Fucking 18-wheeler."

"I need you to skip that dinner and stay home with Kelsey so that I can go back to the hospital."

Alex's facial muscles tightened, sharpening his features, making him even more handsome. He stretched the belt between his hands. For the first time in their relationship, Diana felt uncomfortable, but he had never struck her.

"Alex, be reasonable," she said. "The late hours you put into that law firm downtown—all the Saturdays and Sunday afternoons. The hard work is what's important to your career—not whether or not you show up for some stupid cocktail party and dinner at the country club."

"How would you know what it takes to make it in the corporate world outside of a hospital, Diana?" He slid his belt into place and buckled it against his firm abdomen. He felt his pockets. "Yeah, got my wallet and keys."

She followed him through the den toward the garage. Her pager sounded again: the ER.

"Are you really going to leave for that damn party and not stay home with Kelsey? Not relieve me so I can save lives?"

"Relieve you? What kind of a mother are you? Is taking care of your daughter shift work?"

"You really are an ass, Alex!"

He jerked open the den door and pounded the button on the wall just inside the garage. The electric door obeyed.

"You know what, Diana? You're the one who wanted to have a baby. You're the one who wanted to do it every night. So you deal with it."

*   *   *

134

"Something wrong?" Brad asked and lowered his feet to the floor.

"Huh?" Diana had been staring into the fireplace and took a longer sip of wine.

"No, nothing's wrong except I'd like to have a full glass and then another, but I'm on call, as you know. Besides, I need to stay sober, get home, and check on my baby."

"How is your daughter?" Brad asked. "How's Kelsey holding up with an absent mom?"

"Since there's no *Kid Club*, I tipped the new babysitter a couple of appendectomies to take a break from school and move in with us while you've been out."

Brad nodded and saluted with his wine glass. "Now that's thinking." The boots and the jeans returned to the coffee table. "New babysitter's smart. Junior college will let her make it up."

They both nodded and took a sip.

"I'll be in the office tomorrow afternoon. I called my appointment secretary yesterday and asked her to open up my schedule."

"Got your doctor's clearance on that?" Another sip. "I don't think so," Diana said.

"You're right. But I know how my doctor thinks."

"Your doctor will look forward to seeing you around the office, seeing you carry your own weight."

Brad grabbed his left thigh, close to the groin. "But where that guy stabbed me. It's still sore." He laughed. "I thought I'd ease myself back into the grind: no night call until next week."

"Figured as much," Diana said. Her glass was nearly empty.

"Just kidding. I'm down to Tylenol for pain." Brad raised his glass in toast. "I'm ready to take the plunge, a whole weekend of call . . . this weekend, in fact. Congrats, Dr. Bratton."

"Cheers!" Brad finished the toast, a long sip.

Diana reached for the bottle and poured another half glass of wine. She answered the toast. "Good chance your entire schedule will be booked your first full day back. If not, I'll share."

"You're a great girl, you know."

"But your day's sure to be interrupted."

"By the ER?" he asked.

"Right. And when they call me about a 'drop-in' at the office,

135

I'm going to share those, too."

Diana finished her drink.

They both laughed.

Brad pulled the bottle from the table and poured. Diana covered the top of her glass. "No, no, I can't have any more," she said. She set the empty near Brad's left boot, still propped on the coffee table.

"OK, OK. I know you're overworked. That's why you need to have another drink and really relax."

"Brad . . ."

"I can call one of the other practices and get them to cover for us. They'll feel sorry for me."

"Like John Haynes feels sorry for you," Diana said, and then regretted it.

"We—I—should have called in the troops already. Haynes would be glad to do it. He'd get off on that."

"John Haynes might be a little stressed this evening, at least he should be."

"I've never seen Haynes stressed. Cool as a cucumber."

"He lost a patient last week in the SICU," Diana said. "A CODE was called, but couldn't bring the guy back. The case was the hot topic at today's M&M Conference."

Brad thought about the text he received while leaving Metropolitan Hospital with Cossar. "That was Haynes' patient?"

"It was that guy who jumped you in the hotel—that Iraqi student. He was still unconscious."

"You answered the CODE, too?"

"First one there. Lucky me."

"What happened? PTE?"

"Not sure. An embolus was first on the list, and I think Haynes agreed. Autopsy came up negative though."

"Haynes was probably glad to get Amarah off his hands. No doubt he's out on the town, relieving his stress."

* * *

Diana was waiting in the bedroom for Alex. She lit the bedside lamp when he turned the doorknob.

"Three – thirty. A little later than last year's country club party," she said.

"I thought you'd still be up at the hospital, shit deep in that 18-

136

wheeler shit," Alex said.

"Did you drive yourself home?" Diana asked.

"Nope, I wanted to take a taxi, but they shut down so damn early in Jackson."

"So, you did drive yourself home? That was a stupid risk, Alex. A DUI wouldn't look so good on your climb to the top."

"No DUI for me, Sugar. Got a ride home."

"Who gave you a ride home?

"Not important."

"And the car?"

Alex stopped in the middle of the bedroom, trying to think. His body swayed. "Still in the parking lot at the Country Club of Jackson. Safe and sound. Look." He held up the car keys. "Still got 'em."

"You're plastered, Alex. God. I'm sure you impressed the hell out of that managing partner at your law firm."

"Managing partner likes shots, too. Really likes the bar at Hal and Mal's. Likes the one at George Street, too."

"Don't you want to know what I did about our baby, Alex— your baby?"

"I knew you'd figure something out."

"I talked to Melinda's husband. Got him to babysit for several hours while I took care of everything at the hospital."

"Like I said, I knew you would take care of it. You're a smart girl."

"Melinda's husband left his sick wife to come over here and fill in for you, to take care of it."

"That's my girl."

"Then once I got all of the acute stuff taken care of at the med center, I talked one of the staff doctors into taking my pager for the rest of the night."

Alex removed his suit jacket and tossed it on a chair—the crispness of his white shirt long gone, his tie wrinkled.

"The staff doc could help me out since he was on vacation today but wasn't leaving town until the afternoon. Made me look really good, didn't it, Alex? Doubt if I make chief resident now."

"Still got faith in you, Sugar."

Diana wished Alex were not so attractive, even when drunk. "Where's your belt, Alex?"

137

"Dunno," he answered and disappeared into the closet, returning with a replacement.

"What do you need that for?"

"For this," he said as he popped the belt across her chest, stinging her ribs and breasts.

*   *   *

Diana felt the left side of her chest, just under the lowest rib. The blow had barely broken the skin, the scar long-faded, the sting remaining.

"You OK?" Brad asked.

"I sure could use another glass of wine, but I think you've had enough for both of us, Brad."

"Maybe so," he said.

"If you're going to be in the office tomorrow and not too hung over, then I might call in sick. Today was hard."

"Oh, don't do that. It'll be fun having us both there—working side-by-side."

"Not only did I have to deal with Haynes at M&M, but that Detective Martin came by the office earlier. His intro was that he had only a few questions."

"The guy seems pretty benign to me."

"I'm not so sure, Brad. My assistant had to practically throw him out.He already had the answers to most of his questions."

"What kind of stuff did he ask?"

"He even went into my financial situation with the clinic."

"Maybe that's just routine, like he's trying to get the whole picture about the Cummins Surgical Empire," he laughed and finished the glass. "Did you tell him that you needed a raise?"

"You're making light of this," she said.

"Martin's a policeman. He's supposed to ask a lot of questions."

Diana reached for the wine bottle, then decided not to lose her medical license. "Martin's looking for a motive, trying to put the two murders together."

"That's what he's paid to do," Brad said.

"He tried to throw sex into the picture."

"The play-by-the-book detective put a move on you?"

"No, he's not tall enough for me," she said and grinned. "His angle was that maybe I had a thing for you."

"Do you?"

"And that my sexual attraction for you figured into Leslie's death."

"Sexual attraction?" Brad asked.

Diana looked away. "But I don't see Martin's angle. How could a thing between you and me figure into your brother's murder?"

Brad said nothing.

"Maybe if your brother was after me, and you got jealous. Then you took him out yourself . . . "

"Diana!"

"Sorry," she answered, turning back to him.

They each waited for the other to laugh, at least chuckle; then it was simultaneous. Brad put his arm around Diana and patted her shoulder before a playful squeeze, then swung his boots to the floor. He walked slowly to the kitchen bar and opened another bottle of wine, Shiraz this time, two fresh glasses.

"The detective's theory is blown because I haven't had the time to plot anybody's murder, much less carry it out," she said as he returned.

"Yeah—no time," Brad said, sitting close enough that she sank in the couch toward him. "You've been too busy keeping the Surgical Center of the South open." He filled the two glasses. "Thanks, Diana."

* * *

"You bastard!" Diana grabbed the neck of the bedside table lamp, suppressing her scream for fear of waking the baby. Alex blocked the blow with his forearm, the lamp falling to the floor and crushing the shade. Light draped the bedroom chair near it, projecting a distorted shadow on the wall.

Straddling her while he pulled apart her pajama top, Alex pressed his arm into her chest covering the welt of the belt. She did not fight as he tore away the bottoms and wrenched apart her legs with his other hand. Alex moaned as he pushed deeply inside her.

Despite the night's alcohol, he finished quickly.

* * *

"What in the hell are you doing, Brad?" She hesitated a second or two before moving away, pressing her body into the arm of the couch.

"We're friends. Aren't we, Diana?" He stretched to put his arm around her again, no playful pat this time. He drew her closer.

139

"Professional associates should be friends," she said, pushing harder away from him, against the arm of the couch.

"I'm going to make you a full partner in the practice. My lawyer advised a hold on your new contract until I was discharged from the hospital, to make sure I wasn't mental."

"Brad, you are mental if you think there could be a thing between us." Diana reached behind her and removed his arm, but stopped there. She stared at the full glass of wine waiting for her on the stone coffee table.

*   *   *

Diana slept little after he finished, although the cruelty of the 4:30 phone alarm shocked her: another work day. She turned to Alex, motionless on his side of the bed, but breathing. He lay nude just as he had landed after rolling off her, his male physique as attractive as the night she first saw it and felt it, although she hated him now. She massaged the mark on her chest, now spreading beyond the width of the belt. Diana was thankful that the reddish-blue streak was well below the neckline of her scrub suits. She thought about Alex's missing belt. It was wider than the one he had used on her.

Diana slid from the bed, grabbed her robe, and walked to the nursery. The door was ajar and she peeked in. Her baby girl was beautiful, peaceful.

"Still asleep," she whispered. "Thank God."

Back up the short hall to the master bedroom, the bed was empty. The last sounds of a flushing toilet came from their bathroom. Diana felt him from behind.

"I didn't get enough," he said, sliding his hands below her waist and pulling her closer. He pressed himself against her.

"I did, Alex. I got enough for a long time."

He spun Diana around and kissed her.

"Get away from me." She pulled back, wiping her mouth. "Your breath—like something dead."

"You don't need to worry about my breath," he said as he pushed her toward the bed.

"I've got surgery and clinic patients today. My attending will can me if I'm late again. I need time to shower and . . . "

"You can either do it with me here on the bed, or I'll take a shower with you, and you can do it with me in there. Your choice."

140

"My choice is no. *Diana broke free toward the dressing area. I'll shower later this morning in the call room. Besides, Kelsey needs to be fed and dressed for daycare."*

Alex knocked her to the floor, stinging the bruised area of her chest. He covered her with his body and opened her. She screamed. Diana felt a heavy wetness between her thighs and imagined blood.

Forcing herself to move with him to lessen the pain, she considered reaching over her grunting husband and slamming her fists into his back. Instead she thought about an upward blow to his hard, rippled stomach, but was no match for his height and build.

When they had resumed intercourse after Kelsey was born, sex quickly progressed to playful force and she craved it. Diana felt such relief each time, giving herself completely to him, imagining that she had no control over what he would or could do. Her professional life was so different. But now her marriage was different.

Her marriage was over.

*   *   *

Brad's arm draped Diana's shoulder, this time tighter. There was no resistance.

"You know, I've got a shrink. We can talk to her about it."

"About what?" she asked. His finger tips were on her chest, near the reach of Alex's belt. She felt the sting.

"Our relationship," he answered.

"What relationship?" Diana asked.

"We're partners, professionals, and now we're involved in a doctor-patient relationship on top of the doctor-doctor relationship."

"I can send you a letter, dismissing you as a patient—or better yet, an email."

"Why don't you go ahead and do that—send me that letter."

Brad leaned into her slowly. She tilted her lips toward him, and he kissed her.

"Email is too impersonal," he said.

Brad pulled away as Diana's cell phone vibrated along the surface of the end table. She grabbed it for the text: a call back number from the answering service.

"You still have to buy into the practice, Diana, no matter how good that lip lock was," he said as his head sank into the sofa pillow.

"OK, I'll go ahead and write you a check, boss, but aren't you worried about my charging you with sexual harassment? Until that new business contract is signed, I'm just a clinic employee."

"A willing employee is always appreciated," he said.

Brad reached for the blanket throw draped across the other end of the couch and wrapped it around them. She unbuttoned his shirt, then lifted her blouse over her head. Brad stroked her breasts.

"And as my doctor," he said, "you'd better not raise my blood pressure. My concussion could explode into a subdural hematoma."

"I'm not your physician anymore. Remember, the letter?"

He looked under the plush throw. "I see the letter." Diana had lifted her skirt. He helped her with his belt and zipper. Brad lifted her onto him.

"Instead of worrying about getting a hematoma, you should be worried about my ex-husband," she said. Diana braced herself with her arms against his shoulders as she straddled him. She had not felt a man inside of her since Alex.

"He'd be jealous of your new relationship?"

"No." Diana took a deep breath. "I mean—he got around."

Brad lifted his hands to her hips and slowed her.

"There wasn't any time for me to get a condom from my shaving kit. Maybe we should stop. I usually keep one in my wallet."

Diana laughed and pulled the blanket closer around them. She pulled his face into her breasts. "Don't worry." Another deep breath. "After I figured out the situation with Alex, I got out of there. I'm clean: passed all the tests."

"What about . . ." Brad cupped his hands behind her and groaned as it was over. She seemed to follow.

"What about since then?" he managed to ask.

She bent down to his ear and whispered, "When would I have had time for a 'since then'?"

"I hear ya," he said. "We'll need to see what we can do about that."

Diana rolled away and fluffed the pillow behind her head. She reached back to him and put her hand between his legs, touching him.

He pushed up against her hand and said, "I'm not sure I'm good for a second round, not this quick."

"Men surgeons . . . all talk." Diana released him.

"So I guess you want some history from me," he said.

"This was really reckless of us, although I have kept up with my pills."

"That's good. Leslie was on the pill during our entire relationship, so I haven't thought much about birth control."

"But do I need to start some zithromycin and Rocephin?" Diana smiled.

"No, I'm clean, too. I was true to Leslie over in Iraq, although there was this older nurse—Cossar—that had the hots for me, I think."

"Wouldn't surprise me. Maybe she thought she could teach you something."

"It was strictly platonic. She came by to see me the day I was discharged."

"No problem with the old chick. But what about Leslie? Three months overseas was a long time."

"While I was gone, she was too busy opening up that new bookstore and planning a wedding to screw anybody," he said.

Diana frowned. "That was crude, Brad. Sort of spoils the moment."

"Sorry. You're right." He looked toward the wine but didn't pick it up. "Her looks got me first."

"Leslie was awfully young," Diana said.

"I was happy that she wanted a career and started that business. But her friend Caroline was the brains behind it."

"I met Caroline at the office after Leslie died. The girl seemed together."

"I had hoped that Leslie would mature after marriage and owning a business, but my doubts were growing," he said. "I wasn't sure that our relationship was going to make it—not for the long haul."

Diana put her arm around him. Brad was admitting what she had thought all along about Leslie, and he was now freeing himself from guilt.

143

And Diana had felt it.

What she did not feel, what she did not know, was what to do next.

24

Brad skipped his parking spot near the garage elevator and pulled in near the stairs next to Diana's Honda. Since his brother's murder, he had avoided the elevator except for approving the job of the cleaning crew and the replacement of the carpet. The cleaning service made good on its guarantee that all blood residue would be removed. A black fluorescent light exam of the elevator car proved it.

The exterior of Diana's vehicle was filthy. Dried mud accented the tire rims and peppered the lower body of the vehicle. Several smiley-faces decorated the dirty rear windshield. He assumed Kelsey's work.

Diana will be able to upgrade soon he thought. *BMW or a Lexus? Probably a black one, sleek—her style. Maybe she can afford a car wash, too.*

Brad removed his key from the ignition and popped his sunglasses into the overhead compartment. He had held onto the SUV, considering that he and Leslie would probably start a family soon and need a larger vehicle. He looked over to the front passenger seat, seeing her, remembering how she fumbled through her purse the night they found Brian. He could hear her screams, along with Bullet's barking. Both had been terrified.

He thought about the sex with Diana and wondered what kind of guy could replace a dead fiancée so quickly.

Brad grabbed his white coat from the backseat and stepped out of the SUV. He ran his forefinger along the dusty back fender of Diana's vehicle. The dirty car was evidence of an overworked, single mom, a busy doctor still on a strict budget.

He hoped that she saw some substance in him.

I'll surprise Diana and spring for a car wash he decided.

* * *

"Excuse me, Dr. Cummins."

"Shit! What the hell?" Brad's keys clanged to the pavement.

"Detective Martin, sir. Sorry if I startled you."

"Detective Martin! That you did. Sorry for the language." Brad found his keys next to a tire and slipped them into his coat pocket. Pushing past Martin, he asked, "Can I help you with something? Do we have an appointment?"

"Nope, too hard to get an appointment. You docs are too busy. Thought I'd just stop by."

"This is a lousy time to 'stop by'. It's my first afternoon back at work. A packed schedule is waiting for me upstairs."

"Funny, your associate, your partner, Dr. Bratton, told me the same thing . . . busy, busy, busy," Martin said, trailing Brad.

"Right. Diana—Dr. Bratton—did mention that you had come by the office yesterday and interrupted her work, too."

"Wouldn't call it an interruption, Doctor. That's how my line of work plays out. It's the only way for you to find out who killed your brother and your fiancée."

Standing at the door to the stairs, Brad punched in the security code, an upgrade since his brother's murder. He turned the door knob at the signal to enter, then released it. The door eased to close. Brad took a deep breath and turned to the detective. Brad was taller and better built.

"You bet I want to know who killed my brother and Leslie. And remember the attempt on my life? Any idiot can see that the Iraqi guy took Brian for me. Then with Leslie's murder—you were heavy on Leblanc."

"Didn't have enough to hold Leblanc."

Brad forced calm. "I could have told you that, Detective. Minor Leblanc's not the murdering type."

"And about your being attacked at the hotel? Better thank your partner . . . could have been more than just an attempt on your life."

"Listen, Detective. I'm not sure what's going on here, but you're bordering on harassment. First barging in on Dr. Bratton and now me. We have work to do." Brad reopened the door to the stairwell and stepped inside.

"Doctor, you need to talk to me."

Brad stiffened. He paused at the bottom of the stairwell.

"Were the two of you working last night?" Martin asked.

Slamming the door behind him, Brad came at the detective. Martin met him half-way.

"What's that supposed to mean?" Brad asked, his voice echoing throughout the garage.

"I'm not convinced that we have your brother's killer, Dr. Cummins, much less solved Miss Coachys' murder. I believe you're still in danger. We've been trailing you ever since that Iraqi fellow came at you."

"Trailing me?"

"I even put one of my deputies on Dr. Bratton. I know that she visited your hotel last night."

"So what? The King Edward's a fairly big place."

"My guy followed her to a unit on eleven. He watched her enter. We checked; that's your place. I guess she was making a house call—an apartment call, you might say."

"She had discharged me from the hospital, needed me to come back to work. So she came by to check on me."

"And I guess she found you to be in pretty good shape," Martin said.

"I think she did, Detective. I think she did."

Brad stepped back into the stairwell and Martin followed. The door slammed behind them. Brad ascended a few steps.

"Oh, and there was another woman at your place several days ago, an older woman."

"Several days ago? What's going on here, Detective?"

"We've got two unsolved murders here, Doctor Cummins. And there could be more."

"Detective, you need to call off the dogs. As far as I'm concerned you've got the killer. Amarah was probably looking for me and surprised Leslie."

Brad headed up the stairs, then turned to call to the detective. "And if it were any of your business, that older woman is Elizabeth Cossar, and she was dropping me off after my release from the hospital."

Two more steps up. "And if you need anything else, check with the receptionist. She'll be glad to make you an appointment."

"Well, I do have this hernia-thing going on, Doc," Martin called to Brad's fading footsteps.

When Brad reached the top of the landing, Charlie greeted him as he opened the door into the rear hallway. A divorced male in his early thirties, Charlie worked as a personal fitness trainer at the Y when not a physician's assistant.

"You're running way behind, Dr. Brad," he said.

"Sorry, I was detained downstairs."

"Anything wrong?" Charlie asked. "Need me to take care of anything?"

"Just get me through the day," Brad answered.

"You're double-booked. I'll see if I can get someone to help triage the patients."

"Don't get me wrong. I'm glad to be busy, particularly since I've been out. But I don't want to stay late anymore than you do."

Brad plowed through his clinic schedule: examining each patient, then pounding the findings and prescriptions into a laptop. He ran across a few left over dressing changes and suture removals from Diana's stand-in cases. He let Charlie handle those.

Brad sought an emotional rush during the afternoon, counting on the thankful folks he treated to heal the turmoil of the last weeks and months: *I'm so sorry for everything you've been through, Dr. Cummins—So glad to have you back as my doctor, Dr. Brad—Don't the police have some good leads by now?—Are you safe—you sure?—Got a new girlfriend yet?* greeted him in almost every room.

The emotional therapy never came.

By the end of the afternoon, a dull headache swelled to match the pain of his aching leg. "I may have come back to work too soon," he told Charlie.

"No matter when you made it back, Dr. Brad, the first day was gonna be a killer."

"I suppose you're right."

"I know I am." Charlie removed supplies from a hall cabinet to restock the examining rooms. "Did that patient from up in Flora mention his colon problems to you?"

"In great detail," Brad answered, without looking from his laptop. He hit *Enter*, submitting the last office note of the afternoon to the server. "We need to sign him up for surgery next week."

"Got it." Charlie made a note on his own laptop.

"The hospital census doesn't show anything for me, so I'm headed home. I'm dragging." He checked his pockets for his keys and cell. He wondered if Diana had finished her schedule, too.

"Sorry, but your day's not over, Doc," Charlie said.

"Not a call from the ER, I hope."

"Just a couple of walk-in consults. Triage nurse is holding 'em in ER observation. Don't sound all that urgent."

"Sure it's just two?" Brad asked. He felt his thigh. It throbbed.

"Yes, sir. That's what she said. Just two, so far."

"I'll try to get over there and clean things up before they stick me with more garbage," Brad said. "Maybe tonight's ER physician will leave me alone."

"Hope so," Charlie said. "Early night would be good for you, 'specially after this hard afternoon."

Brad wondered if Diana had plans tonight after work; then he remembered Kelsey. He thought about tipping the babysitter to stay later.

* * *

"This is the train wreck we paged you about, Doctor." The triage nurse handed the psychiatrist a stack of ER forms blackened with handwritten notes.

"I don't remember ever getting a call to the ER before I moved to Jackson." Twila Crockett, MD, was new to the psychiatry staff. She flipped through the pages of medical records. "I went into psychiatry to avoid stuff like this."

"We do get a few in here," the nurse said. "The ER physician usually makes the call to specialists for consults, but we've been real busy: a CODE, lots of lacerations. A husband and wife got after each other with beer bottles. We even had this lady show up in labor, crowning . . . didn't even know she was pregnant. And I delivered the baby!"

"I have tickets to the play at New Stage," the psychiatrist said. "If I hurry with this, I could make it by intermission."

"I don't know, Dr. Crockett. I thought the couple with the beer bottles might just be drunk, but I think they're a psych case."

"Try to talk them down first, won't you?"

"Yes, ma'am. We'll try," the triage nurse said.

"Please—*Yes, Doctor* would have been better than *ma'am*." She studied the patient information sheet. "I see that this first patient is from out-of-town? Tennessee?"

* * *

A mixed crowd of smokers milled about the entrance to the Emergency Department, unimpressed by the fifty-thousand-dollar

149

new landscape and signage job. Crepe myrtles, azaleas, hydrangeas, and live oaks accented stone walls inscribed with *Jackson Metropolitan Hospital*. Yellow and white chrysanthemums were starting to bloom in the flower beds.

Dodging the patients standing outside to smoke while clad in hospital gowns and attached to IV poles, Brad held his breath in the still humid, warm air.

He made his way through the throng that included patients' visitors and returned the nod to an elderly woman standing immediately outside the sliding glass doors. She was holding her pole and a lit cigarette with the same hand.

So much for that script I wrote her last month . . . still didn't kick the habit he thought as a thick cloud rose from her nose and mouth to encircle her head.

She waved good-bye and smiled.

* * *

"Glad you're here, Dr. Cummins," the triage nurse said. "Your patients are in rooms 4 and 9. I think you may be with us for a while."

"Don't take this personally, Renee, but I hate to hear that," Brad said.

"Radiology says the guy in 4 has an appendix the size of a hot dog, the wiener part, that is, and the lady in 9 has decided she wants her incarcerated hernia fixed. She's left AMA at least three times before with the same findings. The thing looks horrible."

"So far, doesn't sound so bad," he said. "If anesthesia cooperates, I should be in and out of here in a couple of hours." He wondered what time Diana put her daughter to bed.

"I hate to ruin your night, Dr. Brad, but the skin over that hernia looks almost rotten. And she's a diabetic, uncontrolled."

"And the appendix?"

"Had a heart attack last year. Spent two weeks in the ICU."

John Haynes brushed between Brad and the nurse. "Back at work, Cummins? About time, don't you think?"

"It's good to see you again, too, John," Brad said.

"Bro, busting my butt. Looks like we're both stuck with the duty tonight. If you need some help, just have one of these people page me," Haynes smiled back toward the triage nurse. "It'll be just like old times."

150

* * *

"I would have had you come by my place and go through my closet, but I'm afraid there's not much to work with."

Minor Leblanc fanned his arms to the side with palms upward. "As elegant a woman as you? Jesus! That can't be true."

Diana suppressed a laugh. She had witnessed the same mannerisms through the observation window at the police department. However, watching the self-proclaimed personal shopper/stylist through a two-way mirror and listening to Minor through a cheap microphone and speaker did not do him justice. A personal appearance was so much more entertaining.

She had reached him through one of her female patients. *"Minor did wonders for me and my daughter during her wedding. My daughter looked beautiful, and, by the way, so did I. What a character!"*

"Do you mind if I sit down, Doctor?" Minor nestled into one of the upholstered chairs across from her desk. Beads of sweat erupted on his forehead.

"Are you too warm, Minor? Thirsty perhaps? There's water in the cooler down the hall, and we've got soft drinks in the lounge."

"Aren't you sweet, but I'm fine." He wiped his forehead dry with a linen handkerchief.

"I haven't had anyone call me *sweet* in a longtime. Surgery residency takes out the sweet," Diana said.

"Nonsense. I think you're sweet, sweeter than sweet. But with your looks, you can get away without it."

Diana felt a bead or two on her own forehead. Minor Leblanc had found another new client who needed tons of work. However, how far would he push?

"We just need to bring you out a little. Underneath that medical diploma you are beyond gorgeous!"

"Let's back up a minute. I'm not trying to come out anywhere."

Instead of the leather chair behind her desk, Diana eased into the upholstered one opposite Minor, crossing her legs as femininely as possible. "I gave you a call because I've met someone. He's a physician, too, but after hours he's accustomed to something a little less professional."

Diana thought about the makeup and clothes that defined Leslie Coachys. She watched Minor study her office, scan the certificates

151

and diplomas on the walls. He stopped at the framed photographs of Kelsey that decorated her desk.

"Dazzling little thing. Your daughter? Proud, proud, proud. I just know it!" He moved on to the desk lamp and tapped the shade. "You look drained, exhausted, and much too pale. It might be the lighting in here."

"Work has been pretty hard, particularly over the last several weeks, months, really. I've been the only doctor here most of the time."

"Don't worry, Gorgeous, it's nothing that a couple of visits to the tanning bed won't fix."

Diana eyed her faded reflection in the face of the desk clock, displayed beside a thrilled Kelsey, photographed riding a pink Barbie bike. The bike had matching training wheels.

"Minor, I'm glad you don't think that I need plastic surgery," she said, and turned the clock to face the wall. Diana wondered if the patient with the information about Minor meant to do her a favor or play a joke.

"You don't look horrible—just need a little freshening, Dr. Diana, a little updating. I have clients out there a lot worse. Believe me."

"Good to know," Diana said. "I've gone from gorgeous to not horrible?"

"Don't you worry about one thing, Gorgeous. We're going to go all the way to fabulous!" Minor clapped his hands and stood. "Now, is there a special occasion we need to work toward? A trip maybe?"

"Look, Minor, I've sort of let myself go—haven't thought about clothes, makeup, or my hair in a very long time. Thank God my weight is still under control."

"You poor thing. You've worked yourself to the bone." He reached for another tissue and wiped his forehead.

"Working. That's the issue. This guy I'm seeing. I work with him. We've sort of been drawn together by all that's happened. I think I'll be seeing him more—outside of the office, I mean."

"No doubt, you will," Minor said.

"I think he's more accustomed to women being . . . the best way to say it . . . *fixed up*."

Diana thought again about Leslie—hair framing her face

152

without looking coiffed, makeup flawless but not overdone, stylish clothes that predicted the next *Vogue* spread.

"I'm not sure why I'm so worried about this—about how I look," Diana said. "I don't have to snag him. I've already slept with him."

"Oh, my Jesus," Minor said, another swipe of the forehead, his large, full eyes twitching. He sprang from his chair and clapped his hands again. "But I'm sure you want him coming back for more."

* * *

Renee Smith, the triage nurse, followed Brad down the hall of the ER to his waiting patients. A laboratory technician carrying a tray of blood-filled vials and urine specimens scurried by, followed by a few visitors from the smoking club outside. Several physicians were paged overhead. There was a STAT call for respiratory therapy to the intensive care unit.

"I've got another staff nurse coming in to assist you later, Dr. Brad," she said. "Computers are down. Lab results are coming off the printer really slow."

"No problem, Renee," Brad said. "Anesthesia won't need anything but electrolytes and a CBC. Type and screen will do for me. Probably won't need to give any blood." He pulled open the metal door to the first patient's room and closed it behind him, leaving the triage nurse in the hall.

"Someone call security. Call *911*!" Trying to balance her loaded tray, the same lab tech ran by Renee, the woman's coat torn at the sleeve, a trail of printed laboratory reports left behind.

Renee grabbed the tech's arm, scattering the remainder of the reports. "Man's got a gun on that doctor down there!" the tech cried. "Somebody's got to do something!"

"Which doctor? Down where?" the nurse reached deep into her uniform pocket for her cell. She had left it at the nurses' station.

"That new lady psychiatrist." The vials teetered. "I walked into the wrong exam room and saw the gun."

"Just tell me what happened?" Renee asked.

"Let my arm go, bitch! This job ain't worth getting shot at, not for what this joint pays."

The tech shoved the tray at her and disappeared. A piercing alarm sounded, indicating she had run through the emergency-fire exit at the end of the hall. An announcement from the overhead

153

speaker system followed:

SECURITY TO THE ER. STAT. SECURITY TO THE ER. STAT.

Renee felt the door behind her fling open.

"What's all the commotion?"

Brad stood in the doorway, wearing examination gloves, his assistant left at the patient's bedside to calm the helpless-looking man. The man was clinging to his sheets.

Two gunshots sliced through the screeching alarm as the hospital operator continued to broadcast the call for security. The man with the near-ruptured appendix yelled from his stretcher, "Doc, I need my clothes. Is there a fire?"

"Bobby, you stay here with Mr. Vitolo. Get him to sign consents for the OR." Brad darted past the triage nurse into the corridor. Losing his footing on the slick papers left in the wake of the fleeing lab tech, Brad slammed his shoulder into the wall.

"Got it, Dr. Brad!" Bobby called out.

Renee ran into the examination room and set the tray of lab specimens on a counter. "Bobby, you let me stay with the old guy."

"Hey!" Mr. Vitolo yelled. He pulled his sheets even closer.

"No thanks, Renee. *Lunatic with a gun* sounds like something for triage," Bobby said. "You go check things out with Dr. Brad. I'll stay here."

Brad steadied himself and rubbed his shoulder before stumbling over the patients and hospital employees cowered along the walls of the corridor. He called into Mr. Vitolo's room, "Renee, you coming or not?"

The nurse hurled her clipboard at Bobby, landing it in a corner of the room, barely missing him. "You jerk!" she yelled. "I'll get you later." She ran after Dr. Brad.

Two hospital security guards were standing outside an exam room. Brad recognized one of them from the smoking group outside.

"Doc, we think somebody's been shot in there," the guard said. "Better stand away from the door."

The other guard's tall spiked hair waved in rhythm as he nodded agreement. "We can hear some lady in there moaning," he said. "Not sure who she is."

"Regardless, we need to get in there and help her," Brad said.

Renee was close behind, breathing deeply from the sprint down the hall. "I put a patient in there for the new psychiatrist to see: a man in his early sixties, maybe late fifties. I can't remember the date of birth."

"What was his complaint when he signed in?" Brad asked. A third shot, the bullet piercing the door and shattering the glass of the framed print hanging on the opposite wall.

There were several screams.

The security guard without the spiked hair radioed, "Call JPD again. Where in the hell are they?"

"Seems like hell's right here, officer."

Detective Martin produced his badge and waved his sergeant to take the other side of the door. "Dr. Cummins, nice to see you again. Although I'm not surprised."

Ignoring Martin, Brad said, "Renee, tell me again what you know about the patient in this room."

"His chief complaint was depression. He's from Tennessee, doesn't have a local doctor; so he came to the ER."

"Detective, I believe one of our physicians, a female psychiatrist, is with him and may have been shot. She hasn't called out," Brad said.

"Is there any other way into this room?" Martin asked. He motioned for the sergeant to press closer to the exam room door with his weapon drawn.

"No other way out. The exam rooms don't have windows," Renee answered.

"Everybody stand back against the wall, away from the door!"

Martin thrust a heavy boot against the door. It flew open. With weapons raised, the sergeant followed his boss through the opening.

To the intrusion, a wide-eyed Chadwick Giles again shot aimlessly with his forty-five. His self-inflicted scalp wound only superficial, this bullet pierced a wall in the exam room. Martin grappled Giles to the floor as his sergeant handcuffed him. Giles' pistol slid across the floor, twirling to a stop at the heel of the psychiatrist's shoe.

Renee screamed and Brad yelled. "Are you all right?" They both ran to Twila Crockett.

She was crouched in a corner, her right hand gripping her left

155

arm, blood oozing between the fingers. There was a dark red pool beneath her.

"This man pulled out that gun," she said. "And he started waving it in the air . . . clearly psychotic, rambling about the death of his grandson . . . then the gun went off and then he shot himself."

Brad felt her pulse: weak, thready. He found a thick roll of gauze in a cabinet and used it as a tourniquet. The detective and the sergeant pulled Giles from the floor.

"I don't think he meant to shoot me," she said. She kicked the forty-five across the room toward the police and then fell limp.

"Call the OR, Renee. We better get her to surgery now," Brad said. "And notify the blood bank that we're gonna need 'em after all."

Renee retrieved a stretcher from hall storage and rolled it into the room. She and Brad carefully lifted the bleeding woman onto it. A respiratory therapist appeared with portable oxygen.

Welcome to the medical staff Brad wanted to say to Dr. Crockett.

25

Chadwick Giles pulled against the hand restraints, shaking the bedrails. "Hey, somebody help me! Somebody's got me tied up!"

Sunlight streaming through a break in the drapery bore into his eyes. He feared his head would explode.

"Mr. Giles, I was the nurse in the ER last night. My name's Renee Smith."

Giles tugged again at the restraints. "Why am I here? Nurse, why am I here?" He wanted to massage the side of his head. "Nurse, I need to touch my head. It hurts."

"No, sir. You don't need to do that."

Renee straightened the white sheets and bedspread and checked the IV. "We had to restrain you 'cause you might hurt yourself again." She checked the white turban bandage held in place by burn netting and anchored to the right side of his chin. "The psychiatrist said you tried to commit suicide."

"I don't remember," Giles said.

"The doctors said you were lucky; the bullet only grazed your scalp. There'll be a scar, but you'll be OK," Renee said.

Key Martin observed the exchange through the observation window. He swung open the door to Giles' room and produced a badge, then flipped the case closed.

"Chadwick Giles, I'm Detective Martin. You might remember me from last night."

The sunlight hurt. The bandage hurt. His whole body ached. "Yes, you're one of the policemen who pushed me down," Giles said.

"We had reason to arrest you. Shooting up an emergency room is against the law," Martin said. "You purchased that forty-five at a sporting goods store in Memphis."

Giles pulled again at the restraints. "I always carry a gun."

Martin said, "Last night, your doctor claimed that you shot her and then shot yourself, or at least tried to. You were both bleeding when we busted in on you."

Giles twisted his wrists and looked in anger at the gauze. "I don't remember."

"Doc says you're psychotic."

"Maybe I am."

Renee stepped between the detective and her patient. "Detective, Mr. Giles isn't feeling well."

"Neither is the doctor he shot last night," Martin said. "Do I need to talk to one of your superiors, Miss?"

Renee stepped back. "Mr. Giles, the doctors have put you on some medication but go ahead and try to talk to the policeman."

"What sort of medication?" Giles asked.

"Something to calm you down. In fact, I can give you another dose."

"Nurse, don't sedate Mr. Giles. I need to ask him some questions."

"Doesn't he need a lawyer?" she asked.

"Maybe he does; maybe he doesn't. That depends on how he answers the questions."

"What do you want to know, Detective?" Giles asked. He relaxed his arms. There was some slack in the restraints. "It's OK, nurse," Giles said.

Renee adjusted the blinds and again checked the sheets. "Mr. Giles, you call if you need anything. You can reach that buzzer right there, even with your hands—you know—tied."

Both Martin and Giles studied her shape as she left: the curvy, white dress uniform cut above the knee, the sleeves just long enough for an embroidered nursing insignia of some sort, her long, thick, dark hair falling gently at the shoulders. She had a tempting, yet confident swagger. The nurse shut the door behind her.

"I would feel a lot more comfortable talking to you with my hands untied, Detective," Giles said.

"No way. You seem pretty sane to me, Mr. Giles, but like I said, the doctors around here say you're psycho."

"Been through a lot, Detective."

"When that doctor you shot last night woke up from surgery, she told me that you were waving the gun around the room at her, rambling about your grandson."

"Yeah, Chad died over in Iraq."

"Sorry for your loss, Mr. Giles. Any kid who dies for his country dies a hero, but that doesn't give you license to shoot someone."

Giles looked toward the window through the opened blinds. The light no longer bothered him. "My grandson didn't die on the battlefield. The doctors in that military hospital in Balad killed him."

"What evidence do you have of that?" Martin asked.

"Chad made it through hell, lived through one of those fucking roadside bombs. They flew him to Balad for treatment. He wasn't supposed to die."

"So you say doctors killed him?"

"My boy made it through the operation and then died right after. Military never would tell me why. Just that his heart stopped."

"Was the doctor you shot in the ER one of those doctors?'

"No, I didn't really mean to shoot her. I need to offer my apologies."

"I'm sure she would appreciate that." Martin spotted his sergeant through the glass door and waved him in.

"Let me see if I understand, Mr. Giles," Martin said. "You came down from Tennessee and decided to shoot up the ER to avenge the death of your grandson?"

The sergeant said, "Mr. Giles, sir, we sorta agree with the doctors. That does sound crazy."

"You see, the doctors over in Iraq, the ones in charge of my Chad . . . they live around here."

"But you already told me that the doctor you shot last night didn't treat your grandson overseas."

"Right, but Dr. Brad Cummins was one of them, and I think there was another one that lives around here."

Martin rolled his eyes at his sergeant. *Cummins, again.* He remembered learning of the trouble with a medical tribunal in Iraq. "So you shot the lady psychiatrist because Dr. Cummins couldn't save your grandson?"

"I've been hanging around this area for awhile, wanting to talk to Cummins face-to-face, just waiting for the right time. I needed to know why Chad had to die. One night the TV news in my motel said that Dr. Cummins had been injured and was in the hospital. He was all doped up from pain killers, probably doesn't even remember that I visited him. He seemed like a really nice guy. I was surprised."

"But where does the psychiatrist come into all of this?" the

159

detective asked.

"I wanted somebody to talk me out of killing Cummins." Mr. Giles pulled at the restraints. "That woman doctor said that wasn't her job."

"So, that's why you shot her?" Martin asked.

"Just got frustrated, I guess. Needed help, but no one would help me." Giles reached to wipe a tear, but couldn't.

"I got all confused in the ER. Even though Cummins didn't save my grandson, I hated for his pretty girlfriend to be alone, too."

"When did you see Dr. Brad Cummins with the girlfriend?" Martin asked.

"Outside of Memphis. Recognized him from the Internet." Another tear. "Nice-looking couple."

"What did you do next, Mr. Giles?" the sergeant asked, looking at Martin for approval. He got it.

"I followed 'em in my truck to a motel. Waited over night in the parking lot while they shacked up. Then followed 'em down here to Jackson."

"Stalked 'em, you mean." Martin said. "Got your jollies off."

"I'm not some kinda pervert."

"What you are, Mr. Giles, is headed for charges of attempted murder for what you did last night. And when I fit you completely into this puzzle, you may be looking at murder."

Mr. Giles ignored the detective. "Chad had someone, too. He met her over in Iraq. That's what made it so hard for me: seeing Cummins happy."

"Fact is, Giles, once those nurses put you in a wheelchair to roll you out of here, we'll push you right over to our place," the sergeant said. "You'd better line up a lawyer."

"The girl Chad liked in Iraq was a nurse. Guess she's still over there."

"A nurse?" Martin asked. "Did your grandson have a picture of her, maybe a picture of the two of them together?"

"No, he never sent me a picture."

Renee returned with a small paper cup and water. "Your afternoon medicine, Mr. Giles."

"Miss, could you could get Mr. Giles' wallet for him, so he can double check for a picture of his grandson and his girlfriend?"

160

Renee looked to her patient for approval.

Giles started again at the restraints. "Looks like a crazy man's got no rights. Don't it?" he said. "Go ahead and show these people what they want to see, nurse."

"If that's what you want. Personal effects are locked away at the nurses' station."

26

"It seems I missed all the fun," Diana said.

She looked into the rearview mirror. Minor was correct; Botox would be a good option.

"I was lucky that all three procedures went smooth, real smooth," Brad said. "I extracted the bullet from that psychiatrist's arm before I started the other two cases from the ER. Anesthesia really pushed to get her taken care of. No delays. That's what professional courtesy gets you."

"I'll have to remember that." Diana pushed her hair back. She imagined it with highlights.

"The bullet missed the bone and the major vessels. Crockett was fortunate."

"You might say that," Diana said. She let her hair fall back in place.

"Glad your babysitter could take Kelsey for the weekend, especially last minute."

"The extra hundred you slipped her didn't hurt," Diana said.

Brad and Diana waited in traffic on Canal Street in front of the Ritz Carlton Hotel. A black Lexus and a red Jaguar finally disappeared ahead of them into the motor court. The uniformed attendant dressed in matching hat and gloves stood at the cave-like entrance and waved through Brad's SUV. There was no shortage of waiting valets and bellmen.

The silver Nissan behind Brad slowed nearly to a stop at the entrance, but then drove on. The driver was to take the next right onto Burgundy.

"The special weekend rate didn't include parking," Brad said.

"You mean well-paid physicians like you worry about the small stuff?" Diana said. She smiled.

Brad's monthly draw from the practice still dwarfed hers.

"I guess I shouldn't keep putting off the money talk, as in your new salary," he said.

"Not this weekend," she said. "That's a subject for office hours and professional time, not play time."

"Ok, then. It's on the calendar for Monday." Brad triggered the rear door hatch below the dashboard and the nearest bellman came to attention.

"It's strange you never mentioned hiring a locum to relieve me when I was alone on the front lines," Diana said, checking herself again in the rearview mirror after gathering her purse and the paperback novel she had been reading. She had finished nearly half of it during the three-hour trip south from Jackson.

"Take one more look at yourself in that mirror. You'll see the reason," Brad said. "You were able to handle it."

Diana had worked hard, and the makeup and new hair style created by Minor Leblanc hid the fatigue. "I sure hope that guy you flew in from LA isn't over his head," she said. "He's got the four post-ops I left him plus there were three calls from the ER just as we were leaving the clinic."

Brad walked to the passenger side. He preempted the bellman from opening the door for her.

"Piece of cake as long as none of them were about some man shooting up the place," Brad said. "Besides that locum is being paid a ransom to cover the practice this weekend."

"Welcome to the New Orleans Ritz," the bellman said. He handed Brad separate receipts for the car and luggage and pocketed the ten-dollar tip. "Check-in is up on third floor. Elevator's 'round the corner."

Brad led them through glass doors into the hotel and around to the bank of elevators. Diana studied her image in a series of mirrored panels scattered between columned walls and floral arrangements. Minor's change to a shade lighter hair color had dropped a few years, although she missed the extra fifteen minutes of sleep lost to applying redesigned makeup. She had eventually said *no* to Botox, but as she reached to smooth the beginning cleft between her eyebrows, she decided *yes*. With the parting of the elevator doors onto the third floor and with another glance, she decided to order her own medication and inject the ditches herself.

* * *

"There's only so much these new jeans can do, Dr. Diana," Minor said. "They're tight, just right for you: fabulous and dazzling. But, my Jesus, those crow's feet, no way these fabulous jeans can hide them. Look what all that studying in med school did to you."

163

Diana stood beside Minor outside her closet, massaging her temples, staring with him into the mirror on the rear of the door. The wrinkles were from much more than medical school.

"Not even this Bobbi Brown can hide those awful things." He pulled a case of the makeup from the next shopping bag. "Those patients have worried you to death, saving all those lives! And you are too young, too fabulous, Doc. Do you hear me? 'Fab-u-lous!'"

Diana massaged harder.

"We have got to do something about the worry lines on your forehead," he said. "You can only apply so much Bobbi in those ditches. Those hot lights in the operating room will melt Bobbi all over your patients."

*   *   *

As they left the elevator and walked toward lobby check-in, Diana ran her hands from smoothing her forehead down the sides of the designer jeans and then patted her abdomen.

"Brad, where's dinner?" she asked.

"We could drive back over into Metairie to the original Drago's or go to the one over at the Hilton. Can't beat the chargrilled oysters."

"I don't think I want anything heavy, maybe a dinner salad or a piece of grilled fish. Why don't we walk into the Quarter and find someplace. I haven't been here since a college girls' trip."

"We might not need reservations since it's just us two. That is, if that Martin fellow doesn't show-up. But I think we gave his guy tailing us the slip."

"Remember, something light," she said, another pat to the abdomen.

"Could try dropping by the Pelican Club or Muriel's or even one of the newer places," Brad said. "After check in, I'll get with the concierge for a suggestion."

As he took his place behind three other guests in the registration line, Diana walked up the steps to the open-air courtyard. Empty tables scattered among miniature trees suggested the hotel had plenty of vacancies. The afternoon light streamed down onto her face. For the first time since her divorce, Diana felt truly beautiful, truly desirable. She was happy.

She felt a twinge of guilt for replacing Leslie Coachys, but Brad deserved to be happy, too.

"Can I get you something, Miss?" A waiter appeared from the adjacent Library Bar.

"No, thank you," she said. "Not yet."

The waiter disappeared.

"Concierge was on the phone, so dinner's still up for grabs," Brad said, joining her in the courtyard and holding a small, heavy-paper folder. "But got us eleventh floor, Canal view."

"Adjoining rooms or am I down the hall?" Diana asked, then grinned.

"Adjoining as *in the same room*," he answered. "That's how I was able to spring for the locum."

"I'm sure the clinic bookkeeper will be all over that," she said.

The bellman from the motor court waved to them from the lobby area. Brad and Diana walked from the courtyard toward him. "I'll be right up with your luggage, Dr. and Mrs. Cummins."

"Sure, buddy," Brad said. *Three more bucks will be plenty for that guy* he thought and walked Diana toward the separate bank of elevators leading to the guest rooms. "Guess I'll have to carry you over the threshold now, Mrs. Dr. Cummins," he said.

"You're in luck, Mr. Dr. Cummins, 'cause I worked off ten or so pounds while covering for you. But since we're not legal, I can handle myself."

They stepped inside the first elevator. Diana moved to the rear as Brad slid the laminated key into the slot for upper-floor access. He noticed the small gold-colored placard by the control panel. "For the safety of our guests, elevators under video surveillance," he read aloud. The doors closed and the car responded.

Diana reached to touch the small sign, and said, "What that means is: *No screwing in the elevator.*"

"I hate that rule," Brad said.

The elevator opened on 11. They walked toward their room.

"I think the last time I was in an elevator with you was when Brian was shot," Brad said.

Diana reached to put her arm around his waist and pulled him near.

"I feel like I've been treading water since. Dodging bullets, literally," he said.

"That's why I agreed to this weekend. You needed a getaway."

"You do, too. That's for sure." Brad smiled and leaned closer to

165

her. They turned at the sign pointing in the direction of their room number. "You saved my life, Diana. I owe you."

"You've made me feel good about myself, Brad. That's enough." She kissed his cheek.

"I wish I could have known more about what was going on with that Iraqi."

"Sorry I tossed him out the window," Diana said.

"No problem." Brad returned the kiss, a lingering one, and not on the cheek. They were around the corner from their room. "You've done much more to take care of me than the police ... in a lot of ways."

"Excuse me, Dr. and Mrs. Cummins?"

Brad recognized their bellman's voice.

Diana's body was responding to Brad's hand placed halfway up her back and pressing her into him. The silk of her blouse felt smooth against his fingers.

"Hate to interrupt, but I'm here with your things," the bellman said.

The three-dollar tip dropped to a buck. "Sure, fella, here's the key. Just put everything in the room."

"Yes, sir." He tipped his hat. "Would you like me to fill-up your ice bucket?"

"Don't worry about it, and you also can skip the room tour. We'll figure it out," Brad said. They watched the bellman and cart disappear down the hall.

"How much time have we got out here before he comes back through?" Diana asked.

Brad cupped her buttocks with his left hand and pulled her even nearer. "Hate to admit it, but I don't think we'll need much time."

"Then think about something else until we get into that room." She slid her hand down between them, following his hard abdomen, slipping her fingers between the buttoned areas of his cotton shirt. She tugged at his belt buckle.

"Better slow down," he said but did not pull away.

"As long as I have enough time in that room to freshen up and change clothes before we go out to eat, I'm good," Diana said. She looked forward to wearing her Nicole Miller slacks selected by Minor Leblanc, promised as fabulous with the new Theory blouse and Kate Spade shoes.

166

* * *

From Burgundy, the Nissan had worked through the narrow streets of the French Quarter, past an empty spot along Royal near an antiques shop, to the busy, uncovered parking lot behind Canal Place. Bordering the Mississippi River levee, the lot offered both hourly and by-the-day parking. She wasn't sure how long this would take.

Before taking an empty spot, the driver waited for three noisy women with Saks Fifth Avenue shopping bags to load their car and pull away. She stuffed the metered parking ticket into the glove compartment. After unfolding the tourist map provided by the rental company in Jackson, she traced the several block walk to the rear entrance of the Ritz Carlton.

A horse-drawn carriage went by as she stepped from the curb to cross North Peters onto Iberville Street. A couple sat tightly in the rear of the carriage, kissing. Stacy Lane could see herself snuggling there with Chad. They had talked about New Orleans; they had talked about a honeymoon in a lot of places once their tours were over—anyplace but Iraq.

Over the clacking of the horses' hooves against the pavement, she heard the driver call over his shoulder: "Ahead is Canal Street. Too much traffic. Need to circle back into the Quarter."

The two lovers didn't look up.

Stacy escaped across the street, focusing on the sidewalk leading up Iberville. If there were other approaching vehicles, she missed them. All she could see was the pleasure on Chad's face when they last kissed, when they last slept together during a few off duty hours in Iraq. The next time he returned to her in Balad, he was to die.

She worked through the revelers on Bourbon, party goers lingering from the night before or gathering for a new one. The rowdy lines crisscrossing the street smothered Stacy. Deafening music and laughter assaulted her from every direction. She bumped shoulders with a heavy woman wearing a Saints football jersey draped with over-sized black and gold beads.

"Hey, bitch, watch where you're going!" the woman cursed. "You made me spill some of my hurricane!" The woman took a long pull at the tall glass as though inhaling, her beads and breasts rising with the motion.

Stacy faded into the crowd, ducking into the nearest tee shirt shop. Stooping between racks of *Who Dat?* and *Geaux–something or other* designs, she watched through the window while the woman with the hurricane finished the thick, red beverage, squeezed her mate's buttocks, and stumbled with him into the margarita shop next door.

She slid out the front door, waited for several metallic-painted mimes to disperse, and then crossed the narrow intersection back onto Iberville. Stacy forced a walk. She could see ahead to Dauphine Street and the Ritz-Carlton.

There was no foot traffic at the corner rear entrance, no marquee, only a series of tinted glass doors. A single hotel attendant greeted her. "Welcome back to the Ritz, ma'am."

Stacy stepped into the receiving area. She smoothed her hair and slacks. Her shoes had escaped the spill of the woman's drink. She fumbled through her purse, holding it near her chest.

Zarife Amarah had convinced her to do this.

"Hi, I'm meeting a friend in the lounge," Stacy said to the attendant. "I was going to show you my key, but I can't seem to find it." The barrel of the gun tented the side of her leather purse as she snapped the purse shut.

"Be with you in just a minute," the attendant said. He turned to a woman standing next to him, studying an opened map. "I wouldn't try to walk it," he said to the woman. "That restaurant is way, way down on Magazine. Better let me call you a cab."

"Really sorry to interrupt again, sir," Stacy said, "but I checked in a few hours ago and don't know my way around the hotel yet."

"No problem, ma'am."

The woman with the map rustled it for attention. The effort was hopeless.

"The elevators are right through there." The attendant pointed down a short corridor. "Jazz lounge will be to your right once you exit the elevator. You'll find the front desk on the other side of the bar. You have a nice night, ma'am."

They've probably already checked in Stacy decided. She imagined how the cold hard metal would feel in her hand.

"Oh, I'm sorry. Just one more question. Is there a place I can make a call without having to go all the way up to my room? My cell battery is dead."

"Sure is. Take another right at the front desk, go past the elevators up to the guest rooms, and you'll see a house phone. There's also phones in the business center over to the left." Stacy was at the first elevator before he tipped his hat and returned to the lady with the map problem.

"Now you better get to those reservations on Magazine," he told her.

* * *

The business center was deserted—not much business on a Friday night. There were several telephones scattered among flat screen computers. A printer waited in each of the two far corners. Stacy sat at one of the phones. She checked the opened door; no one was outside in the hall. She studied the face of the phone and punched the two digit number for room service.

"This is Mrs. Cummins, Mrs. Brad Cummins. I'd like to order room service," Stacy said.

"My pleasure. What would you like, Mrs. Cummins?"

Stacy groped through the sheets of paper left scattered around the work space as though a menu would appear. "Ahhh, we will, Mr. Cummins and I, that is, will take the cheese plate … and some crackers … nice crackers … wheat ones with sesame seeds."

"We have a very nice cheese plate, includes fruit. Anything to drink?"

"Of course." She scattered the papers some more. "Champagne. We'll take some champagne. Good champagne. And two glasses. And some ice."

"Some ice? It's my pleasure. And your room number, Mrs. Cummins?"

Silence. Stacy picked up a couple of the discarded sheets of printer paper and flipped them over again.

"My husband checked in earlier this afternoon. He wants to surprise me with the room, so I don't know the number yet. But I would like to return the favor and have something special waiting."

"Our pleasure," room service said.

"So you'll have everything ready for us when we make it up to our room? I can't wait to be with him. It's our anniversary." Stacy giggled. She was proud of herself, her imagination.

"Be assured that everything will be ready for your special weekend at the Ritz, Mrs. Cummins. And happy anniversary."

"Thank you so much," Stacy said.

"With pleasure," room service repeated, then disconnected.

Stacy slammed the phone receiver into its base. She clutched her purse, pulled it against her chest, and kicked back from the desk. The chair flew from under her and across the aisle, striking the opposite work area. She was able to stand without falling.

"Oh, 'cuse me," said a dark-skinned man with a thick Spanish accent. He carried a large plastic bag from the common area outside the business center. "Sorry, but I need to get the trash." He slid Stacy's empty chair out of the way and emptied the waste can into his bag.

Collecting her composure, "Sir, could you tell me where the kitchen is?" Stacy asked.

"Don't work in the kitchen—housekeeping. See?" he held up the emptied waste can and carefully placed it under the desk.

"Don't they ever send you to the kitchen to pick up the trash?"

The man ambled out of the business center as Stacy brushed past. "Fine!" she grunted. She needed to find the kitchen before drawing any more attention to herself. Stacy reached deep into her purse and felt again for the hard, cold metal. She traced the lines of the barrel down to the grip and squeezed it. The purse dropped to the floor, scattering wallet, pens, hairbrush, and a few coins across the carpet. She still held the gun.

Drawn to the commotion, the man from housekeeping bent to help her.

"Hey, lady. Why you got that gun?"

Stacy pointed it at the center of his forehead. She surveyed the area for hotel guests or more employees. She saw no one, then thought about a security camera and pressed the muzzle against his skin. "Stand up," she said.

The housekeeping employee stood. He was a couple of inches shorter than Stacy. "Lady, I got no money."

"I'm not interested in any money, you idiot. Get back in that room."

"No Problem, lady. No need to be rough."

"Quit talking. I can barely understand you with that Mexican accent," Stacy said, pushing him back toward the business center.

"You hard up for a little sex or something? They give me a pill at the clinic, but I took the last one last week," he said, the accent thicker, excited.

She shoved him into a recessed corner supply cabinet that ran floor to ceiling, the gun now pointed at the back of his head. Stacy thought about Chad dying in that military hospital in Balad, a facility run by the strongest nation on earth. How could the United States let her love die? What price she had paid for the incompetence of Major Cummins.

She pressed the gun hard against the Mexican man's scalp. No one could replace Chad, not even John. John was too old, good for sex, but too old for a family. She tried to steady the gun by pushing even harder.

"Lady, you hurting me. If you want me to drop my pants, I'll do it. We can see how it goes."

Stacy steadied herself. She turned her head toward the entrance to the business center. Still no one. "Move back a bit—out of the way of the door to this cabinet," she said.

"Whatever you say, lady. But I need to warn you that my supervisor will be looking for me soon."

"Shut the fuck up!"

Stacy yanked open the full-length doors to the supply cabinet and kicked the man inside, knocking lose a series of shelves.

"Hey!" he yelled. "I said, no need to be so rough!"

Her repeated strikes across his head and chest, alternating the butt of the handgun with the barrel, splattered blood across the rear of the cabinet. The man crumpled to the base of the cabinet, whimpering, the shelves bent and clanging off their supports to cover him.

Stacy panicked with the noise. One more lashing stopped the whimpering. She checked the doorway. The hallway remained clear: no security, no horrified hotel guest. No one had heard the beating. The room was suddenly fraught with silence, broken only by the faint hum of the computer hard drives.

Stacy used the man's trouser legs to wipe clean the smeared blood from the barrel and butt of the gun. He did not move. She kicked the limp leg into the cabinet and gently shut the doors. Her own clothing was free of blood. She smoothed the few wrinkles, took a deep breath, and stuffed the handgun into her blouse

"Mind if I join you?" A man in a dark suit with briefcase appeared in the doorway. "Nice business center, but a little small for a Ritz. Don't you think?" He set the briefcase near the house phone. "At least it's quiet," he said.

"You got the whole place to yourself," she answered. "I'm all finished." The businessman was already absorbed in a spread sheet and one of the keyboards. She grabbed her purse from the chair and slid the gun inside. There was no sound from the supply cabinet. She realized that another person had seen her, but there would be others.

Outside the business center, she fought to calm herself by breathing deeply, taking in the brightly-lit, black-metal wall sconces, the oil paintings, the flowers arranged extravagantly on an antique sideboard. Another man hurried toward her: this one taller, with broad shoulders. He wore a dark-blazer, pinned with a gold-colored name badge on the front pocket. He seemed headed toward the bank of guest room elevators and check-in.

"Excuse me," she said.

"May I help you?" the man asked.

The man carried a leather folder. He looked important.

"I'm looking for the kitchen," she said.

"The kitchen?"

Stacy felt the man's steady eyes take in every curve, every seam of her dress, the style of her shoes—all without a flicker.

"Miss, if you're here to apply for a position, you'll need to go online and fill out an application."

"I'm not looking for a job. I've heard so much about the food here—that I shouldn't miss eating—dining here before I leave—before I finish my weekend here in New Orleans."

"If you're looking for the restaurant, follow me."

They walked to the lobby. She pictured the man from housekeeping stuffed in the cabinet of the business center, left crumpled, unconscious, and bleeding—probably dead. *I should get rid of this guy, too.*

"Miss, take a left up those few steps, then through the lounge. The maitre d' will be waiting. Enjoy." He passed behind three clerks studying computer screens at the reception and check-in desk, then disappeared through a door behind them.

Stacy climbed the short steps only to find several more leading down to the lounge. She ignored the smile of the bartender and a waitress who approached with a half-empty tray of nuts and

172

several empty wine glasses. A thin banister separated the lounge and bar from the restaurant.

The hostess stood behind a Louis XVI style desk that abutted the banister. "Do you have a reservation?" she asked.

"Don't need one. I'm meeting friends here. They're supposed to have a table." She waved at a busy group surrounding a table across the room. There was an empty chair. "Look, there they are. Thanks."

Stacy hurried into the dining room; a busboy cleared the table next to the group.

"Enjoy," the hostess said, redirecting her attention to a couple holding hands and looking at the posted dinner fare. "Good evening. Do you have reservation?" she asked the two men.

Stacy looked back at the hostess. She was escorting the men to the other side of the dining area. The busboy placed the last water glasses from his table into a plastic bin and disappeared with it behind a partition. Stacy followed. She heard voices and kitchen noises as she slipped through the swinging doors and crouched in a corner behind a tall metal rack. The rack was stacked with china.

A voice startled her.

"Got this cheese plate for *1139*."

Stacy narrowly missed falling forward into the rack.

"Order don't call for no certain champagne."

Stacy peered unnoticed through the stacked dinner and salad plates with cups dangling from small hooks in between. A young girl about her height and dressed in a starched white uniform had stopped in front. "I got that fancy ice bucket. Whatchu want me to stick in it?"

"Let the bartender pick out something. Make it middle-of-the-road," the chef answered. "And, hey, make sure it's cold this time."

"Got it," the girl said.

"And check the glasses. Wipe off the spots if they need it," the chef said.

"Like I said *Got it!*" The girl went out through the swinging doors with the room service order, and Stacy followed. The chef was deep into chopping vegetables. She stood at the edge of the partition, allowing the girl time to reach the bar before passing the hostess for a seat on an empty lounge sofa.

"Did you decide not to join your friends after all?" the hostess asked.

"No, I'm good," Stacy answered.

"Can I ask that server to get you something to drink?"

"I already said *no!*"

The hostess stiffened. They both studied the bartender as he nestled a bottle of Louis Perdrier into the bucket. The room service attendant filled it with ice, a few cubes at a time.

Again Stacy forced calm, shielding her face so the girl from room service wouldn't see it. "I'm sorry. The server seems so busy. I don't want to be a bother."

"Well, perhaps you're right, Miss." The hostess spun away to face two hungry-looking teenage girls, standing at the Louis VI with their father. She squared her shoulders and repositioned herself behind the desk. "Three?" She grabbed menus from a drawer.

The girl with room service carried the oval silver tray on her shoulders and maneuvered toward a narrow corridor. Stacy followed, approaching the service elevator. The girl pushed *Up* and turned to Stacy. "Lady, the guest elevators are around through check-in. You're supposed to use your room key to go up."

Stacy scanned the interior of the service elevator car as the doors parted. The girl stepped in, carefully balancing the silver tray; the bucket of iced champagne; and the plate of sliced cheese, fruit, and sesame seed-peppered crackers.

Stacy kicked the girl in her lower back, jumping into the elevator as the doors closed. She pushed the lighted *11* button and kicked the girl in the face, planting her heel under the chin and popping the head backward. A faint red spray marred the wall behind the girl as her body went flaccid, the bucket falling to the floor. The bottle of champagne spun among scattered ice cubes and clipped the bucket.

"Dammit! What a mess!" Stacy took another blow at the motionless girl as the elevator closed. The first six floors flew by. Stacy hit the *STOP* button. There was no bell or a buzzer when the elevator halted. Reaching across the girl's chest, she unbuttoned the hotel uniform and slid it free of the limp arms. The back of her hand brushed across blood running from the girl's nostrils.

Careful to keep the white cloth of the uniform clean, Stacy

wiped her hand on the girl's pants, saving the pristine linen napkin that landed nearby. She held the jacket against her and admired the reflection in the mirror at the back of the elevator. Smoothing the fabric, "Not too bad," she said. Stacy set her shoulder purse to the side, clear of the blood, and dressed in the jacket.

"I was right. She was my size."

Stacy gathered the bucket, the bottle, and the tray. Except for a small chip to the rim and a tight crack across the middle, the china plate had survived the fall. She arranged it on the tray and scooped up the few surviving crackers. There was blood on most of the fruit, but the cheese slices were passable. Fanning the cheese and crackers across the center of the plate, she covered the crack.

"Appetizing, for sure. Since there's an opening on the staff, that chef ought to hire me," she said. Stacy released the *STOP* control and the car jolted upward.

Seven, eight, nine, ten. The elevator opened into the service area of the eleventh floor. A cart of soiled linen waited in the corner near a rack of folded clean towels and fresh toiletries. Stacy saw no one. She rushed to set her redecorated tray on the rack, retrieved her shoulder bag, and dragged the room service attendant from the elevator into an adjacent closet, knocking free the hanging mops and brooms. The utensils toppled to the floor, the mop heads covering the girl's face.

The elevator doors shut. "Room 1139," Stacy repeated as she smoothed the lapel and front of the jacket, deciding that her solid dark slacks against the white jacket created the right look. Only the high heels seemed out of place although the shine had survived. "Glad my heel didn't break when I kicked that bitch."

She worked the purse strap under her jacket and over her shoulder then shifted the purse to her back. The contents felt heavy. Stacy grabbed the tray from the supply rack, nearly loosing the ice bucket. She steadied it against her chest and walked into the hall.

A man and women were outside a room struggling with their key. "Miss, these plastic card things never seem to work for us," the man asked. "Can you help us open our door?"

"Get lost. I'm with room service."

Stacy held the tray high and kept moving.

"Last time I stay here," the man mumbled.

"George, shut up. Let me try it," the woman said.

Stacy forced a slow pace, but lost to her adrenaline. A cracker fell to the carpet, and she left it. The plate looked skimpy but would have to do. A wall sign ahead pointed left to rooms numbered below 1150. She rang the bell at room 1139.

"Room service."

* * *

"I thought we were going into the Quarter for dinner," Diana said as Brad fluffed his pillow.

"We are. Must have the wrong room."

Brad sat up. The sheet slid away from his body.

"Room service for 1139!" A loud knock this time.

"Better answer it," he said.

"First, you better put on that hotel robe I saw hanging in the bathroom, or she might jump you." Diana reached for his shoulders and pulled him back to her. She wanted him again.

"Room service!"

"OK, OK." Brad found his shorts on a chair. "Hold that pose, Diana."

"Meet me in the shower—I'll pose there," she said, pulling the sheets after her as she walked into the bathroom.

"Won't keep you waiting long, that's for sure," Brad said.

He opened the door and said into the hall, "Sorry, but we didn't order anything."

"Compliments of the hotel," the server said.

Stacy stopped before barging into the room. "Honeymoon, right? May I set this over on the desk?"

Brad backed away. "Why not? Free is good." He checked the offering as she brushed by. The tray looked skimpy, unappetizing: the bucket lacked ice, champagne label torn, crackers cracked. "Yeah, free is about right," he said just before the edge of the silver tray slammed into his gut.

"What the hell?" he grunted, falling against the closet door. Brad lifted his head to the barrel of a handgun while the remainder of the purse contents spilled to the floor.

"It's OK. It's OK. I'll get you my wallet. It's by the bed. No need for that." Brad steadied his back against the door as he pushed to his feet, the raised ridges on the wooden panels scraping his flesh. He staggered toward the walnut bedside table.

176

"I don't want your wallet, Major Cummins."

"*Major* Cummins?" Brad turned to the gun still pointed up at his head. "Do I know you?" He studied the girl's face. Immediately behind her, the bathroom door cracked open.

"You were the trauma surgeon at Balad."

Brad stared more deeply. "Balad?"

"You murdered my friend in the base hospital, my boyfriend," she cried. Stacy was surprised that the revolver shook; it felt heavy, the barrel dropping to point at Brad's feet. "We were going to spend the rest of our lives together."

Brad considered a lunge forward, but the girl steadied herself, the gun back in his face. "You were one of the surgery nurses," he said.

"You didn't know me over there. You didn't care about me," she said. She cocked the hammer of the revolver, again nearly losing grip of the weapon. Then the shaking stopped.

"Where's your girlfriend?" she asked.

"Girlfriend?" Brad was ten inches taller. His shoulders dwarfed hers, but there was little distance separating them.

"Yes, you asshole ... *girlfriend*."

"Do you see anybody in here but me?" Brad waved his arm across the empty bed toward the window. "I'm alone."

"I'm not falling for that, Doctor. A great-looking guy like you alone in a hotel room in New Orleans?"

"I needed to get away, a little R & R." Brad threw his arms up.

"You're a better murderer than a liar, Doctor."

"I'm not a . . ."

"Shut up! I followed you and your whore down here from Jackson. Right behind you the whole time—so wrapped up in yourselves you never even noticed. Besides I see her fucking suitcase over in the corner and her panties on the floor. "

Brad saw a tear slip from the corner of the girl's eye.

"You didn't even notice me when you stopped at that convenience store in McComb. I was at the pump right next to you. Your whore didn't even acknowledge me in the check-out line either."

The bathroom door behind the nurse eased open a little further. "OK—I give up. I am here with my girlfriend. She's—getting a massage—be back any minute."

The bathroom door moved slightly more.

"That massage won't help her when she finds your brains blown all over this room. I want that slut to feel what I felt in Balad." The barrel of the pistol remained firm. "After I shoot you, I'm going to wait here. I want to see, to enjoy, what the sight and smell of your blood does to her. I might even kill her, too."

"Look, miss. If you would tell me your name I might be able to put all this together."

"You are truly one arrogant sonnavabitch, Major Cummins, Dr. Cummins. Don't worry your intelligent brain about remembering my name. I'm just one of the little people—just a nurse."

"Look, you're wrong about me. I'm not like that."

"Shut up!" She popped her support hand against the left side of the gun, stretching both arms to push the pistol inches from Brad's face. My name is Stacy. Stacy Lane … as if you cared."

"Thank you, Stacy," Brad said. "Now, what are you talking about? Who are you talking about?"

"Chad Giles, you bastard!" She pushed the tip of the pistol even closer.

"Giles? This is about Giles?"

"Yes. My fiancé, Chad Giles!" she shrieked.

"I tried to save that lance corporal's life."

"You're lying. You're lying!"

Brad tightened his calves, his bare feet firmly against the floor, his ribs still aching, his back still on fire. He stared into the barrel of the gun.

"Maybe I should shoot you in your stuff, let you bleed out down there while I watch."

Brad kept focused on the end of the gun, ignoring the edge of the bathroom door as it inched toward Lane.

"Better yet: I'll shoot you in the face, too, and leave you alone to drown in your own blood, let the whore find you and your bloody balls all by herself."

In a second he could be all over her, Brad decided, her face buried in his chest. The gun—who knows where.

"Your girlfriend will go ballistic when she finds you in all that blood, clutching yourself one last time. That's all she really wanted from you anyway." Stacy Lane waved the revolver over her head.

Behind her the bathroom door parted slowly. Brad forced his

attention to Lane's face and the revolver.

There were more tears. Brad's heart was racing.

"I wonder if she'll cry as hard as I did when Chad died."

Brandishing the top of the toilet tank, Diana burst through the bathroom door, barely missing the girl. She pounded the hard ceramic into Stacy's head. Stacy sank under the adrenaline, the piece falling to the floor intact, a wad of bloody scalp and brunette hair smeared across its shiny surface.

Brad leaped onto the bleeding girl as the gun fired, shattering the plate glass window that overlooked the garden courtyard. He threw Stacy to the floor, her contorted body twitching under his weight.

Diana's scream muffled the sound of the glass falling back into the room.

As Brad pulled himself up, he heard a gurgle deep within Stacy's throat and felt another seizure. Then there was no motion, no carotid pulse. Brad stared down at her. The gun lay a couple of feet from the body. He felt the girl's blood on his chest and abdomen.

"Brad, my God! She's dead!"

"So, you want to be the one to pronounce?" he asked.

They stared down at the eyes: fixed, glassy. For Brad, there was a vague familiarity from Balad. He again reached to the young woman's neck, still warm, but nothing.

"I'd say 'Dead, very dead,'" he said.

" OK, then, who the hell is she?"

"I don't know. I don't remember anyone by that name." Brad looked at Diana. "And by the way, I'm good."

"Spectacular," she said. "But you've got some explaining to do."

Brad assessed the brain matter oozing from the jagged depression in the scalp. He instinctively wiped his hands across his chest, leaving bloody gray smears.

"And, I might add," Diana said, "this is the second time I've had to knock a pointed gun off of you. Only difference is the perpetrator didn't fly out the window."

"Yeah, you're getting better, not as messy," he said. He looked down at the blood on his hands, chest, and abdomen and at the stains on the carpet. "Well, almost."

179

"So, I guess this means we're definitely dating," she said.

"Fine with me."

"Security!" followed a pounding at the door.

"And I guess I won't be getting that shower after all," Diana said. She studied Brad. "But it looks like you need to rinse off more than I do."

The door to their hotel room flew open. Two husky men in dark navy suits rushed in and pushed Diana aside. The first one stopped over Lane's body and shouted into a head piece. "Get NOPD up here and call an ambulance. He looked up at Brad and back down at the body. "Hold the ambulance."

"Looks like no one is getting a shower tonight," Brad said.

27

Color 8x10's covered the desk.

Brad was frozen near the center of one photograph, holding his arms high as though having just been strip-searched. His Jockey boxers were more than wrinkled, blood stains soaked into the creases, dried blood on his arms and breasts. Near the pen set of Key Martin's desk, Stacy Lane's body was shown just as Brad and Diana remembered it—the gun lying between the dead nurse and the broken hotel window. Scattered pillows, wrinkled sheets, and a bedspread turned inside-out were in the surrounding photos. The silver serving tray lay overturned, propped diagonally against the dresser with its contents scattered beneath.

"NOPD was already in the hotel when a guest next door reported the shot. Some suit trying to print out a last-minute presentation in the business center had called them about a beaten-up janitor locked in a cabinet."

The detective held up a photograph of the sniveling janitor from the Ritz. "You two didn't run across this poor soul, too? Did you?"

"No, we never saw that guy," Diana answered. "We hadn't left the room since check-in."

"Figured as much. They found this gal's fingerprints all over that janitor," he said, putting his on the photograph of Stacy Lane. "Same thing for a waitress from room service. She was stuffed in a service closet on your floor." Martin pointed to the still of a second dead woman. "Don't guess you ran across this young lady?" he asked. "Either of you?"

"No, detective." It was Brad's turn. "Like Dr. Bratton just told you, we checked in and went to our room. And we answered all these same questions in New Orleans. Didn't NOPD provide a report?"

"And you never called for room service?" Martin asked.

"No, just like we told 'em in New . . ."

"OK, OK, Doc, relax. I'm on your side, but I shouldn't have dropped the tail on you. He returned to study the photograph of Stacy Lane. "This Miss Lane went to a whole lot of trouble to get at you. My buddies in the Big Easy think she faked the room service order and took down the real server just to get your room number. That was pretty smart, don't you think?"

"Lane said she was a nurse in Iraq with me. And if she was an RN cleared by the military, that sort of speaks for itself, doesn't it?" Brad said.

"I checked," Martin said, "graduated in the top ten percent of her class."

"And look where that got her," Diana said.

"Dr. Bratton, Stacy Lane was there on a mission, a well-planned one, it seems to me."

"She blamed me for killing her boyfriend," Brad said, "when I was trying to save him."

"Detective, Brad's already been through hell over that serviceman's death. He told me that he was cleared of any wrongdoing."

"That's not what this is about. Your boyfriend—I mean, Dr. Cummins—has been the target, I suspect, of three attempts on his life."

"Three?" Diana asked.

"Yes!" Brad clenched his fists. "Somebody finally believes me: whoever shot my brother was after me." Brad grabbed the photograph of Stacy Lane then threw it back to Martin's desk. "This bitch killed my brother."

"Don't think so. Ballistics don't support it," Martin said.

"The gun Lane had at the Ritz Carlton was not the one used to murder Brian?" Diana asked.

"Right," Martin said.

Brad shook his head. "So this still isn't over."

"Different gun, plus evidence says the bullet's trajectory matches a taller assailant," Martin said. "Lane barely topped five two."

"Then who shot my brother and my fiancée, Detective?" Brad asked. "Are we back to Amarah?"

"I don't know, Dr. Cummins. At least, not yet."

Martin thought about Mr. Giles and the shooting in the ER. "Why don't you two take another little trip?" he asked. "This time with me and not to such a fancy place."

28

Brad felt more at ease in Detective Martin's squad car, a vehicle less imposing than the NOPD version that whisked him through the streets of New Orleans. He wondered if Diana felt the same and thought about turning to ask her, then decided against it. She had chosen the rear seat, yielding the front to him. He glanced around the dark, plain, unmarked sedan for the manufacturer's insignia. Finding none, he assumed Chevrolet, or maybe a Buick.

"The website says male patients can refuse visitors in the Acute Services Department, but I expect the front desk will let us in—perks of the profession," Martin said. "Plus, I got some paperwork from a judge."

"Twila Crockett was a little hesitant to fill me in at first, but she got the guy admitted out here. I guess she knows the same Chancery Court judge," Brad said. "She's trying to get Giles transferred to some shrink in Tennessee."

"You docs, you snap your fingers. If you want it, it happens." The sound effect followed. "My stepsister's a real wacko ... been on the waiting list at Whitfield for over a year and still can't get in."

"Then get her an appointment with Mr. Giles' psychiatrist. She's not going anywhere. She's propped up in her office over in Hilltop Village, her arm in a sling," Brad said.

"No way I can treat Sis to that. She'll just have to stick with the free mental health center in South Jackson." Martin stopped before turning onto Highway 475. "That lady psychiatrist is bound to charge 200 an hour, maybe even more. Chief doesn't dole out that kind of cash to the hired help."

Three female trustees uniformed in white slacks with wide green, circular stripes sweated over a flower bed lining a section of the highway. One of the three worked a hoe, the other two pulled weeds. An obese male in a grey supervisor's uniform sat sideways behind the wheel of the pickup parked along the shoulder, his stubby legs dangling through the open door, his ear pressed into a cell phone. He tipped his hat to Martin's vehicle as it entered the tree-lined drive to the hospital entrance.

"I haven't been out to Whitfield since medical school," Brad said. "We had to do a three-week rotation in psychiatry here in addition to spending time at the VA." A red-brick column displayed the plaque: *Mississippi State Hospital-Founded 1855.* "The crazies I took care of that summer cured me of ever wanting to be a psychiatrist."

"All these white buildings, the columns—reminds me of Mount Vernon," Diana said.

Martin pulled the police cruiser under the portico nearest the check-in station. A smiling male guard with a clipboard leaned toward them as Martin presented credentials through the opened window. "Well, Doc," Martin said, "you better hope this Giles fella ain't too crazy, or we won't get much out of him."

* * *

A stone-faced nurse in a starched white uniform stood in the reception area of the Acute Services Department. Her lapel was heavy with round- and square-shaped metal badges. Brad recognized one of them as a nurse's graduate pin. The badge hanging from a front pocket read *Maria Tugwell, RN.* The picture under the name was from an earlier year.

"Which one of you is Detective Martin?" Tugwell asked.

Brad felt the short vibration of a new cell phone text. After he stepped back to read it, he leaned forward to whisper, "Diana, the locum's got a couple of appendixes and a bowel obstruction for us to do when we get back. They're established patients and want to wait on you or me to do the surgery."

"Be my guest," Diana said.

"Beg your pardon?" the nurse asked of the young couple. "If you need to talk privately or use your cell phone, you might want to go back outside."

"Ma'am, I'm Detective Key Martin." He produced the same credentials from his blazer pocket and flipped out the badge. "I'm with these two physicians here. They've got patients back at their office waiting for them."

"We have more acute patients in this ward than these two doctors could possibly have waiting for them back home. In fact, I could be tending to my own patients now instead of wasting my time with you."

"We're here on a legal matter, Miss Tugwell. We need to talk with one of those patients."

Diana stepped forward. "Tugwell, you're the one wasting everyone's time. We're here because people have died."

"Relax, relax. I know why you're here. The judge in charge of the commitment called me. This way, please. Mr. Giles is down the hall—in group therapy."

They looked through the window into the activities room. Brad leaned closer. "The old guy doesn't look so manic now," he said. "Lithium?"

"Yes, lithium," Tugwell answered. "Our psychiatrists have heavily medicated him."

"I hope not too heavy. I need some answers," Brad said.

* * *

The group therapy session was over a few minutes later. "You people need to let me go, let me go home," Giles said. "I've been to all your hokey group sessions. All those people in there are crazy."

"Mr. Giles, these people are not here to treat you. They just want to talk. The aide will stay in case you need anything." Tugwell turned away for her office.

The nurses' aide guided Giles across the hall. He shuffled into the private consultation room, the image a sharp contrast to what Brad remembered from third-year medical school: male psychiatric patients dressed in faded house coats, pajamas, and ill-fitting slippers—the set of the Jack Nicholson movie. Giles wore khakis and leather loafers, similar to that night in the ER.

"You're that doctor!" Giles yelled. The aide stepped forward, took his forearm, and flipped open a cell phone.

Detective Martin sandwiched between Brad and Giles. "Like the nurse told you, Mr. Giles, we just came here to ask you a few questions," he said.

"A few questions?" Giles asked. "All I get in this prison are 'a few questions.' I'm tired of questions." The aide motioned for him to take the nearest chair at the table. She stood behind Giles and dropped her phone back into her jacket. Brad and Diana sat across from them.

Martin paced the room.

"Did you know of a young woman named Stacy Lane?"

185

"I think that was the name of my grandson's girlfriend," Giles answered, "from his letters," still watching Diana. "Hey, Doctor, this isn't the same girlfriend you had in Memphis."

"No, Mr. Giles, this is Dr. Bratton. She practices surgery with me."

"Didn't know I knew so much about you; did you, Cummins?"

Detective Martin," the aide said. "Mrs. Tugwell wouldn't like Mr. Giles getting so agitated. It's too soon for his next dose."

"Tugwell doesn't need to worry about me," Giles said. "I keep telling you people that I'm not crazy, I'm just pissed. I've lost everything."

"Mr. Giles, we did everything we could for your grandson in Iraq."

"No excuses, Cummins. I looked you up on the Internet," Giles said. "I recognized you at the air show. I followed you and that girl to your motel afterwards." Giles grinned. "Don't suppose that dog got too much in the way?"

"Psychotic or not, fella, you're outta line!" Brad jumped from the folding chair, lunging across the metal conference table at Giles. He felt Diana's firm hand on his thigh.

The aide popped open her phone. "I'm calling security."

"No, no," Martin stood. "No need for that, Miss. He glanced across to her name tag, but did not read it. "Dr. Cummins, please sit down."

Brad slid down into his seat. Diana relaxed.

"Mr. Giles, the reason we came here was to learn a little bit more about your grandson's relationship with his girlfriend over in Iraq. We know her name is . . . was . . . Stacy Lane."

"What I can tell you, Detective, is that my grandson sure didn't get to shack up with her in a Memphis motel room."

"That's it!" Brad popped again from his seat. "Martin, if you won't drive us back into Jackson, I'll call a taxi. I'm sure there are bunch of them lined up over at the airport."

"Sit down, Brad. We're not going anywhere," Diana said.

Brad sank into his chair, catching the aide's grin.

"All we need is a little more information about your grandson's relationship with Miss Stacy Lane. Isn't there anything you can share with us?" Martin asked.

"He wrote me that he had met a girl over there, a young nurse,

186

who worked at the military hospital. Said her name was Stacy. You're right: *Stacy Lane*. Never saw her picture or anything, but I knew that she had to be beautiful."

Brad ignored Giles' glare.

"My grandson liked to write letters. He didn't do much email, I don't think, so I wasn't surprised with all the letters they sent me with his things."

"What letters?" Martin asked.

"Letters the girl wrote him, Detective, and one that he had written her—but never got to mail. And if I had those letters, you would want to see them, I guess?"

"We're just trying to find out why there have been so many deaths, Mr. Giles," Diana said.

"Why don't you ask your boyfriend there, Doc? He's good at killing people."

Brad again felt the pressure of Diana's hand on his thigh.

"I burned the damn letters. They were Chad's personal business."

"Didn't read any of them? Not even a few?" Martin asked.

Giles looked into his lap. "I was lonely, Detective. I did read a couple of them."

"Perfectly natural thing to do, Mr. Giles. Any parent or grandparent would do that."

"Chad must've met the girl on furlough, at a restaurant. He talked about how good the food was, really-good American style. I'm surprised they have anything like that in that desert."

Brad looked at Diana and then at Detective Martin. *Waste of time.*

"Anything else in the letters?" Martin asked.

"The girl must've been dating someone else when she met Chad. She said the guy still wanted to, you know, be with her. The girl wrote real mushy stuff. Said she loved my grandson but couldn't let the other guy go. Seems Chad was desperate for her to be with him."

"Who was the guy?" Diana asked.

"None of the letters said, but I think he was older. Seemed like she was afraid to spell out the guy's name in a letter, like someone in the service might intercept it and tell him. Anyway, why is that so important?" Giles asked.

"There must have been a lot more than *love* going on there, Mr. Giles," she said.

"What do you mean by that?"

"It seems that Stacy Lane was obsessed with your grandson. She tried to kill Dr. Cummins."

"I wanted Dr. Cummins to die, too."

Brad stood again. This time slowly. "I'm ready to leave, Martin. This was a bad idea. We're just opening up old wounds."

Diana shook her head. Brad slid back into his chair.

"It was in her last notes to Chad. She said that she was afraid of the other guy, afraid of what he would do if she left him for Chad."

29

"Look, man, I'm already really behind. Patient schedule is packed."

"Doc, you always say that when I drop by. I guess detective work doesn't pay like cutting on people."

"Martin, we call it *surgery*."

"And being a *detective* is more than riding out to a psychiatric hospital to talk to a distraught old man," Key Martin said.

"Diana and I should have stayed at the clinic and gotten some of these patients seen. Let you do the interrogating out at Whitfield."

"I'm not so sure that questioning that sad Mr. Giles was interrogation," Martin said.

Brad pulled up the next patient's lab results on the computer screen in the hall. " 'Crit's come up since he was discharged. That's good. Lot of blood loss on that case," he said, clicking to the next page.

"Those letters Mr. Giles talked about, the ones between the nurse in Iraq and his grandson," the detective said. "There was a serious relationship going on there."

"Guess Stacy Lane couldn't handle that boy's death—sent her over the edge," Brad said. He retrieved the paper chart from outside the door to the next exam room. "But we already knew the girl was more than a killer—she was nuts. Remember? New Orleans?"

"So you think she was crazy? Psychotic?" Martin asked.

"She was definitely crazy."

"At least the girl knew she was nuts."

Brad looked up from the patient chart. "Psychotic killers don't know they're psychotic, or at least they ignore that they're crazy."

Martin tossed a small vinyl pocket purse into the air. Brad caught it. "That turned up in a search of Lane's rental car," Martin said.

"What do you want me to do with this?" Brad asked.

"Look inside."

Brad popped open the purse. Several white pills were scattered through it.

"Have you got one of those new, fancy medication ID programs on your computer?" Martin asked.

"Yes, I do." Brad returned to the computer. "But I still find myself referring to that heavy *PDR* over in my bookcase." Brad tapped in the two digits and the letter imprinted on one of the tiny white pills.

"Alprazolam," he announced. "It brought up Alprazolam, the generic equivalent of Xanax. It's for anxiety. It would be easy for a nurse to get her hands on this," Brad said.

"Xanax," Martin said. "My ex-wife used to take that. She took a lot of it, in fact."

"Bet she did," Brad said.

"Doc, I need you to help fill in the blanks in this case."

"You've already got blanks filled in, Detective. It's obvious that Amarah killed my brother and Leslie. You just can't prove it. And Stacy Lane was just another psycho."

"There's more going on here, Dr. Cummins. Like I said, dig a little deeper. Work with me."

30

After work Brad slid his key into the door of his old place at the Plaza Building. It looked just as he had left it before Leslie was attacked. The same cleaning service that sanitized his brother's murder scene had removed every blood stain. The place had been listed with a realtor for weeks, and while units in the building generally flipped quickly, there had been little interest. The real estate agent assured him that once news of Leslie's murder faded, potential buyers would materialize. Brad questioned the optimism.

The apartment smelled musty, felt cold. He left the door open for air. The listing agent suggested that Brad leave the place furnished, so his mahogany desk still stood in the study. He opened the bottom drawer. The manila file folder he brought home from Iraq had survived the police search. Martin had admitted yesterday that his investigation was going nowhere—no new witnesses and no new persons-of-interest. The detective still believed he had two unsolved murder cases: Leslie Coachys and Brian Cummins. Brad wasn't so sure; he needed some answers.

He slid the stack of reports from the folder. On top was the letter from the Balad medical tribunal summarizing its findings and exonerating him of medical negligence in the death of Lance Corporal Chad Giles of Tennessee. *Guess that ass John Haynes got one of these letters, too* he thought. Following the letter was a photocopy of Giles' medical record made available to all interested parties during the inquest. Brad scanned the first and second pages: nothing but the medic's emotionless first assessment of the scene where the IED detonated and the same notes from the helicopter transport that he first reviewed in the ICU.

He flipped through his notes and Cossar's nursing notes, then some lab reports, then lists of medications administered and supplies used until he located the autopsy findings. Brad pulled the leather chair to his desk, turned on the floor lamp beside it, and studied.

"Nothing," he said. "No congenital heart anomalies. No missed head trauma. Liver OK. No PTE. My sutures at the spleen held even through the attempted resuscitation. There's nothing here." Brad went back to the blood chemistry reports. "Even his 'crit was up after the last unit of pack cells was transfused."

"Why the hell did this kid die?" Brad asked aloud.

"I don't know—why did he?"

A woman's voice came from the foyer.

"Cossar? What are you doing here? I thought you had left for Atlanta."

"I've been thinking about moving from Atlanta to Jackson. A place downtown comes close to what I have over there. The realtor showed me around this building a couple of days ago."

"I can make you a great deal on this one," Brad said. He closed the folder.

"She showed it to me. Nice. I didn't put two-and-two together until I saw you down the hall. Actually, the one for sale around the corner is smaller and better suited for me, but I'll probably stay in Atlanta.

"Maybe I should move to Atlanta, and stay with you, Elizabeth," Brad said. "Hide there since the police think that there's still a killer on the loose."

Cossar walked the length of the foyer, past the library, and into the living room. She looked out the same windows framing the area where Leslie's wedding gown was fitted. "Maybe I can afford this place," she said.

Brad produced a couple of boxes from a nearby closet. "Here. Help me unpack this desk, and maybe I'll give you a discount." He placed the folder in a box and began to empty the other drawers.

"It would have to be a mighty big one for a nurse to swing this," she said. "But we've had that money talk before."

"Maybe I'll just drop the mortgage payments, let the bank have it. They'll make you a good deal."

Cossar thought about her brother's reaction should she move to the area—the screaming, the profanity. *It would almost be worth it* she decided.

* * *

Brad left Cossar at her car and drove back to his apartment at the King Edward. Diana met him there. "Do you see anything I might have missed?" he asked as he unpacked the second box.

"No, Brad. I don't think my looking through this a fifth time

192

will help." Diana dropped Giles' medical records on his new desk. "Why do you still have this stuff anyway?" she asked.

"Should have shredded 'em, I know. Nobody asked for this stuff back."

"Forget it, Brad. You did your job. That guy was a casualty of war and the poor guy's girlfriend was a fruitcake, a real fruitcake." Diana walked to Brad's mini-refrigerator inside his home office and was surprised to find a bottled water.

"There's got to be more to all of this," Brad said.

"You shouldn't have called off Martin's people, Brad."

"Gee, now you tell me," he said.

Diana twisted off the cap and drank half. "That Lane girl was stalking us—stalking you, that is." She finished the water.

"The rental car the police found in New Orleans, she rented it in Jackson," Diana said. "I wonder how long she had been around here? I wish Martin could place her at your clinic the day Brian died."

Brad asked, "Instead of Amarah thinking Brian was me, you think Lane made the mix up, don't you? Remember, Martin thinks the shooter was taller."

"I'm not the detective, Brad."

"You might as well be," he said.

31

"Get a promotion, Detective?"

Key Martin stood up from his desk, letting a short stack of papers slip to the surface. "I'm usually the one to interrupt you."

"Beat you to the punch, I guess," she said.

"Guess you did, Doc," he said. Diana's hair fell against her shoulders, a more textured style and a shade lighter than he remembered. Several of the better-paid precinct secretaries sported the same look. Key wanted to study the doctor more closely but dropped his eyes back to the papers on his desk. He first found her attractive in the blood-splattered elevator below the surgery clinic.

Over the following weeks of interviews, the shock had disappeared from her face, the pallor of fatigue faded … or at least was better disguised with makeup. The appeal grew each time he saw her: a smart, strong woman, yet one so attractive. The detective lifted the first two sheets of paper from the stack as though to review them. He thought of his ex-wife and the girlfriend that followed. Both were heavy into makeup, gobs of it. They wore it to bed. The stuff got all over the pillow case and the sheets and on him. But the pretty doctor wore just the right amount—just enough to show off her thin lips, her green eyes.

"Detective, I want you to share some information with us," Diana said.

"Come right on in, Doctor. Have a seat. Water?"

Key gestured to a wooden chair near his desk. "I'd get you a Diet Coke or something, but we just went to a pay machine."

"No thanks." She tossed the dirty notebook and police journal from the seat of the chair, landing them on a shelf in the near corner. A small cloud exploded above the space.

"What'd you do? Bring the dust from the old office with you?" Diana wiped her hand across the seat as she slid the chair under her. "I'm really not thirsty, grabbed a freebie from the fridge in the doctors' lounge on the way out."

Her legs were longer than Martin remembered. Today more of them showed.

"What happened to your partner? I'm used to dealing with the two of you as a team."

"Brad seems close to giving up on the criminal investigation."

"You're not saying that he doesn't want to solve his fiancée's murder? Or his brother's murder?"

"No, it's not that. I think he's tired and ready to move on. He needs to practice medicine."

"To me, it seems like he's set," the detective said. "Got you as a partner—I mean a medical—surgical partner—and a great big, profitable practice."

Diana shifted in the chair. As she crossed her legs, her back stiffened. "This partner finally earned a day off. I'd be at the mall with my daughter, but she's in school." Diana checked the time on her cell. "I need to pick her up at three."

"I'm curious, Dr. Bratton. How much bling does that big practice churn a month, anyway?"

"Why is that important?"Diana asked.

"It's something I've never asked before."

"Then why are you asking now?"

"No particular reason. I get the feeling that you, and maybe your doctor buddy back at the office, think that I haven't been asking enough questions, so I thought I'd ask a different one ... that one."

"My question is can you tell me, us, a little more about your investigation? I don't think you've shared everything about Stacy Lane."

"Everything about Stacy Lane?" he asked.

"I agree with Brad. The little drive out to Whitfield was a waste. Nothing out there but a broken old man," Diana said. "The grandson's girlfriend, the nurse, was the one who threatened Brad, not Mr. Giles."

The detective pulled a file folder from his desk drawer. "Let's do it like they do it on TV," he said. Martin slid a glossy of a dead Stacy Lane from the folder. He walked to a bulletin board mounted on the wall opposite his desk. "Let's see. Where'd that secretary put those thumbtacks."

"No time to watch TV, Key. Where is this going?"

"You wanted to talk about the deceased Stacy Lane, RN—the one with the cracked skull. So, let's talk about her." Martin pulled

195

a plastic thumb tack from the bulletin board, releasing a yellow message slip to flutter to the floor, barely missing a waste can. He pushed the tack through the top border of Lane's autopsy photo.

"Doesn't look the same, huh? Eyes all swollen shut. Hair tangled, matted."

"I never saw her face before I …"

"Took her out?"

"I heard her threatening Brad. Her back was to me the whole time."

"No doubt she was attractive before you split her head open. Must have been smart, too. They say nursing school isn't all that easy." Martin stepped back to his desk and lifted a coffee cup to his lips. "But I'm sure it was easy for her to hook up with a boyfriend," he said, taking a sip.

"That's why I'm here, Key. I know Lane was devastated over her boyfriend's death. But she was more than just heartbroken."

"Most people kill for a reason, Doctor." This time he took a drag on the coffee. He planted the cup on the desk. "Damn stuff's gone cold."

Diana moved closer to Lane's photograph and ran her fingers across the glossy, bloated face. "I think there's more to this. I just don't think that this girl acted alone."

"You don't, huh?" Martin cleared papers and books stacked on the counter under his office window. A miniature microwave appeared. He popped it open and slid the coffee cup inside. "Damn thing's been on the blink." The machine whirled and groaned.

"Doctor, remember that there has been a police investigation into this case—a lot of tax dollars spent."

"I'm not sure that your department has looked at all the angles."

"We've got security camera footage from the Big Easy. I showed it to you and Dr. Cummins myself." The microwave chimed at 30 seconds.

Diana stepped back to the chair opposite Martin's desk. "Apparently Lane was alone in the rental car when she pulled into the parking lot in New Orleans and when she entered the Ritz," she said.

"You left out the earlier video from the convenience store in McComb, Doctor. She was alone then, too. Remember? Only person she spoke to was the pimple-faced teenager behind the cash register."

"Bet the boy had the hots for the hot nurse," Diana said.

"We talked to that kid," Martin said. "He admitted to hitting on her while counting out the change. Told me he was really pissed off when she turned him down, wouldn't meet him after his shift was over in fifteen. She claimed she had something she had to take care of down in New Orleans."

Despite the bloated face of the autopsy photo and the strands of dark hair left matted across the bruised forehead, Martin could still appreciate the attractive, feminine features.

"I don't argue with that horny kid," Martin said. "No doubt she could have gotten another boyfriend, easily gotten back in the scene after that poor guy from Tennessee died."

"In that hotel room, her voice, her screaming: more than just anger. She was delusional."

"The girl was real mad; that's for sure." He reached again for his cup of coffee, then remembered it was likely still cold. "Delusional? I think she was just acting out a vendetta, but you're the doctor." He reconsidered and took a sip. A grimace followed the swallow. "It's obvious she was a stalker, a really good one," he said.

"Any idea how long Lane had been in Jackson before she followed us to New Orleans?"

"How long?" he asked.

"Yes, how long. You said that there has been an investigation, an ongoing one. So, what was she doing in Jackson besides stalking my partner—my practice partner?"

"We have credit card and cell phone records."

"Then you know more about Lane than you're telling Brad and me."

"Maybe so," he said. "But there's no obligation for me to tell you or Dr. Cummins anything about the investigation." He returned to his desk and dropped into the chair. "That is, unless sharing information would help to solve these cases."

"We won't get anywhere with this, Key, unless Brad and I know what the police know."

Martin pushed a button on the keypad of his desk phone. "Cassie, bring me a cup of coffee, and make sure it's hot." He pushed the button a second time. "And thanks."

"OK, Dr. Bratton." He opened another paper file lying on the desk. "I guess since the patient's dead and might be twisted up in a murder investigation, the HIPAA folks won't come down on me if I fill you in."

"HIPAA?"

"Guess the nurse realized she was nuts, but she still knew how to use a credit card."

Diana checked the time again on her cell. "I promised my daughter I'd pick her up at school since I'm off today." Diana stood to leave. "Detective, are you going to fill me in or not?"

"Just hang on a minute. Sit back down, Dr. Bratton. Please." He referred again to the file.

"There were multiple charges from a psychiatrist's office in her credit card history. We even found bills in Lane's purse," Martin said. "Looks like she had several appointments with the doctor. I guess the credit card got maxed out a couple of times. A late payment fee was tacked onto some of the visits and one no-show."

"Which psychiatrist? Someone in Jackson?"

"Yeah, in Jackson. You asked me what Lane was doing hanging around in Jackson."

"The psychiatrist?" Diana asked. "Name? Maybe I can talk to him."

"The shrink's the same one that Giles shot in the ER," Martin said. "NOPD searched the rental car again and came up with more Xanax." He handed the plastic medication container to Diana.

She rolled it in her palm, then read the label. "Alprazolam, Xanax."

"I showed a few of the pills to Dr. Cummins, but that was before we knew where they came from."

"You gotta give Stacy Lane credit for seeing a psychiatrist." Diana flipped through the medical bills and credit card receipts. "It's obvious that the sessions didn't do much. The girl needed more than medication for anxiety."

"The final statement from Twila Crockett, MD, was unopened, evidently the last date Lane was treated."

"When was that?" Diana asked.

"Three days before she visited you and Dr. Cummins in New Orleans. The doctor's secretary must have been real efficient. Got the bill in the mail the same day. Check the postmark."

32

Twila Crockett's psychiatry office was on the second level of Hilltop Village. It was the smallest of several suites that overlooked the rear parking lot.

"Thank you for sparing a few minutes, Dr. Crockett." Diana took the chair across from the psychiatrist's desk as the receptionist shut the door behind her.

"Dr. Bratton, if you're looking for some surgery referrals, I'm afraid I can't be of much help. The only patients with abdominal pain that I see are the hypochondriacs, the narcotic withdrawals, and an occasional Munchausen syndrome." She swiveled in her chair to the miniature refrigerator behind her desk and winced as she leaned down for a diet Coke. "And, call me Twila. I'm not much older than you are." She opened the can and adjusted the strap of her arm sling.

"Thank you, but I'm not here looking for someone to operate on. I'm here to get some information. And I'll pass on the Coke." Diana surveyed the room. There was no couch.

"Information?" Twila asked.

"You've met my partner, practice partner, Brad Cummins."

Twila pushed a short stack of files to the side and set the soda can on a coaster. "Brad and I renewed our bond that night in the ER." She pointed to her injury. "First time I've been shot by a patient."

"A lot has happened since the two of you graduated. A young woman recently tried to shoot Brad."

"That can't be true. Wasn't his brother killed recently?"

"His fiancée, too," Diana said.

"I thought I had heard that." Twila stood from her desk and walked to the window overlooking the parking lot. It was as empty as the day before.

"Why are you here, Diana?"

"The girl who tried to kill Brad was one of your patients."

"And how would you know that?"

"The police know it. The detective in charge of the case told

199

me. She paid your bills with her credit card."

"I don't think I should talk to you about one of my patients if you're not involved in her care."

"Ex-patient now, Twila. The girl is dead."

The psychiatrist returned to her desk. She raised the can of Diet Coke. Her fingers quivered and she spilled on her suit. "Shit!" She tried to dab away the spots with a Kleenex.

"I was there. The girl was out-of-control, psychotic," Diana said. "Toxicology reports were negative. She wasn't even drunk or high."

"You're not saying much for my medical management skills." She made one last pass with the tissue and tossed it into the waste can.

"No worry. I'm sure you're at the height of your field." Diana remembered the sparsely filled rack of chart files framing the receptionist in the front office. "I'm not sure why JPD hasn't subpoenaed her medical file."

"It's not uncommon for psychiatrists to testify at trials, to be interviewed by the police. Why didn't your detective himself come talk to me?" She looked to her drink, shook the can, but decided against another sip.

"I think Detective Martin assumed I might be able to find out more," Diana said.

"Then what is it you want to know?"

"If Stacy Lane was making legitimate threats, like planning to murder someone, then physician-patient confidentiality flew out the window."

"I know HIPAA as well as anyone," the psychiatrist said. "We see very little true psychosis in the urban office setting." Twila shuffled a few of the paper files along the surface of her desk.

"And you didn't think she needed to be committed?"

"I told you. I see very few psychotics in the out-patient setting, particularly in an upscale place like this. The ER? That was another story."

"Stacy Lane certainly seemed out of touch that day in New Orleans," Diana said, "screaming, rambling, waving a gun around the …"

Twila said, "I can tell you one thing: that poor, poor girl was obsessed with her lost love."

200

"Yes, the boyfriend. It seems it was all about the boyfriend."

The secretary tapped on the door, then opened it. "Dr. Crockett, your two-thirty is here." Diana glanced into the empty front office as the secretary closed the door and returned to her post.

"Diana, you see that I am busy. Just what in the fuck do you want from me?"

"We need to know if Stacy Lane was acting alone. If there is still someone out there bent on killing."

"Bent on killing whom?"

"Brad. Brad Cummins."

Twila Crockett stood. "This entire conversation is an insult. If Stacy Lane had shared any real intent to kill anyone or serve as an accomplice in any crime I would have been duty-bound to report the threat." She walked to the door and winched as she first opened it with the injured arm. "What kind of person do you think I am?"

"Brad just needs some answers. We thought you might be able to provide some closure."

"On second thought, I'd rather you address me as Dr. Crockett, Dr. Bratton," Twila said. "See you around the hospital."

Diana nodded thanks to the receptionist and left the office suite.

The psychiatrist stared into the empty waiting room as the exit door snapped shut.

"What kind of person do you think I am?" she repeated.

33

"Dr. Cummins says your wife's surgery is going great. He's removed that piece of colon and is putting everything back together. Shouldn't be much longer, he says."

The nurse, Christine, hung up the phone.

Brad kept his eyes pressed into the surgical console. He had said little during the robotic case. His sock-covered feet worked the foot controls while two fingers of each hand controlled the surgical instruments inside his patient. Diana sat on an elevated stool a few feet away, directly beside the anesthetized patient. She studied the video monitor while using a separate hand-held laparoscopic instrument to assist Brad with tissue retraction.

"Thanks for repositioning that monitor, Christine," Diana said. "Now my eyes won't get so tired."

After the colon resection was completed, Brad visited with the patient's family in the post-op unit and rounded on a couple of patients on the fourth floor. He found Diana in the surgical scrub area located between the operating suites. She was prepping for her upcoming case. Brad was to assist her.

"You haven't asked me about my visits with the detective and with Twila Crockett," she said.

"Seems like on a day off you could have found something more fun to do—something more productive."

"What's more productive than finding out what's behind all this? Or who's behind all this? The police are dragging their butts."

"What I meant was that for once you should do something for yourself: like play tennis, go shopping for you or Kelsey, work out, or just take a nap."

"You're not serious, are you?"

"Hell yeah, I'm serious. You took out the killer. You and that commode top. As far as I'm concerned, the case has been solved," Brad said.

"I think you're wrong," Diana said. She scrubbed her arms with greater force.

"I think Martin was just giving you lip service," he said. "He would have already questioned Twila if there was reason."

Diana's brush strokes grew brisker, more directed, her forearms glowing under the lather.

"They've got their man, or woman I should say," Brad said. "Passion and revenge shoved that girl over the edge. It's just that my poor brother got in the way." He tossed the used scrub brush into the trash and pushed through the swinging doors into the operating room. Diana propelled her brush into the sink and pressed ahead of him.

"Here you go, Dr. Bratton. It's your case; you go first." The waiting OR technician assisted Diana with a sterile surgical gown and gloves as Brad stood to the side.

"My wet hands are getting a chill," he said.

"You'll survive, Dr. Cummins," Lee Ann, the tech said.

"Maybe not," Diana said.

*   *   *

Elizabeth Cossar's unannounced visit to her brother satisfied the hasty invitation issued during their tour in Iraq: "When you get back home, just give me a call when you're coming through town," John had offered between patients. "I'll have some people out to the house. Maybe fix you up with one of the widowers in Jackson. It's never too late to catch a doctor, Sis. Maybe you can do better than that bastard lawyer you divorced."

The match-up never came, neither did the party.

When she arrived at the John Haynes mansion, she had followed the housekeeper's instruction and rolled her suitcase the 200 yards or so down the grand hall to the guest room in the north wing. Her brother showed up just in time to help her into the room. Now it was time to leave, but not before one last stroll through the manor. She left the suitcase packed and propped against the walnut armoire. Its next home would be the trunk of her rental car for the trip back to Atlanta.

Cossar walked toward the grand foyer that divided the Madison County mansion into north and south wings. She passed the collection of oil paintings interspersed among a parade of Greek figures that lined the walls, each piece of art worth more than the annual salary of a registered nurse. The display climaxed with the headless Roman nude guarding the entrance to John's master suite, which was separated from her room by two smaller bedrooms and a media center. Their bedrooms had been adjacent in their parents' home, where they shared a bathroom.

Nearer the foyer, the smiling antique Blackamoor French figure greeted her, still holding the service tray high above his head. It no longer held her brother's empty from last evening's nightcap. The housekeeper had already made her rounds.

She continued through the foyer to the south wing and a walkway plain by the Haynes standard: only a few paintings and a colorless statue or two. A single, large bedroom ended the hall, the door ajar. Cossar ambled inside.

Bright light streaming through the opened curtains struck her face as she crossed the deep Stark carpet. The air was fresh. Cossar doubted that her brother's housekeeper was that diligent. She pulled open the doors of the closet. A pair of silk pants and several blouses hung carelessly above black patent sandals tossed at the bottom. There was no suitcase. She tried the nearest blouse against her chest and turned to search for a mirror. A pink-colored slip of paper floated to the floor. Cossar picked it up and crumpled the paper in her palm.

"What were you doing in here?" John said from the hallway.

"What are you doing home?" she answered.

He slurped the remainder of his coffee and entered the room. "I could use a refill." He walked into the dressing area, installed an unused brew packet into the personal coffee maker, and flicked the switch. The machine sputtered on. The smell emanated throughout the room.

Haynes filled his cup. "Going in a little late today."

"Don't bother, Brother. I don't care for any," Cossar said. "Looks like I took a wrong turn at the emperor's statue."

"Your end of the house is a lot nicer than this, Sis. You're lucky the housekeeper put you over there."

"Whose blouse is this?" she asked.

Haynes stirred in a packet of sweetener. He took a loud sip and swallowed. "You're a grown woman, Liz. I'm a grown man."

"No argument from me, John. You've always had girlfriends, so why stop now? But these clothes are more like what a daughter would wear."

"I sent that slut packing," John said.

"She must have taken you at your word, and left in a hurry. I'm surprised your housekeeper didn't box these things up."

"No reason to. I knew the little tramp wouldn't come back for that crap. And I haven't called her either."

"I would try on her things, but they really are a little young for me," Cossar said.

"Yeah, *a little young.* I'm sure that's the problem," John said, another slurp of coffee.

"You know, you really are an a-hole," she said.

"Like you said, Sis, nothing new. Nothing new." Haynes finished the cup and left. His voice boomed back into the room from the hallway. "I thought you were driving back to Atlanta today."

The thunder startled Cossar, and she dropped the blouse -- the same reaction felt when they were kids. However, at night when he walked through their shared bathroom into her bedroom, his tone was much softer.

"Can't believe you haven't heard from this sweet thing, Bro." Cossar replaced the blouse on a hanger and lifted the pink and white top beside it. She stood in front of the mirror over the dresser. Haynes stepped back into the room.

"Still no way that stuff's gonna fit you, Sis."

"You're still such a character builder, John." Cossar threw the silk piece against her brother's chest. The garment slid to the floor.

"*Character builder?* I build character every day in the OR."

"Chew 'em up and spit 'em out. Isn't that old school medicine?" Cossar retrieved the silk top. She ran her hands over the material to smooth it.

"Who are you to talk, *Florence Nightingale?* I saw the way you bossed around those lower level nurses in Balad."

"Somebody has to take charge, even if we're just nurses, *Doctor* Haynes. And can't you think of a more contemporary comparison than Florence Nightingale? Heck, I'd take *Julia.*"

"Chip on your shoulder, Sis?"

"You're right. That's the whole issue here." Cossar pushed past her brother into the hall. "I need to get on the road. Thanks for the hospitality, John."

"Hold on a minute." Haynes followed Cossar back to her guest room. "Remember, I tried to push you into applying for med school, even after you got your RN. You would have blown away the MCAT."

"I needed to keep working. I couldn't go back to school—too many bills." Cossar pivoted in the doorway, losing her grip on the pull of the roller suitcase behind her. The handle slammed to the floor, followed by the suitcase. Cossar hesitated before bending to retrieve the suitcase pull.

Her brother did not budge to help.

"If there had been someone to pay the baby's medical bills and the funeral home, then maybe I could have considered medical school."

"I always said you wasted yourself on that trash you married. Why the hell you kept his name, I'll never know."

"You never give up; do you? Like I said, John, thanks for the hospitality."

Cossar bounced her suitcase over the Orientals that lined the grand foyer, the rollers catching the edge of each of the carpets as they popped off the wide, century-old planks of hardwood.

Her brother followed slowly, and then disappeared into his room.

*   *   *

The housekeeper met her at the front door. "Miz Cossar, you leavin' so soon?"

Cossar grasped the doorknob. The pink laundry tag fell from her hand to the floor.

"Don't worry about that, ma'am. I'll get it."

"That was in the guest room on the other side of the house. Let me see that again."

"It's just trash. I guess that young girl left it." The housekeeper dropped the laundry tag into her apron pocket.

"It was on one of the blouses I found hanging in the closet. I didn't know that anyone else was staying here."

"I left those things, in case the girl came back," the housekeeper said. "Dr. Haynes is a grown man. I don't mess in his business."

"Give me that piece of paper," Cossar said.

"Yes, ma'am." The housekeeper complied and turned away.

Cossar unfolded the crumpled piece. She righted the blurred print and read *Lane, S.* "Lane, S," she repeated.

"Ma'am, you've been visiting here long enough to know it's *Linda*, not *Lane*.

"Of course. Excuse me, Linda, but can you wait just a minute?"

"Yes, but Dr. Haynes wants me to run out and pickup some sushi. People are coming over."

"Tonight? What a coincidence." She remembered seeing fresh strawberries, kiwi, and seedless purple grapes piled in the bin at the bottom of the refrigerator. Several wheels of brie were stacked in the back behind the bottled beer. The beer was chilled by now.

Her brother, the doctor, the surgeon, the rich surgeon, had always liked cheese, the indulgence belied by his physique, a look he somehow preserved as they had both aged. He liked scotch and Jack, too. Same game.

"Don't worry," Cossar said. "I won't ruin my brother's party. Just need to ask you a couple of questions." She moved closer. "What did this young lady look like?"

"Look like? Pretty. But they're all pretty."

"I'm sure they are." Cossar stared again at the piece of paper and stepped even closer to the housekeeper. "Short hair? Dark hair?" She peered into the woman. "Blond, maybe?"

"Got to go. Dr. John needs his sushi."

The housekeeper slipped away toward the kitchen.

"Wait, you need to describe that girl for me. The rear wheel of Cossar's suitcase again caught on the edge of an Oriental rug as she tracked the housekeeper.

"OK, OK. Let me think." Linda ran her hands up and down her cheeks. "No, not light hair," she answered. "Brunette." The housekeeper stopped by an antique mahogany cabinet and withdrew an ornate silver tray. Her arms sank under the weight as she turned into the arched hall that led into the kitchen.

"And I heard that girl say something about being a nurse," Linda said and then disappeared.

* * *

Cossar tossed her suitcase into the trunk and drove down Highway 463 to the upscale shopping development near Interstate 55 in Madison. She remembered the restaurant offering free wireless Internet and parked near the entrance to Beagle Bagel. There was an empty booth toward the rear of the café. A busboy who looked about sixteen was clearing an adjacent table.

"Can I get you anything?" the busboy asked, holding a plastic tub filled with small plates, coffee cups, and scraps of flavored bagels and condiments.

Cossar flipped open her laptop and waited for it to power up. She grabbed a menu card from the display against the wall. "I'll take the chicken salad." She tossed the menu back toward the wall. Her laptop monitor was coming to life.

"Wheat or sourdough?" he asked.

"Whatever's easiest. Make it wheat."

"Coffee with that? A Coke?" He reached across her table to tidy the napkin dispenser and return the menu to its display rack. "Or how 'bout a sweet tea?"

"You pick," Cossar answered. She entered her password and launched the search engine, then typed in the web address that accessed the Balad Hospital personnel records. A few clicks and she pulled up the nursing division. "S. Lane. Stacy Lane," she said. The headshot of a young, attractive brunette popped into the upper right-hand corner. She enlarged the photo.

"No way to forget her," Cossar said. She studied Stacy Lane's fair, wrinkle-free complexion and the hint of large breasts at the lower edge of the photo. "My brother, he was screwing one of my people over there."

"Uhh, excuse me, ma'am. I've got your sandwich." the busboy said. "Didn't mean to interrupt, but the kitchen's turnin' stuff out pretty fast this afternoon."

"Just leave it right there," she said, gesturing to the side of her laptop.

He placed the sandwich as directed while Cossar scanned Lane's personnel file. "Here's your silverware. Enjoy!" he said.

"Good grades in nursing school," she said. "Looks like she had some promise."

"Ma'am? Did you say something? Need something else?"

"Some privacy. Maybe?" she answered, eyes not leaving the laptop. "Go check on that couple over by the cupcakes."

Cossar waved him away.

"Sure that you don't need anything else?" the teenager asked.

"I want that couple to eat some cupcakes."

This time Cossar pointed across the restaurant toward the confections. "Take a hike, kid."

34

"You made it to Birmingham yet?" Haynes said. He answered his cell after several rings.

"No, stopped for a sandwich before I left town," Cossar said. "I'm not half-way to Meridian."

"Linda would've fixed you a bite," he said. "Should've told her you were hungry."

"She was too busy with your stuff to worry over me. But I'm not calling to comment on your lack of hospitality."

"Whatever." He spoke over the loud voices in the background. "I'm getting ready to scrub into a case, so what do you want?"

"Were you nailing one of my nurses back in Iraq?" Cossar said. "A young one?

"Too many to keep up with. Young ones, old ones."

She heard the water splashing in the surgical scrub sink.

"You were screwing the girl that tried to shoot Brad Cummins."

"I was?"

"For God's sake, John. It was in the paper, all over the news. Her name was Stacy Lane. The girl that tried to shoot Brad Cummins in New Orleans was staying in your guestroom! More likely, hanging some clothes in the guestroom and sleeping in your bed without them."

"So?" Haynes asked.

Christine, put my phone on the equipment cart over there Cossar heard him say.

"The girl needed a place to stay during her furlough, and I was happy to oblige," Haynes said. "See ya, Sis."

"Bet you were. And I bet you *obliged* her all over your damn house!" Cossar yelled into her cell before someone in the OR punched *End Call*.

Cossar tossed her phone onto the passenger seat.

"Talk was that she had hooked up with some young recruit, not you!"

Her brother's keeping secrets was no surprise, and growing up the two never exchanged any emotional love between them.

209

Although she and John worked side by side during his residency in Atlanta and later in Iraq, they did not discuss their relationship with peers. Her placement at the military base in Balad was a long-term assignment; her brother's concurrent service there, a coincidence, and one she regretted.

Cossar's hopes to change things were dashed. Not only did the visit to her brother's home fail to kindle a healthy sibling bond, but she now understood John Haynes even less than before. She decided to come clean with Brad and reached for her cell. *No, face-to-face is better.* She took the next exit off Interstate 20. She gambled that Brad would be working late.

An hour later Cossar was on Lakeland Drive in the direction of the Cummins building. A couple of cars remained in the parking lot. A young man and woman were leaving as she approached the front door. Cossar overheard the man say something about his bill. There were two patients in the waiting room.

Brad stuck his head through a door behind the reception desk and said something to the receptionist. He spotted Cossar and smiled. He motioned for her to come through the opening to the hall that led to patient exam area.

"Shouldn't you be more careful about working after hours alone in this place?" she asked. "Maybe even lock the main entrance after five?"

"Why would I do that, Elizabeth? I've got Jessica out there at the desk." Brad hugged her. "The police don't agree, but seems to me that all the folks intent on taking me out of the picture are out of the picture themselves—all revenge thwarted." He felt a vibration against his right hip and checked his cell phone. There was a text message asking for a call-back to the surgical ICU.

"Need to get that?" Cossar asked.

"I know what they want. I'll tell 'em to go ahead with the antibiotic order." He began to type a response.

"Did you know that John Haynes and I are related?"

Brad stopped in the middle of his text. He stared at Cossar. "You're kidding. How close?"

"Brother and sister."

"Shit. Brother and Sister? How was it growing up in the same house with that asshole?"

Her laugh did not surprise him.

"Sorry," he said.

"Sorry for insulting my younger brother and lone sibling or sorry that I grew-up in the same house with the asshole?" They both laughed. "I didn't see him much after I married and then even less often after Momma and Dad died. There are no military regs against relatives working together on the same base, so I didn't question his assignment to Balad."

"He treated you like shit over there, just like the other nurses: no better, no worse," Brad said. "John's definitely not one of my favorites, but I've learned to tolerate the guy."

"I believe there was one nurse in my Balad unit that he treated very well, or maybe I should say that she treated him."

"Don't take this personal, but there wasn't much temptation over there except that nut case Stacy Lane, and I didn't know her."

Cossar reached up and back-handed Brad softly on the shoulder. "You're so right. I was too busy serving my country." They both laughed a second time, and she repeated the back-hand with enough force to sound.

She followed Brad to his private office as he rubbed his shoulder. "What about those two patients in the waiting room?" she asked.

"They were waiting on a ride home. Jessica will lock up." He lifted his white lab coat from the hook behind the door and felt for his keys in the lower right hand pocket. He jiggled them among the index cards, post-it notes, and tube of Chap Stik.

Stacy Lane: that's who my brother was screwing over there she wanted to say but suddenly couldn't. *I know he was nailing the thing because he brought her home with him.*

Brad pivoted back into the hall from his office doorway, his lab coat draped across the shoulder. He slid it around to his back and put his arms up the sleeves, then pulled his car keys from the pocket. "You must be parked out front?"

"Yes."

"I'll drive you around to your car."

Cossar followed him to the physician elevator.

He pushed the *Down* button on the control panel, but backed away. "On second thought, let's take the stairs."

Brad stopped before opening the door to the stairwell. "Cossar, you came over here just to confess that John Haynes is your

211

brother? There are worse crimes."

"I just wanted to say good-bye," she said. "I'm leaving for Atlanta tomorrow."

"When I saw you out in the waiting room, I hoped that you were here to make an offer on my apartment."

"No way. It's a motel for me tonight, Major, and a six-and-a-half-hour drive home tomorrow to a dumpy house."

"With my luck, my old place will wait for you to change your mind, Elizabeth."

They got into his SUV and drove up the incline to the outdoor parking area. Brad headed toward the only vehicle left in the lot.

An uncomfortable need to protect her brother enveloped Elizabeth Cossar, but Brad deserved to know everything. Her brother had watched TV and read the newspaper. *Why had he been so secretive about his relationship with Lane?*

"There was another reason I came to talk you," she said.

Brad asked, "What's that?"

"Why do you think Stacy Lane went so berserk over Chad Giles' death? Post-traumatic stress?" Instead, she had planned to say: *"John was having an affair with Stacy Lane in Iraq and has been living with her in the States."*

"Wow, that takes PTSD to the extreme, but I guess we'll never know," Brad said.

"I think you need to find out," she said.

35

"So, I shouldn't have hammered the girl with the toilet seat."

"No, I didn't say that." Brad poured a second glass of chardonnay for Diana as he fell into the couch beside her. His arm fit nicely around her as she moved closer. "The time you've spent in the gym saved me once again. But if you're so aggressive, why can't you take yourself beyond chardonnay to *pinot grigio*?" he asked.

She held the glass of wine into the light. "I pick my battles." She took a sip and another. "Detective Martin is digging into Stacy Lane's background, like where she was living while she was in Jackson. So far there's no clue, no hotel receipts in her things, nothing."

Brad tasted more than a sip of her Kendall Jackson as she kissed him. His change to Jack Daniels was no match. "Why don't you send Mr. Cop an email next time he has questions or wants to discuss the case?" he said. "I don't think I want you to spend any more time with that guy."

"Actually, Boss, I don't have another day off. No more trips downtown for me."

"Boss? Who's the boss?" Brad pulled her over onto him. Diana bent her long legs to clear the coffee table as she straddled him. As though on cue, Bullet sprang from his spot on the upholstered chair catty-corner to the sofa and bounded away for the guest room comforter.

"Didn't you have a bunch of security cameras put in this place?" she asked as he unbuckled and slid up her skirt. "And wasn't there something about a digital recording of everything that goes on in your apartment?" She pulled open his jeans.

"We're just two adults, alone in a private residence." Brad's kiss went beyond the taste of the wine, the liquor.

"How much longer can the practice afford these surgeons you keep bringing in to fill in for us?" Diana braced her arms with the back of the sofa. The only sound was the movement of the cushions beneath them until she climaxed. Her foot knocked over the near empty bottle of wine.

"Let it spill," Brad managed.

Diana pulled off him and ran to the kitchen for paper towels to mop up the wine. "Those locums have gone up to almost $200 an hour!"

"It's nothing that my brother's insurance policy can't handle." Brad said, redressing. He took his glass and toasted the dim beam falling on them from the recessed lighting fixture. "Brian was such a planner." Brad downed the last of his cocktail. "A really great brother." He kissed Diana after she took care of the spill and returned to the couch. He again savored the taste of her wine mixed with his whiskey.

"Do you miss him, Brad?" she asked.

"Why do women ask so many questions?" Brad reached for his glass and swirled the ice. "I need a refill."

She studied the rear movement in his jeans, the subtle creases in the dark blue fabric that appeared and disappeared as he left for the kitchen bar. "Do I?" she asked. "Do I really ask too many questions?" She finished her second glass of wine and stared at the empty, twirling it in her fingertips. "Gee, I'm a real girl."

"No doubt about that." Brad paired another chilled bottle of wine with a new bottle of Jack Daniels. Both stood against a heavy piece of McCarty pottery that centered the piece of furniture, a gift from a grateful patient from Merigold, Mississippi. Having stuffed it with fresh flowers, the lady presented the piece last week, happy to be absent an inflamed appendix.

"Aren't you going to pour me another glass?" Diana asked.

"In a few minutes, I will." Brad leaned into the sofa and kissed her, nearly covering her with his body.

"Wait, wait, wait..." Diana slid out from under him. She straightened her blouse and skirt again. "We need to talk about my visit with Twila Crockett."

"OK, Diana, you really are a girl," followed a deep breath. Brad over-filled the glass, splashing a few drops of chardonnay on the still wet carpet, then reached for his bottle. He filled his own glass with the whiskey, thought about walking to the kitchen for the ice he had forgotten, but decided against it. He sank into the couch.

"Dr. Crocket practically tossed me out of her office, or she would have if she hadn't taken that bullet."

"Dead end? Not surprised," Brad said.

Diana set down her chardonnay. This time a few drops splashed on the surface of the coffee table. She was beginning to feel light-headed. "Martin could always have Stacy Lane's psychiatry records subpoenaed."

"Why would he do that? What more do we need to know about her?" he asked.

"Don't you want you to know more about this girl, Brad? She was dating the guy whose death almost cost your Air Force commission—and then she tried to kill you."

Brad finished his drink and stared at the bottle. He rocked the empty glass in his right hand. "Look, Diana. I need to put this behind me. Put this behind us." He stared into the bottom of his glass and felt his head swim. "Think we better order take out from Bravo—one of their pizzas and add chicken. They'll deliver if I tip hard." He rested his head on Diana's shoulder. She got a whiff of deep, alcohol-ridden breath.

"Better add double-chicken to that," she said, reaching for her purse and cell phone. "And maybe add dessert—brownie with ice cream."

"Sounds good. Do it." Brad's upper body fell into her lap. His empty glass fell to the carpet. Diana kicked it under the coffee table as she brushed the thick black hair from his forehead and leaned down to kiss him. She ran her hand down his chest and abdomen and stopped at the belt. He was out.

Diana scrolled through her contacts, hit *Bravo* and ordered the pizza. An extra charge would arrange delivery. She would brew coffee, and Brad would revive just in time to pay when the hot food arrived, forty-five minutes max. She felt the bulge of his wallet in the back pocket of his Polo jeans. The delivery boy would plop the box of pizza on the coffee table. More wine, more whiskey. The locum was in charge of the practice for the night.

Diana slid from under him, watching Brad as she walked toward his study, his body firm, still. She came back for her glass just as he rolled his head and right shoulder deeper into the back of the sofa.

"Brad, you are a great looking guy, a terrific surgeon, but so naïve," Diana whispered. "And you need to stop drinking so much."

His only response was a deep, long breath, too far away for her

215

to smell the alcohol.

She looked into her own drink, swirled the liquid for a few seconds, then decided she would not finish it. She crossed under the glass transom above the doorway to the study. The base of her wine glass fit snuggly on Brad's desk in a coaster branded with the emblem of a pharmaceutical company. The surface of the new desk was no more than a sheet of polished granite supported by simple cylindrical steel legs, the only other feature a narrow drawer mounted under the center. Diana sat in Brad's leather chair and opened the drawer. Inside was a tangled pile of paper clips and ink pens inscribed with names of other pharmaceutical companies.

There was no noise from the living room. Diana studied the contemporary oil painting of trees growing somewhere in the Mississippi Delta that hung on the wall opposite the desk. Brad's medical school diploma and framed board certification were instead displayed in his clinic office, along with more oil paintings. She considered her own plain office space in the Cummins surgical clinic. Brother Brian had not specified the same expensive wall coverings for the new associates' offices. While university and medical school diplomas and training certificates were hung on her own non-descript walls, the only artwork was Kelsey's cheaply-framed pre-school finger-painting and a professional school photo.

Against the far wall of the study was a shallow bookcase with a darkly striated, faux wood-grain finish. The space was filled with leather volumes, mostly antique books purchased for the bindings, the rows interspersed by small mahogany and quill boxes. She stepped to the bookcase and ran her fingers across the top of a section—no dust, not in place long enough to gather any. This display and all of the surrounding furnishings were masculine and expensive-looking, a sharp contrast to what she had at home and in her own office. She had never seen Brad's old apartment and wondered how much of a hand, if any, Leslie Coachys had played in selecting that décor—and if it had been recreated here.

Diana checked the opening into the living area: still quiet. She worked her way to the end of the bookcase to a recessed stack of drawers, some larger than others. The bottom drawer was empty, the same for the next one up. Inside the drawer just above waist level was a hanging section divider labeled *Balad* in Brad's neat printing. It contained several files, the thickest hung near the back:

216

Mortality Review Tribunal.

"This is what I'm looking for," Diana whispered, withdrawing the file folder while looking over her shoulder—still nothing from the living area. Reaching for light from the sleek, painted desk lamp, she removed the papers from the folder and spread them across Brad's desk. The initial page was a letter from the tribunal chief officially clearing Major Brad Cummins of any wrongdoing in the medical treatment of Lance Corporal Chad Giles. Brad's personal notes followed. Annotations in Brad's block print were in the margins of the testimonies of John Haynes and Elizabeth Cossar: not one question mark, no exclamation points. She read through Brad's notes—no elements of surprise, no shock. He agreed with every detail, every recount.

"You may be an aggressive doctor and surgeon, boyfriend, but you are such a pushover."

"Did you say something?" Brad stood leaning against the door jam.

"Good God, Brad!" Diana slammed the folder shut.

"Diana, I don't have any secrets. If you need to know something, ask."

"I have, Brad. I have asked questions." She sat on the edge of the desk. "It's just that you never give any answers, and someone else is going to get hurt."

Brad exchanged his empty glass for what was left of Diana's wine and collapsed into the desk chair.

She looked away. "Am I the next one, Brad?"

"The next *what*? The next fiancée?"

Diana shoved the closed file at Brad and pushed away from the desk.

"What nurses say about male physicians is true," she said to Brad's amusement.

"If anybody is the example of the anti-stereotype, it's you, Diana." He reached for her and missed, then spun the chair 360 around on the hardwood floor. "I've never known any professional with more self-confidence, male or female."

"We need to talk about this tribunal investigation, Brad." Diana pressed her left hand firmly against the thick stack of documents. "I needed to study it again. There's got to be something here."

Brad watched her move into the living room. "Bring me another

217

whiskey, Dr. Bratton." He took another spin in the desk chair. "Especially since there's no nurse around to get it for me."

"Bigot." Diana frowned. "And, no, I won't. You've already had too much." The front door buzzer sounded.

Brad called from the study. "Diana, was that the door?" He flipped open the file and then let it drop closed. "Did I tell you that Jeremiah got hired last week to fill the doorman job over here?"

Diana walked toward the door. The buzzer sounded with more urgency.

"Must be the pizza," Brad said, joining Diana under the transom between the study and the living room as he rubbed the back of his neck. "The doorman is supposed to call up first. But Jeremiah might not know the ropes yet."

Brad held the empty cocktail glass carelessly at his waist, his wrinkled shirttail extending past. He wobbled, bumping against the wall of the passageway, but still managed to juggle the glass in one hand. "What about pouring that drink you promised?" He raised the glass. "Kinda thirsty." He returned to the desk chair and swiveled.

"Like I said, you've had enough," Diana said. "I need you to assist me tomorrow with a BKA. And the guy tops 350 pounds."

Still frowning over her shoulder at Brad, Diana opened the apartment door to the aroma of mozzarella cheese, tomatoes, basil and grilled chicken.

"Detective Martin?"

"On my way up, I stopped the delivery boy in the lobby. You can pay me back later—and include the tip."

He handed the pizza to Diana.

Brad met them in the foyer. "Isn't it enough you hound us at work?" he asked, then leaned against a wall.

"Don't blame your doorman. Poor guy wasn't too happy to see me again. Besides, a police badge is the universal ticket in," Martin said. "By the way, Dr. Cummins, JPD is behind budget on DUIs, so don't tempt us tonight."

He took a seat in the living room and Brad followed.

Diana returned from the kitchen with three plates, napkins, and the pizza box, along with a Diet Coke for Brad and the detective. "Why are you here, Martin?"

"I talked to the ICU nurse who took care of Amarah the day he

218

died. The guy explained that Dr. John Haynes was the attending physician."

"Yes, he was," Diana said. "Haynes and I ran the CODE."

"Amarah's nurse said that Amarah tried to talk to Haynes right before he died. Nurse thinks he heard something about 'some unfinished business.' " Martin helped himself to the first piece.

Diana offered him a plate and napkin. "The guy had just woken up. Maybe he just wanted to know about his condition."

"Don't think so," Martin said. "The nurse said Haynes seemed rushed, not interested in what the Iraqi had to say."

"Not surprised," Brad said. "Haynes is not much on bedside manner." He started his second slice.

"Have you talked to Dr. Haynes about this?"

"No, I did something better, Dr. Bratton. I showed his housekeeper Amarah's visa photo. She remembered seeing him at the house."

"Haynes' house? Why?" Brad asked. He had finished the canned drink.

"The housekeeper spotted Amarah around the back of the property. She was about to report a prowler when Haynes' houseguest invited him up onto the porch."

"Who was the guest?" Diana and Brad asked almost in unison.

Then Brad said, "Must have been his sister. I just found out she's been in town."

"Don't think so," Martin answered. "The housekeeper said a young woman had been staying on that end of the house, but she didn't know her name. The girl kept out of the way, but the description matches that nurse who came after you—Stacy Lane."

"That psycho was staying with Haynes?" they both said.

"Like I've said before," Martin said, "I really need some help in figuring this thing out. JPD's already blown its budget on the Cummins saga."

"You think the Iraqi set up Stacy Lane to kill Brad, don't you, Martin?" Diana asked. "Maybe as back-up?

The detective's cell phone rang, and he walked back into the foyer to take the call.

"Looks that way to me, too," Brad said. He started a third slice.

Martin returned. "That was Haynes' housekeeper. I gave her my cell in case she came up with something else.

219

"And?"

"She said that Haynes just fired her because she talked to me. Not sure why she told him, but he was gonna find out from me sooner or later."

36

The following morning Diana struggled through a few post-op patients in clinic but took the afternoon off, leaving Brad solo in the office. She wanted to take another look at the tribunal documents. The file was just as she and Brad had left it in the study, still open with the medical tribunal's conclusion staring at her. The wording was crisp, the tribunal's summation exonerating Brad absent of lengthy medical jargon.

She flipped back to the testimony of Lieutenant Colonel Elizabeth Taylor Cossar, identified as the head charge nurse in the acute care and ICU area. Diana read the report, the nurse's words emotionless but clearly supportive of Brad's actions. Brad's own interview mirrored what he had shared with her about the pre- and post-operative care of Lance Corporal Giles.

Colonel John Haynes was next. Without hesitation, he followed Major Cummins' lead during the emergency surgery. He described Brad's fluid surgical movements: a systematic exploration of the internal organs, quick identification of the bleeding vessels, and expert removal of Giles' lacerated spleen. Massive bleeding was encountered, but constricting blood vessels and an expert splenectomy halted the blood loss. They had conversed little during the case. In Haynes' opinion, Major Brad Cummins ordered appropriate blood replacement and systematically managed the care of Giles to the highest standard.

Diana envisioned Brad sitting stiffly, glaring at Haynes in the witness chair as the lead investigator pushed deeper:

Lead investigator: Colonel Haynes, the surgery was a success, but as they say 'the patient died.' If Major Cummins is such a flawless surgeon as you say, then why did the patient die?

Colonel John Haynes, MD: Lieutenant Cossar paged both of us to post-op when there was a concern over Giles' condition. He had become unstable.

Second Investigator: And you arrived first?

Haynes: Yes, I did. I must have been in closer proximity.

Second Investigator: Were there others in the recovery area.

Other patients?

Haynes: No, Giles was the only one.

Lead investigator: Medical staff?

Haynes: Yes. Cossar, Lieutenant Colonel Cossar, along with another nurse, a younger nurse.

Second Investigator: Another nurse? Lieutenant Colonel Cossar testified that she positioned the crash cart at the bedside immediately after calling the CODE. She didn't mention getting help from anyone.

Haynes: I didn't recognize the other nurse. She stayed clear, looked to be stocking supplies or making a delivery of some sort to the recovery area when I arrived. She did not assist in the resuscitation efforts.

Lead Investigator: Someone check the personnel file for that serviceperson. Let us know when you have the name. Continue, Colonel Haynes.

Haynes: Major Cummins arrived to the unit, and I believe the younger nurse then left the area.

Lead Investigator: Let's see.

Diana imagined eyeglasses tightened for a closer look at the notes, followed by a wrinkled brow, then a raised head.

Lead Investigator: Colonel Haynes, Major Cummins testified that he left Lance Corporal Giles in stable condition in the post-op unit to check the status of the other casualties brought in that day. Is that what you recall, Colonel Haynes?"

Haynes: I understand there was a local brought in with Giles and the others injured in his unit. The local was a young Iraqi male.

Lead Investigator: Let me flip through these pages. Yes, I see that here, a Mr. Zarife Amarah. Please continue, Colonel Haynes.

Haynes: Cummins was just following protocol. Maybe he went out to check on that guy.

Second Investigator: 'That guy'?

Haynes: The Iraqi. I don't have any problem with what Cummins did, checking on that Iraqi after treating him. If I had been the primary on duty, I would have gone out to make rounds, too.

"Imagine that. A cooperative John Haynes," Diana said, closing the file. "Complete with compliments."

37

Diana reached above the stainless steel sink and slid a surgical scrub brush from the dispenser above the shelf. She ripped away the plastic covering and tossed it into the trash on the other side of the corridor.

"Nice aim, Dr. Bratton," a passing scrub tech said. "Nice, very nice."

"Thanks, Mallory," Diana said, pushing the side of her thigh into the below-sink lever and halting the flow of water. This would be the second surgery for her patient in six months: first, a successful face lift by the plastic surgeon around the corner on Mirror Lake and now the overweight woman needed her gallbladder removed.

Diana held her dripping fingers at breast level as she turned the corner, almost colliding with John Haynes.

"Dr. Haynes, well, how are you?"

Haynes was rubbing his hands together, working sanitizer solution between the fingers before smearing it up his forearms. "If you had joined my group, Diana, you'd be doing more than a gallbladder now and then."

"I'm plenty busy, Haynes."

"Don't doubt that. Bet Cummins has made sure of it," Haynes winked. He leaned into the entrance of his surgical suite and started barking orders to the techs. The doors swung closed behind him. Diana pushed through into her own room, her mind on John Haynes' testimony during the Balad medical inquest. She hoped that he had squirmed, even just a little.

Yes, Cossar . . . Lieutenant Colonel Cossar . . . and another nurse ... a younger nurse. I didn't recognize the other nurse. She stayed clear, looked to be stocking supplies or making a delivery of some sort.

Mallory was the OR tech assigned to Diana's case and held open sterile gloves for her. "What are you going to close the skin with this afternoon, Dr. Bratton? Glue or maybe a stitch?" she asked.

A younger nurse. I didn't recognize.

"Dr. Bratton, Derma-glue or are you going to suture? Dr. Bratton?"

. . . a younger nurse. I didn't . . .

"Dr. Bratton, you okay?" Mallory asked.

Diana shoved her dry hands into the gloves. "I'm sorry. Better use the Monocryl today." She nodded toward the anesthetized patient. "Also a 0-polyglactin for the fascia. Whatever brand the hospital's got on contract this month."

"Yes, ma'am." The OR tech helped Diana into the surgical gown. "Will Dr. Cummins be assisting today?"

"No. He thinks I'm a big girl now—thinks that I can do gall bladders all by myself," Diana answered. "And he's going to let me take call again tonight, too."

*　　*　　*

The confrontation with her brother and the turn-around to Jackson for the talk with Brad had exhausted Cossar. She turned down the airline's $750 one-way ticket back to Atlanta. ("Not on a military nurse's salary," she told the unsympathetic agent.) Cossar extended the rental car agreement and spent an extra day resting in the small hotel off Lakeland Drive. After sleeping through her wake-up call, she missed the complimentary breakfast before check out.

Hungry, Cossar found an empty booth in Primos Café around the corner. She recognized no one. Brad would be at work and her brother was above such casual eateries. A late breakfast of home-made buttered biscuit with strawberry jam, bacon, two eggs over-easy, black coffee, and grits renewed her. She lingered over her second and third cups of coffee while reading a copy of the day's newspaper left by a customer in the adjacent booth. The lunch crowd came and went and the servers began to prepare for the wave of early supper patrons. She noticed someone deliver a stack of magazines inside the entrance of the café -- something else to read -- and picked one up.

Her brother's smiling face on the cover of the Jackson *Northside Sun* stared at her.

"Not surprised that John didn't mention this," Cossar said, reading the lead article detailing the Children's Hospital fundraiser scheduled for that night. The Madison home of Dr. John Haynes would be filled with silent and live auction items including fine art, vacations, and dinners for 12 at local and regional restaurants. The magazine promised an extensive menu including shrimp shooters, chipotle fish wraps, spicy jambalaya dip, pecan crusted catfish, Mexican scrambled eggs, rib eye and gorgonzola sandwiches along with sweet potato pancakes complete with pulled pork. There was also something about rolled chocolate pastry and strawberry parfait filling tiny glass cups.

A big party. Not just sushi, beer, and cheese but service out by the pool or maybe in the rose garden among the statues. An invitation to this soiree and another sleepover for a sibling wouldn't have been an imposition she decided.

*   *   *

Diana's cell phone vibrated. "Christine, my phone is in the back pocket of my scrubs. Might be the office. I'm already behind for the afternoon."

The nurse circulating in the surgical suite removed the phone. "It's a text," Christine said. "Want me to read it to you?"

"No, text 'em I'll be there in fifteen. Gotta get this little bleeder stopped."

"But it doesn't look like it's from your office. Somebody named Key Martin?"

"I'll call him when the gallbladder is out."

Mallory handed Diana the next laparoscopic instrument.

"OK, Dr. Bratton—what's going on?" she asked. "New guy?"

*   *   *

Diana completed the cholecystectomy, signed the post-op orders, and pushed through the door into the doctors' lounge. Someone had left the television tuned to FOX News. She eased into a dictation cubicle around the corner and dialed the number from her cell phone.

"Your text said that you had something new?"

"Not really anything new. Just wanted to get your thoughts on that nurse's love life."

"Stacy Lane?" Diana felt another buzz at her waist. This text from her clinic secretary read *Four patients waiting. Two threatening to leave. Hurry.* "Detective, you've called me in the middle of surgery to discuss Stacy Lane's love life?"

"I like your insight, Doc. You're becoming quite a detective,

225

but I hope you're not after my job. Doubt you could live on what they pay me around here."

"The love life?" Diana glanced at the time. She hoped her secretary could work her usual magic and smooth things over with the clinic patients.

"Besides being attracted to military guys like Chad Giles, guys more her age, she had a thing for rich older doctors, especially military ones. I guess that's not so unusual. Is it?"

"She was young. Probably out for whatever came along," Diana answered.

"Colonel John Haynes would fit that bill—the rich older doctor."

Diana heard the chair slide back in the dictation cubicle beside hers and someone fumble with the dictation equipment. A strong voice rose above the partition. "John Haynes, dictating case number 2565."

"Seems as though Dr. Cummins could help me make some sense of this," Martin said. "Did he mention ever seeing Haynes and Lane together over there in Iraq?"

Diana leaned away from the partition between her and Haynes and whispered, "Doubt it. The Giles kid probably kept her busy, or maybe it was the other way around." She paused a moment. Haynes was deep into his description of an appendectomy and colon resection. "But why don't you check with Brad?"

"Dr. Cummins is not as accommodating as you. He never answers his cell. Maybe you could work on him for me."

"I might just do that, Detective Martin," Diana said.

38

Her friendly smiles, excuses about the emergency surgery, and frequent pats on tense shoulders seemed to smooth the ruffled feathers of the afternoon patients. Despite the delayed schedule, they all waited to see Diana, even the last gentleman who spent three hours to have his reflux and weight problems evaluated.

All of the clinic employees had left. Housekeeping had arrived early. Diana retrieved her keys and maneuvered through the trash bags waiting for pick-up in the halls to Brad's office. He was immersed in his lap top, completing medical records.

"Got another call from our detective friend today."

"He's your friend, Diana, not mine. I'm ready to move on." Brad motioned to several printed documents lying to the right of his desk. He flipped through a couple of pages of stapled sheets. "I promised to give this talk to the Rotary Club next week on the topic *Healthy Living and How to Prevent Surgery.*

"You trying to put us out of business?" she asked.

"I'm way behind on my community service. Besides, with Zarife Amarah and Stacy Lane out of the way, it's finally time to put all this detective stuff behind me, behind us."

"I'd like to do the same, but . . ."

"But, what, Diana?" He pushed aside the medical journal and half-closed the lap top.

"Martin is looking into the connection between Stacy Lane and Haynes. He wants to know if they had a history in Iraq."

Brad remained immersed in the laptop. "If Stacy Lane was hooking up with Haynes in Balad, I never saw it. Besides, the freak was supposed to be deep into Giles at the time. Remember our weekend in New Orleans?"

"Don't make light of this. I'm only trying to help."

Without turning to her, Brad opened a paper file on his desk. "Diana, I'm drowning here."

Brad, you've been drowning since you came back from Iraq she thought. "There is one thing I'd like to know. Was Lane around when Giles crashed in the Recovery Unit?" she asked.

"I never saw her," Brad said. "But then I was focused on the CODE. Besides, what difference does it make? With Haynes and Cossar already working on Giles, we didn't need anyone else."

Diana turned to leave, but stopped. "Brad, this thing isn't over. You need to call Key Martin. You were in Iraq with Haynes and Lane, not me."

"Somebody's got to stay around this place and work, Diana. This is the present." Brad slid another chart from the deep stack atop his desk and retrieved his hand-held recorder. "Medical record number G6314. Arnold Payne. Mr. Payne presents with right lower quadrant abdominal pain." He paused the recorder and referred to his laptop.

Diana breathed slowly, forcing control as she moved closer to Brad's desk. She thought about the deeper pile of charts waiting in her office.

Brad finished Mr. Payne's dictation and flipped open the next chart.

"Look, wherever John Haynes is, he's got something going on. And, no, I'm not surprised if he hooked up with a young nurse over there, even if she was screwing somebody else. We all know he's a rich sonnavabitch."

The recorder snapped to attention as he pushed the start button.

"Next chart, Wilma Summerford, number C4."

Diana reached across the desk and slammed the chart closed. "Dammit, Brad! And Haynes just happens to be screwing the same chick as Giles?"

"What are you trying to say, Diana?"

"You know John Haynes just as well as I do. He's a competitive ass. He doesn't like to lose at anything."

"Who does?" Brad tossed the recorder to his desk and swiveled his chair toward her.

"Think back to the recovery area, the ICU." She began to pace the room. "Did you notice anything strange, anything out of order?"

"That's a joke. The whole place was 'out of order.' And quit walking around the room like some a-hole attorney interrogating a witness."

"Sorry." Diana leaned against Brad's desk.

"Day-to-day operations in a military hospital in Iraq," Brad said, "are not the same as a typical hospital here in the States."

"What do you mean?" Diana asked. "We have trauma over here, too. Lots of it."

"I don't mean that. I'm talking about routines, shortcuts, ways to get things done, and get them done quickly."

Brad's memory of that afternoon's chaos remained vivid: ripped open packages of half-used medical supplies, IV poles with dangling bags of fluid and plastic tubing, medical equipment left askew in the corridor.

"We didn't always have a central supply cart for dispensing medication and certainly no pharmacist to fax or email. If we needed something, we looked around until we found it, then grabbed and used it. There was so much going on. I guess I did see a young girl working over in a corner in post op. Hadn't thought about it since. She seemed preoccupied."

"What about the supplies for the CODE?" Diana asked. "When the head nurse, that Cossar woman, called it, where were those supplies?"

"The crash cart was already beside Giles' bed. Like I said, Haynes was already there. I had to push a couple of other carts out of the way to get to Giles. There was an opened jump bag lying on the one nearest."

"Jump bag?"

"I suppose one of the Chinook transport team left it."

"Jump bag?" Diana asked again.

"It's a general purpose bag, a carry-all, stuffed with medical supplies," Brad answered. "An enlisted is responsible for his or her own jump bag. He or she restocks it daily before going out into the field."

"Responsible?" Diana stopped again at Brad's desk, this time leaning further over it. "So what's in these jump bags?"

"Diana, stop this. Your interrogation is getting real corny."

"Please answer the question."

"Of course, medicine for one thing. And there's a narc box."

"You mean a handy, separate container for narcotics?"

"Medics need to keep Demerol or morphine handy. Wound splints, wound dressings, epinephrine pens, a small oxygen dispenser, maybe some suture, too—typical stuff for a medic's jump bag."

"Did you stop to check the opened jump bag?"

"Why would I have done that?" Brad retrieved another chart and kept working. "I'm never going to get out of here tonight." He signed in several places and picked up another. "Besides, the supplies I needed to resuscitate Giles would be on the crash cart, not necessarily in a jump bag."

"That's just it, Brad. There was some reason you couldn't resuscitate Giles. Some reason that even escaped the medical examiner."

"But the ME reported a clean autopsy." Another signature and Brad slid a new chart from the stack. There were some electronic medical records as well.

"They found narcotics in Giles, didn't they?" she asked.

"Sure the hell they did! The guy had just had surgery."

Brad ran his thumb down the edge of the stack of unfinished charts, counting them.

"And a tox screen would show only the presence or absence of narcotics, not an overdose," Diana said. "There's got to be something else." She started pacing.

"Your detective buddy has been through everything; the U.S. military has been through everything." Brad started another chart. "The people after me and my family are dead. What more do you want, Diana?"

"So you just want to give up on this?"

"I want to get on with my life, with our lives."

She studied him. He moved quickly through the paper work. "The babysitter is taking Kelsey over to her parents' house for supper and sleepover. So I'm free tonight."

"Hadn't thought much about tonight. It's gonna take me another hour or so to finish."

Diana said, "You need to work more efficiently." She walked to the door.

"What about stopping by for takeout?" Brad asked. He hurriedly signed several pages of lab and pathology reports. "Go ahead and pick up something for me, too."

"Sorry, Brad. I just thought of something else to do," she said. "And it seems, Dr. Cummins, that you're not as smart as I thought, either."

39

Diana sat in the parking garage for a few moments before starting the ignition. She reached for the thin magazine beside her. The cover sported a stone and brick residence with antique wooden beams melted into the front façade.

"The residence of the famous John Haynes, MD," she said.

She flipped the slick pages to the color feature of a twenty-acre spread in Madison County and reread the feature on Haynes and his home: a climate-controlled barn with stereo system and dance floor, an Olympic-size heated pool with waterfall and outdoor spa, and expensive antiques from around the world arranged among Jane Shelton fabrics and drapes. Haynes was pictured solo, smiling and holding a coffee cup in a manicured garden of blooming plants and walls covered in fig vine. Although Haynes may have missed the true purpose of the *Northside Sun Magazine*, the intent was to publicize his home as the venue for the upcoming children's hospital benefit.

"I need the address for Dr. John Haynes," Diana said into her cell phone.

"I've got a pager number, Dr. Bratton," the answering service responded. "That's all they give us. No other personal info."

"OK, look, I need to reach Dr. Haynes."

"I just gave you his pager number. You want me to dial it for you and then connect you?"

"No, I need his address."

"Tried the phone book?"

"Not there," Diana answered. "Give me your supervisor."

The supervisor for the physicians' answering service was more helpful, particularly when she realized that Dr. Bratton was the same nice, pretty doctor who cured her father of melanoma.

Diana drove home to find Kelsey with the babysitter. The invitation to supper with the sitter's parents had fallen through, replaced by an order of pizza and breadsticks and a rented DVD, something about a mermaid. The babysitter agreed to stay late and spend the night if needed.

Diana tossed her scrub suit into the laundry hamper and exchanged it for the only clean, unwrinkled outfit that could pass for cocktail attire: fitted black slacks and a tight white blouse with beading. A thin black bag and a string of faux pearls picked up at a garage sale complemented the outfit.

"Not bad," Diana said, admiring the image in her bathroom mirror. "But a session with Minor would definitely help. Maybe after tightwad gives me a raise."

A half-hour later Diana stepped from her car onto the winding brick driveway.

"Need a ride?" A young man pulled beside her in an elongated golf cart. "It's free. Comes with your ticket." His only passenger was a middle-aged woman sitting in the seat behind him. The woman checked her watch and fidgeted with her purse. She was attractive and dressed in a larger-sized version of Diana's ensemble.

"Sure." Diana had not considered the need for a ticket. She took a seat beside the woman. "Do I need to give you my ticket now?"

"Oh, no, ma'am," the young man smiled, releasing the cart's brake and easing up the driveway. "I think they'll just check your name off the list up on the front porch."

Diana was aware of the $500-per-couple price to attend the function, 80 per cent of the price tax-deductible. A single was only $300. She thought about the amount she actually cleared from performing an appendectomy. "It's for a good cause," she said, fingering the credit card inside her thin black purse.

"My brother better let me in free," the woman said.

"Your brother is John Haynes?" Diana asked. "He might make me pay double."

The cart reached the bottom of the stairs that led to the porch and front entrance. The driver sprang from his seat and smiled. His perfectly aligned, white teeth reflected the landscape lighting and the recessed lighting from the porch ceiling.

"You ladies have a nice time," he said.

"I plan to," the woman said.

"Me, too," Diana said. "Thank you." She decided that a tip was not expected. Diana handed her credit card to the young girl at the door and stuffed the receipt into her purse—her ticket into the grand foyer.

A server brushed by with a silver tray. "Bacon-wrapped, barbecued shrimp?" he offered, lowering the tray to eye level. "Fresh out of the oven."

"No thanks," Diana said. "But which way's the bar?"

"Through the living room to the back loggia," he answered, bending to share with Diana's cart mate and then moving to another guest.

"I saw these earlier in the back of the fridge. They look better cooked." Cossar bit into the shrimp. A droplet of bacon grease oozed from the corner of her mouth. "Slow down, fella. Give me one of those cocktail napkins."

Diana retrieved a napkin from the server's tray and delivered it to her golf cart mate. "Here, you better get that before it makes it to the collar of that white blouse."

"Thank you," she said. "I ate breakfast late, but no lunch. I should have stopped for something on the way over. By the way, I'm Elizabeth Cossar."

Elizabeth Cossar—Brad's friend, the sister he thought might have been Haynes' houseguest. Diana recalled the medical tribunal report.

"And I'm Diana Bratton," she said. "On the ride up you mentioned that John Haynes is your brother. We practice surgery at the same hospital."

Cossar finished with the cocktail napkin. Another server approached, and she tossed the soiled paper on the tray. "I need to find another one of those shrimp." Cossar looked in that direction. "My brother never mentioned having a woman in his practice."

"And John Haynes never mentioned having a sister."

"I just spotted the bar, finally." Cossar said. "Care to join me? And, yes, I'm the lucky girl." She pushed through the crowd toward the rear of the house.

"Glad to." Diana followed. "Hate to disappoint you, but I don't practice with Haynes. I'm in the Cummins group."

Cossar found an empty spot at the bar and signaled the bartender. "Then you mean Brad Cummins." She ordered a Bud Light.

Diana watched a third of the bottle disappear in one gulp.

"Brad and I worked together in Iraq, at the Balad military hospital," Cossar said.

233

The bartender directed his attention past the older woman to smile at Diana.

"Chardonnay for me, please."

The bartender returned with the wine and lingered a few moments. Diana was surprised, flattered. He was nice-looking. She smiled, took the first sip, and admired his physique.

"Anything else for you, Miss?" the bartender asked Diana, grinning.

"It's *Doctor,* not *Miss*, you ass," Cossar interrupted, pushing between Diana and the hot bartender.

"For a while my brother served over in Iraq with us."

Two-thirds of the beer was gone.

Diana continued to sip her wine as she studied the area. The loggia was overflowing with guests interested in the children's hospital. Men and women were sandwiched between floor plants, oil paintings on easels labeled for the highest bidder, and heavy bamboo furniture. Many of the overweight and older donors sat. All four bartenders were swamped, including the attractive young guy with the hair products. The host was nowhere to be seen.

"Were you there when Brad lost that kid?" Diana asked. She stared over her glass into Cossar's eyes. "I don't think Brad will ever get over it."

"We all did everything we could, and they cleared Brad."

"Who is *we*?" Diana thought back through the tribunal report. "Was your brother there, there in the recovery area when Chad Giles died?"

"Something tells me that you already know the answer, Dr. Bratton."

The voice behind startled Diana. "I didn't see you on the invitation list, Diana."

"Don't worry, Haynes. I paid at the door. Wanna see my receipt?" She waved her purse.

"Would never doubt you, Diana. And all those kids with cancer and broken bones and leukemia thank you."

"Sorry, bro, but I skipped the ticket table," Cossar said. "I figured since my brother donated the house . . ." The beer was finished. Cossar turned to reach over the person who had slipped between her and the bar. "Hey, cutie. Another one."

"Elizabeth, I worked my ass off for this house. You had nothing

234

to do with any of it." Haynes gulped his martini. "Besides, I thought you left. Now you've really outstayed your welcome."

Haynes nodded at the bartender, got a top off for his drink, and moved toward the formal living room. He had spotted someone. With glass raised, Haynes parted the throng blocking his path and shouted above the crowd, "Governor, glad you made it!"

* * *

"Comin' in mighty late, Doctor."

"Had a lot of catching up to do at the office, Jeremiah."

"Just keepin' an eye out for you, Doc—tryin' to make up for the other night." Jeremiah followed Brad to the elevator. "Sorry I didn't warn you about that detective comin' up to your place."

"Don't worry about it, Jeremiah. You've never let me down. Anyway, that detective—Key Martin—he's just doing his job."

"Thanks, Doc. See ya in the mornin'."

Brad stepped into the hall from the elevator and slid his key in the door. *"Diana, you here? Did you pick up some food?"* was met with silence. "I guess she decided to go to that benefit she mentioned last week," he said, tossing his overnight bag toward the floor of the library and home office. The sound brought Bullet running through the apartment from the bedroom.

"Didn't the sitter walk you this afternoon?" Brad managed between long, wet licks across the face. "Go get your buddy and we'll throw it."

The lab bounded to the large upholstered couch in the living room and wedged his head underneath the frame. A stuffed miniature of himself appeared between his jaws.

"OK, OK, we'll go out and toss that thing," Brad said.

Bullet handled the toy until they reached the deserted courtyard. He dropped it at Brad's feet and pointed in anticipation. Brad complied and threw the stuffed animal to the other side of the garden.

"My boy had a lab, too."

Brad turned to the voice just as Bullet sprang in mid-air and grasped the stuffed animal in his mouth. An unkempt older man stood in the dim light outside the ten-foot high wrought iron fence.

"You enjoy tossing that thing to your dog, don't you doctor? Just like my boy Chad did."

"Mr. Giles?"

Brad felt Bullet push the slimy toy into his hand for another throw. He again hurled it across the ornamental scrubs and brick, sending the dog bounding for retrieval.

"You must have been discharged from Whitfield."

Brad studied Giles' jacket and trouser pockets, no bulge to suggest a weapon. The man's hands were free.

"Doctors told me that grief had made me crazy. They finally found a medicine that works."

"So you're not waving a gun around the ER anymore?" Another toss. Bullet sprinted across the courtyard, leaping over several shrubs.

"They taught me to find ways to cope with my loss. The medicine just dulls the pain ... quiets my mind a bit so I think about other things, like eating and sleeping."

"I'm very sorry about your grandson. I've told you that. I know you think that I could have made things turn out differently."

"No, I understand that, Dr. Cummins. Part of my treatment was learning about what happened over there in Iraq with Chad. The doctors and nurses got the medical records. They let me see them; they explained them to me. You didn't do anything wrong. I know that now."

Another pitch of the toy Bullet. The real thing was slowing, more panting. Slobber had covered the stuffed animal. Brad wiped his slimy hands across a thick-leafed bush.

"Can I call you a taxi, Mr. Giles? Do you need some help, some money?"

"I don't need any of your money, Dr. Cummins." Giles gestured to the fancy building and the courtyard. "You've worked hard for it. You keep it."

They were alone. No passersby. No cars on the street. "Mr. Giles, you'll have to excuse me, but I've worn down my dog. Need to take him in for some water."

Giles pulled himself toward the iron posts, his thin, wrinkled fingers tight enough to strangle.

"Doc, I know in my heart that Chad shouldn't have died. I think you know that, too."

"I'm sorry, Mr. Giles, but like I said, there's nothing that I could . . ."

"There's something missing here. Something else. You've got

to find it, Doctor."

Brad tossed the stuffed Bullet to a different corner of the courtyard, watching it bounce off the fountain head to land behind an English boxwood. Bullet was on it. Brad turned to face the old man.

Giles was gone.

Brad moved nearer the fence and checked up and down the street and sidewalk. "Why do I attract so many nut cases?" he asked.

The panting lab stood below him, the stuffed animal soaked and clenched between his teeth. Bullet looked up at his master and tilted his head in answer.

"Sure, you're tired. So am I. Come on, boy!"

Reenergized, the dog ran to the hotel entrance.

Brad called the elevator in the lobby of the King Edward. He glanced around the space: no Elder Giles, no Iraqi National, no sexy young nurse with a gun, no bleeding psychiatrist. *There's something missing here. Something else. You've got to find it* the desperate Mr. Giles had said. He pushed the number to his floor. Bullet stepped inside, then sat to watch the lighted numbers ascend the elevator control panel to their apartment.

There's something missing here. Something else. You've got to find it.

Bullet dropped the toy in the entrance hall for his water bowl in the kitchen. Brad stared into the library. He pulled the file to the medical inquest and sank into the leather chair near the window.

There's something . . . else . . . find it.

Brad scanned the record. There were no errors in the type and crossmatch of blood replacement. The emergency splenectomy went smoothly. Even Haynes had said so. Blood loss during the procedure itself was insignificant. The autopsy found no congenital heart defects, no overlooked life-threatening injury from the IED, no missed diagnoses. Brad again read through the toxicology screen: opiates, routine. The ME's report was clean.

He let the file drop beside him and rested his head against the soft leather. He closed his eyes and thought about the cold beer in the refrigerator. The image of the triage/post-op area in Balad engulfed him. Supplies tossed about, personnel slim. Haynes had been the first to respond. Cossar was there looking busy as usual in control of the situation. Yes, Stacy Lane must have been the young nurse in the corner.

Just as he described to Diana, the air vac personnel's jump bag lay open and abandoned on a medicine cart. "Cummins, get your ass over here and help me figure out what's wrong with this guy!" Haynes had ordered. "No response to Narcan, and he won't ventilate with a fucking face mask!" The IV tubing was shaking. Haynes had tilted Giles' head back, preparing to push an endotracheal tube.

"Didn't know I could still do this internal medicine stuff, did you, Cummins?" Haynes pushed the plastic tubing into the dying lance corporal's throat and compressed the inflated bag to force the flow of oxygen. "Don't just stand there! Start chest compressions!"

Haynes.

Brad stopped to pet the sleeping lab on his couch, then grabbed a black Remy leather jacket from his bedroom closet. He checked it against his jeans, still sharply pressed courtesy of the cleaners. *This will do* he decided, especially with the Frye boots.

Haynes' place was forty minutes away. No text or call from Diana, nothing explosive or confrontational so far at the fundraiser—maybe she was even having a good time. *Just another Disease Party.*

Except the party was at the estate of Dr. John Haynes.

40

"Do you have a ticket?" the girl at the entrance table asked. She brushed the strawberry blond bangs from her eyes. "OMG! Dr. Cummins!" she giggled. "Come on in! No way you need a ticket. Party's half over, anyway."

The waiter handed her another glass of chardonnay that she half-emptied in seconds. "I like those hot jeans. Dr. Cummins," she said. "I like 'em, like 'em a lot." She drained the rest of the glass and called to the server for another.

"Have you seen Dr. Haynes around?" Brad asked her.

"Dr. Haynes? Are you kidding? He wouldn't be seen out front with us low-life!" The girl stamped Brad's left arm with the admission mark ink. "There you go, big guy." She watched the server refill her glass and sloshed some on the invitation list as she retrieved it. "You have a blast, Dr. Cummins. See you in the OR on Monday!"

"Looking forward to it. Glad you'll have tomorrow to rest up," Brad said. This was his second visit to the Haynes estate, the first a political fundraiser for a local congressman held before the deployment to Iraq.

The same pourer approached with bottles of wine. "White or red?" she asked. "Oh, I'm sorry, sir. You don't have a glass. Be right back."

"No problem. Have you seen Dr. Haynes?" Brad asked.

"Who's that?" she asked.

"Like I said, no problem," Brad answered. "Just point me to the bar."

"That way. Toward the back," she said before moving to the next guest. "White or red?"

Brad worked through the donors blocking the bar. "Excuse me. Just trying to get through." He brushed past the tie-less cocktail, the dressy casual, the tacky-chic, and the plunging necklines. The governor, the mayor, and the administrator of Metropolitan Hospital formed the perimeter around the bar.

The hospital administrator delivered the first greeting. "Dr. Cummins, great to see you. And thanks for all your cases." She raised her glass. "The guys at corporate just approved next quarter's budget because of you and Dr. Bratton."

"No problem," Brad said. "Jack and Seven, please." The bartender acknowledged. Brad felt the mayor move closer.

"What would it take to get more of you guys interested in practicing up here?" the mayor said with a swirl of the ice drowning in his scotch. A swallow followed. "We've just zoned another multi-use tract off I-55—the perfect spot for a medical office building."

"Congratulations, mayor." Brad toasted the group. "And it's really great to see all of you good folks, but I've spotted my girlfriend over there." He leaned toward the bartender and tossed him a five.

"I know you, you're Dr. Brad Cummins," the bartender said. "You did my appendectomy. Nice scar. 'preciate it."

"Glad to do it," Brad said, then maneuvered around the indoor plants and statues until he reached Diana and Cossar standing across the room. "Looks like you two have met. I told those jokers back there that I had spotted my girlfriend and needed to talk to her."

"And which one is the lucky girl?" Cossar asked before she drank the last of her beer. She stopped a passing server. "Could you get me another one of these? Just check my brother's fridge if the bar's too crowded."

"I'll claim that honor," Diana said and finished her drink as Brad moved closer. "I'm glad you're here," Diana said.

"Cossar, mind if I ask you something?"

"Sure, Brad. But if that guy doesn't show up soon with my beer, you'll have to get one for me to earn an answer."

"Did you keep up with Haynes while we were in Iraq?"

"Keep up with him?" Cossar asked.

"Like know his schedule or meet him off base for a drink," Brad answered.

She shook her head. "No meeting for a drink. And he ran his own social life, always has. As far as knowing his work schedule, I never knew what he was doing until his name popped up next to a procedure." The server produced a cold beer. " 'Bout time," Cossar said. She took a drag. "You seem so serious tonight, Brad."

"I've been thinking about the night Giles died. I've reread the transcript and confided in Diana. She's read the file several times, too."

"That stuff is old news, history," Cossar said.

"Maybe so, maybe not." Brad tasted his cocktail. He remembered Diana's question about Lane's presence in the Balad recovery unit. "Was Stacy Lane standing around when Giles CODE'd?"

"Maybe so," Cossar answered. "She'd been stocking supplies in there earlier, but I never really paid much attention to her. But as for my brother? There's another story."

"That's what Detective Martin thinks."

"Martin?" Cossar downed more of her beer and checked the amount remaining.

"The detective knows Lane was staying with your brother just before she attacked Brad. He wonders when their affair started," Diana said. "Where it started."

"Affair? Is screwing an affair?"

Most of the new beer was gone.

"Something's missing here," Diana said. "Over in Iraq, Stacy Lane was so deep into Giles that she tried to avenge his death. The girl was obsessed with him."

"And I'm not surprised that the girl would go for my brother, too. He's always been able to hold his own with women, all kinds of women."

"But, Cossar, you just said that you never knew what Haynes was doing until his name showed up on the procedure schedule."

"Running into him on base was always a surprise," she said.

"That day the base was shelled, you woke me because no other physician was on duty. Haynes wasn't around as usual."

"Like I said, my brother ran his own schedule. Our relationship over there was just like over here. We never talk, never have been real siblings."

She drank.

Brad asked, "Was your brother on the procedure schedule the day before Giles died?"

"Yes, he did several endoscopies. Two admits started throwing up blood. I had to get all the supplies together for my spoiled brother: the scope, the IV supplies, the Propofol."

Cossar plucked a pastry from another passing tray.

241

"The Propofol?"

"Great anesthetic for those scopes. Any soldier can handle an M9 or maybe even an M110 sniper rifle, but stick a lighted hose down their throats—another story."

Diana moved closer. "Your job was to clean up after your spoiled brother, right?"

Cossar took another bite. "Not that time. When I went down to where John was doing the EGDs, there was no one there. He had finished the procedures. I called out before I opened the curtains. No John. No patients."

"So you did your duty and cleaned up after him," Diana said.

"Not that time. The place was as tidy as could be—no trashed drapes, no left over supplies. Nothing."

"And Brother John's explanation?" Brad leaned in.

"He told me that some of the cases cancelled. He had some extra time, so he cleaned up after himself."

"What about the unused Propofol?" Diana asked.

"I don't know. What about it?" Cossar held up the empty beer bottle and scanned the crowd. No server in sight.

"Diana, a routine tox screen doesn't include Propofol," Brad said.

"An overdose of Propofol would be simple, quick -- just an IV push," Diana said.

"Irreversible respiratory depression," Brad said.

"No wonder you couldn't revive him," Diana said. A server passed between her and Cossar carrying a tray of bruschetta with goat cheese and cherry tomatoes. "But wait. That can't be it. If Giles was intubated, then you could have ventilated him, kept his oxygen sats up.

Haynes had tilted Giles' head back, pushed the plastic tubing into the dying lance corporal's throat and compressed the inflated bag to force the flow of oxygen.

"Diana, Haynes intubated Giles. I never saw him listen for air moving in the lungs. Maybe he missed the trachea—intentionally."

"How about some of those little open-face tomato sandwiches?" Cossar asked. "There were several trays in the back refrigerator."

She left for the kitchen.

"Silent auction's almost over, you deadbeats," Haynes called across the room. "Get out your checkbooks. Children's Hospital takes plastic, too."

Again John Haynes parted the crowd, a cocktail glass in one hand and a list of donated auction items in the other.

Brad blocked his path. "So, Haynes, helping out little children makes up for what you do to big kids?"

"Cummins, I didn't see you on the sponsor list either. Two hundred would have saved face. A thousand was expected."

"How'd you fake the sweat, Haynes?"

"Sweat? I don't sweat, Cummins. What're you talking about?"

John Haynes turned to smile at the Governor's wife, who lingered a second before rubbing against his blazer.

"OK, everybody. Last call for the big bucks!" he yelled across the room, his hands propped to his face like a megaphone, the martini glass held full in the right and the list in the left.

"You pumped that guy's chest like a madman, Haynes. You called for meds during Giles' CODE like a med student primed for a test."

"Cummins, what the hell are you talking about?" Haynes turned toward the crowd. "OK, five minutes and it's lights out on the silent auction." Haynes finished his drink.

"Hey!" He called to the hospital administrator across the room. "Need to talk to you about that new OR equipment." The administrator ducked into the living room.

"Forever the charmer," Brad said, watching Haynes head into the crowd after her.

"What about a murderer? Do you really think that Haynes would push that leftover Propofol on Giles?" Diana asked.

"There you two are." Cossar returned with a half-eaten tray of finger tomato sandwiches and handed it to Brad. "The girl in the kitchen didn't want to give these up, but I tipped her a five." She grabbed another beer from a passing server and sucked much of it down along with the sandwiches. "Hope my brother's maid, Linda-something-or-other, hasn't changed the sheets in my guest room 'cause I sure can't drive back to Atlanta now."

"You can stay at my place, Elizabeth," Brad said. "But for now," Brad spotted Haynes in the formal living room, "I need to talk some more to your brother." Haynes was no longer conversing with the hospital administrator but had exchanged her for the young redhead planted on the upholstered couch.

"Haynes, you can't hide from this."

"What the fuck are you talking about, Cummins?"

"Excuse me," the redhead said, "I'll go check out the crowd by the pool."

"Haynes, you murdered that guy. You pushed no-telling how much Propofol on Giles in the recovery room."

"You're full of it, Cummins. Get the fuck off my property!"

Haynes followed the girl to poolside.

"I did a little research on your buddy, Dr. Cummins."

Brad turned, surprised. "Detective Martin? Taxpayers must pay you a lot more than I thought," Brad said. "And John Haynes is not my buddy. Earn your pension and arrest that guy."

"Dr. Haynes is not the buddy I'm talking about," Martin said. "Three of my guys are working off-duty security out front. I decided to join 'em on-duty. Nice chance to see how that one percent lives."

He gestured toward the bricked foyer. "Looks like the entertainment's starting."

A woman's scream burst from the entrance as a server took cover. The crash of cocktail and wine glasses along with an empty beer bottle bounced from the brick floor into the living room. "Let me go!" The voice belonged to Elizabeth Taylor Cossar. Brad ran to it. Martin was at his heels.

Two of the policemen were struggling to control Cossar. "Guys, guys. I haven't even gotten in the car yet. No way for a DUI," she growled.

Brad yelled, "Hey, what's going on? Let her go!"

Martin held him from charging the policemen. "Relax, Doctor. I was checking my notes on this case a couple of days ago. You mentioned this nice lady's name during one of the interviews."

"Get your hands off of me. I haven't done anything."

Cossar continued to pull against the officers, one of whom was smaller than she.

"You said that she was in Iraq with you and then showed up around here," Martin said.

"Brad, Brad, do something about this . . ."

"And that she lived in Atlanta when she wasn't stationed overseas."

Cossar kept struggling even after one officer drew his weapon.

A female guest standing near the wrestling match fainted against an antique mahogany breakfront, her cocktail glass joining the mess at Cossar's feet.

Cossar kicked it toward Detective Martin.

"I said, get your grimy hands off me!"

Martin's officers shoved their prisoner out the door, across the porch, and down the front steps. Brad and the detective followed; a few of the curious lurked behind. One who joined them on the porch was a horrified Minor Leblanc.

"I took your advice, Dr. Cummins, and started thinking out of the box," Martin raised his voice to be heard over Cossar. "I checked with some buddies over in Georgia. Seems that twenty years or so ago when this woman was working in an Atlanta hospital, a couple of surgical patients died unexpectedly."

"And what did that have to do with Elizabeth?"

"She was the charge nurse on each case. The hospital investigated, but didn't come up with anything. There were no more suspicious deaths, and the incidents were filed away."

"No other details?" Brad asked.

"Patients just quit breathing and nobody could revive them," Martin said. "Sounded sort of like what happened to that patient you had over in Iraq."

"Yes, it does," Brad said.

"With a little more digging into the whole thing over in Atlanta it turns out that Nurse Cossar and Dr. Haynes are sister and brother."

"I know. I recently found that out myself."

"I decided that Elizabeth Cossar might have the missing piece to all of this. But when I checked again with the brother's housekeeper, she said this lovely lady (He pointed to the cursing, hand-cuffed Elizabeth Cossar down near the police car) had already left, headed back to Atlanta. But as luck would have it, I found her here."

"Detective, I don't see that you have any reason to arrest Elizabeth Cossar," Brad said.

"Wasn't planning to. Just wanted to talk. But now that she's put up such a fight—sorta makes her seem guilty, don't you think?"

John Haynes burst from the foyer onto the porch. He ran down the steps to the police vehicle and Brad followed. "What's going

245

on out here?" One officer was holding open the door to Detective Martin's new cruiser, the other his hand on Cossar's head, prying her into the backseat.

"Elizabeth, what the hell have you done now?" Haynes asked.

Brad pushed between them. "Elizabeth, I need to know—that leftover Propofol in Balad? Are you sure that you didn't put some of it away?"

"Don't say anything, Elizabeth," Haynes muttered.

"Get your stinking hands off me!" Cossar wrestled free from the guard.

"All right, All right. Relax, guys," Martin said. The officers shook their heads and backed away a few steps, although the handcuffs remained in place. The policeman smaller than Cossar massaged his shoulder.

"Elizabeth, you said inside that you didn't find any of the unused Propofol," Brad said.

She looked to her brother. "I never saw what happened to it. John must have put the leftover Propofol in storage somewhere."

The reddish, alcohol-induced complexion drained from Haynes' face, the pallor easy to see even in landscape lighting. "I said don't say anything else. I'll call my lawyer for you," Haynes said.

Brad pushed him aside. "The detective told me about what happened back in Atlanta, that there were some unexplained deaths post-op and that you were the nurse in charge." Brad felt Haynes take a few steps backward. "It was just like what happened to Giles," Brad said.

"You think I'm the one who loaded up that Giles kid with Propofol?" Cossar cried. She rattled the cuffs and an officer grabbed her. Martin shook his head and the policeman relinquished her arm. "You figure it out, Brad!" Cossar shouted. "You know my dear brother was with me in Atlanta, doing his surgery residency at the same hospital. And guess who was the first doctor at each CODE."

"I said shut your blabbering, Elizabeth. Wait for my lawyer!"

Haynes took out the cell from inside his linen blazer and hit speed dial.

"Yeah, you'd like that, John Haynes. I was damn sick of you in Atlanta and still am. I was sick of you the minute Momma and Daddy brought you home from the hospital."

"Elizabeth, you bitch. Shut the . . ."

"I've been keeping quiet for you your whole stinking life, Brother John. You can't make me do it anymore."

The crowd was silent. Brad's face was frozen. He looked to Detective Martin, his question met with a raised brow.

Haynes stepped further back, in the direction of the garage.

"John, you were the doctor that tribunal should have raked over the coals, not Brad," Elizabeth said, her voice now drained, emotion spent. "During the inquest, I was wrong not to tell them about the missing Propofol."

"Officers, get this lunatic off my property!" Haynes ordered.

Martin slid behind him.

"I covered for you over in Atlanta, John. You botched those surgery cases. Those patients would never have lived after you butchered them. Somehow, you made it look like they had an MI or a pulmonary embolus."

"Good God, Elizabeth. You're making this whole thing up to save yourself. Can't all of you people see it?"

"You killed those patients in Atlanta just like you killed that boy in Iraq. I know that now. You killed that boy because he was sleeping with your girlfriend," Elizabeth cried. "You're a freak, John."

Haynes turned to run, bumping Martin's chest. He pushed against the detective. "My sister's always been jealous of me, always making up lies to cover her own screw-ups."

"Martin, don't listen to him. Elizabeth would never harm Giles or anyone else."

"I've grieved over the Balad inquest that focused on you, Brad," she said. "But don't you see? It turned out OK for you. Didn't it?" Cossar stumbled forward, hysterical. "Detective, my brother is the real criminal here!"

Key Martin drew his weapon just before Haynes delivered a knockout punch to his jaw. Minor Leblanc and the other onlookers screamed, then ducked behind the dense shrubbery and over-sized stone urns that framed the motor court. Haynes tore through the guests still standing, fleeing toward the garage. He pointed his car keys, and the door raised to a waiting BMW.

Martin scrambled to his feet, pushing away his officers as they jumped to help him up. "Forget me! Get Haynes," he said, dusting off his jacket. The officers sprinted after the surgeon and Martin followed, leaving the handcuffed Elizabeth Cossar propped against the cruiser. Brad moved to console her, her sobs drowned not by gunfire coming from the area of the garage, but by shouting, mostly from John Haynes.

When it was quiet, Brad heard Leblanc say from somewhere behind them, "Jesus, that show was worth the entire ticket. Next year's fundraiser could never be this fabulous!"

The detective's small force dragged the handcuffed and cursing Haynes back to the police cruiser. Martin followed behind, massaging his jaw, his gun drawn. Haynes' light tan, linen blazer was torn, grease-stained, wrinkled to the point of destroyed. Blood trickled from his forehead and down the side of his face to stain the collar.

"You'll hear from my lawyer about this," Haynes said. "My sister's always been the one with the secrets, not me."

Diana ran down the steps from the porch to Brad. Freed from her handcuffs, Cossar hugged them both.

"Brad, there was one thing that was never mentioned in Giles' autopsy report," Cossar said between tears. "The endotracheal tube was gone when the body made it to the morgue. I think John put it down the esophagus so the boy couldn't get any oxygen during the CODE. Then he pulled it at the end, and none of us ever noticed."

"Haynes also intubated those patients that died in Atlanta. Didn't he, Cossar?" Brad asked.

"I never wanted to believe my brother was a murderer," she answered. "Now I know for sure."

EPILOGUE

"Do you think it's too much?"

"No way," Brad answered. "I've heard what cribs in this neighborhood go for."

"I don't mean the sales price," Diana said, sweeping her arms over the front lawn toward the house. "I mean, the impression this place makes. Doctors shouldn't be so ostentatious."

"Who says?" Brad asked. "With the partnership contract you just signed, you can afford it." He shook his head and smiled. "God, don't I know it."

Brad took Diana's arm and escorted her up the walk toward the two-story, red-brick Georgian-style house in the Eastover neighborhood. They looked at the white archway framing the freshly-painted entrance. A neatly-trimmed grapevine crept up the brick toward the windows.

"I want to talk about this—sort this out. This big place isn't me." She turned back toward the street and dropped Brad's arm. The surrounding homes almost dwarfed her new purchase.

Brad smiled. "Diana." He turned her around to face the front of the home. "Everybody knows you work your butt off. It's a great house, and it's just the right size. You and Kelsey deserve it."

His new partner in surgical practice sighed. "I guess you're right. Kelsey has already picked out her room. I'm going to buy her a new bed and dresser and a big comfortable chair and a desk. And some new clothes, of course."

"Well, then, let's hope you get that production bonus I had my lawyer write into your contract. By the way, my accountant is never going to forgive me."

They moved up the walk to the front door. Diana produced the keys from her jeans pocket.

"You could have afforded this place even with the salary the dregs of the Haynes group offered, Brad said. "With John Haynes out, they're really short-handed. Martin thinks he'll never get out of Parchman."

"What a waste." Diana put the key into the lock.

"Martin's a better detective than I thought. He uncovered Amarah's notes about Haynes hiring him to take me out," Brad said. "John capitalized on the Iraqi's hatred."

"And the Iraqi capitalized on John's jealousy of Giles," Diana said. "I guess you should consider it a compliment."

"How so?" Brad asked. "That Haynes may have been jealous of me, too, but in a professional way?"

Diana laughed. "I wouldn't go that far. Haynes assumed you were smart enough to figure out that he murdered Giles."

"Lucky me," Brad said.

"But I'm really the smart one—holding out for that juicy Cummins counter-offer—a better vacation package and enough for private school tuition."

Brad took Diana's key and unlocked the heavy mahogany door. They walked into the foyer.

"You wouldn't need this place if you and Kelsey had officially moved in with me," he said.

"You don't like to hear *no*. Do you, Dr. Cummins?"

"Seems my success with marriage proposals has dropped to 50 per cent," Brad said. He followed Diana across the narrow marble entry into the living area at the rear of the house. She stopped and turned to him. Her kiss seemed spontaneous, but not a lover's kiss.

Brad reached to pull her closer.

"Hold up a minute. That was meant as a *thank you*," she said.

"A *thank you*?"

"A professional *thank you*."

"Handshakes work for that," he said and stepped closer.

"I think we should slow things down a bit," Diana said. "I was wrong to let things go that far."

"Your partnership agreement with the Surgical Center of the South has nothing to do with our personal relationship."

"You're right. With all those hours in the hospital and clinic, I earned the partnership," Diana extended her right hand. "So let's just shake on it."

Brad took her hand and pulled her to him.

"Professional women appreciate a firm handshake," he said. When she returned his kiss, Brad felt the last of his uncertainty and grief slip away.

"I had decided our relationship should change, become strictly business," Diana said after their lips parted. "Maybe we can keep the relationships separate: one at work and one at play."

Brad kissed her again. "Speaking of play, too bad the movers haven't shown up with your furniture."

"When has a lack of furniture stopped us," she said.

.

###

Author Acknowledgments

Many character names in *Wiggle Room* were sponsored to benefit the following charities: McClean Fletcher Center (a service of Hospice Ministries, Inc.); Jackson (MS) Cancer League; Mississippi Academy of Family Physicians Foundation; Mississippi Chapter of Make-A-Wish Foundation; March of Dimes (Delta Gamma Sorority University of Mississippi); Pete and Weesie Hollis Educational Endowment of the American Congress of Obstetrics and Gynecology; and the UMC Candlelighters (Blair E. Batson Children's Hospital). All characters and events grew from this author's imagination and do not resemble or describe any real person by any name in the past, present, or future. I would like to thank the following who contributed to the research: Huey B. McDaniel, Lt. Col., USAFR, MC, FS; Bill Johnson, MD; Brad E. Waddell, MD, Colonel (Retired), US Army; Mark Webb, MD; Mark Culbertson, Former Chief of Investigations Vicksburg (MS) Police Department; Barbara Bollinger, MD; Captain Farris Thompson, Rankin County (MS) DA Swat Team Commander; Mike Tramel, DDS; and Darrell Wilson. Special thanks to Randy Hines, MD; Sarah Hines, MD; Toni Upton, LPN; Katie Brown; and Stephen Kruger, Esquire. I apologize if I have omitted anyone. Advance readers who critiqued the manuscript include Karen Cole, MD; Bill Johnson, MD; Jan Slabach; Donnie Cannada, Esquire; Evelyn North; Billie Bruner, MD; Angela Scholz; and Christine Newman, RN. I would also like to thank my editors John Hough, Jr., and Aviva Layton as well as publisher James L. Dickerson of Sartoris Literary Group and independent publicist Maryglenn McCombs. *Wiggle Room* follows *House Call*, *Points of Origin* [an Independent Book Publishers (IPPY) award winner], and *Fresh Frozen*. All remain available in print and as ebooks. Please visit my website www.dardennorth.com where I invite reader comments.

Made in the USA
Lexington, KY
26 July 2013